A WHISPERING OF SPIES

A WHISPERING OF SPIES

Rosemary Rowe

This first world edition published 2012
in Great Britain and in the USA by
SEVERN HOUSE PUBLISHERS LTD of
9–15 High Street, Sutton, Surrey, England, SM1 1DF.
Trade paperback edition first published
in Great Britain and the USA 2012 by
SEVERN HOUSE PUBLISHERS LTD

British Library Cataloguing in Publication Data

Rowe, Rosemary, 1942-
  A whispering of spies.
  1. Libertus (Fictitious character : Rowe)–Fiction.
  2. Romans–Great Britain–Fiction. 3. Slaves–Fiction.
  4. Great Britain–History–Roman period, 55 B.C.-449
  A.D.–Fiction. 5. Detective and mystery stories.
  I. Title
  823.9'2-dc23

ISBN-13: 978-0-7278-8163-2 (cased)
ISBN-13: 978-1-84751-421-9 (trade paper)

All Severn House titles are printed on acid-free paper.

Severn House Publishers support The Forest Stewardship Council [FSC],
the leading international forest certification organisation. All our titles that
are printed on Greenpeace-approved FSC-certified paper carry the FSC logo.

MIX
Paper from
responsible sources
FSC® C018575
www.fsc.org

Typeset by Palimpsest Book Production Ltd.,
Falkirk, Stirlingshire, Scotland.
Printed and bound in Great Britain by
MPG Books Ltd., Bodmin, Cornwall.

To Kate and Peter, Cynthia and John

AUTHOR'S FOREWORD

The story is set in the winter of 191–192 AD, when Britannia had been, for upwards of two hundred years, the most northerly province of the Roman Empire: occupied by Roman legions, criss-crossed by Roman roads, subject to Roman laws, and administered by a Provincial governor answerable directly to Rome. (This was probably Clodius Albinus by this time, although the date of his appointment is open to debate.) Latin was the language of the educated, people were adopting Roman dress and habits more and more, and citizenship, with the precious social and legal rights which it conferred, was the aspiration of almost everyone. The Emperor Commodus still wore the Imperial purple in Rome, although he was becoming increasingly deranged, and his lascivious lifestyle, capricious cruelties and erratic acts were infamous. He had renamed all the months, for instance, with names derived from his own honorific titles (which he had in any case given to himself), and officially restyled Rome itself as 'Commodiana' in his own honour, though there is little evidence that anybody used the term except in dealings with himself. Such discretion was obviously wise. Stories about him barbecuing dwarves are (probably) exaggerated, but the existence of such rumours gives some indication of the man who, fearing (justifiably) that there were plots against his life, maintained a network of spies throughout the Empire – as suggested in the book.

Glevum (modern Gloucester) was an important town. Originally a fortress, intended to command the river-crossing of the Sabrina (Severn), it soon became a privileged colonia – a retirement town for legionary veterans, where all freemen born within the walls were citizens by right, and where the council enjoyed sufficient autonomy for the town to be a sort of self-governing republic within the province. The original fortress had long since been replaced and resited a little further south, where the flooding of the river would no longer threaten it – which is the reason, incidentally, that the main road to Londinium ran not from the Western Gate, as one might reasonably suppose, but from the northern one, since it went that way to meet the pre-existing road which had been built to serve the earlier fort. On the former site – so fortunately flattened, cleared and partially drained – a lively 'sub-urb' had grown up outside the city walls, and this is where Libertus's notional workshop is assumed to be.

At the time of this story there was still a garrison in the town, although it was apparently no longer kept at full legionary strength and much of the area formerly occupied by troops had been absorbed into civilian use – there is evidence that the forum itself was built on part of what had been the fort. However, the military presence continued to exist, and the Fourth Gaul Half-Mounted Auxiliaries, mentioned in the tale, was a real unit stationed in Glevum and then posted on, as the text suggests, although the date of their departure is not wholly clear.

The presence of this garrison was not merely symbolic. Although most of the quarrelsome local tribes had long since settled into an uneasy peace, there were still sporadic raids (mostly against military targets) by small bands of dissident Silurians and Ordovices from the west. It seems that (perhaps as a further act of defiance against Rome, since the Druid religion was outlawed by the state) these rebels deliberately adopted Druidic practices, including the macabre ritual of severing the heads of enemies and displaying them in 'sacred groves' as a sort of sacrifice to ancient gods. By the time of this story these rebels had been more or less entirely suppressed and although there were still occasional forays (and the mention of raids in the Rhineland is based on evidence) the events in the story are purely fictional: there is no record that there was any significant rebel activity so close to Glevum at this period.

Because of its status as a self-governing colonia it is possible that Glevum had no appointed lictors; similarly quasi-independent city republics and client kingdoms generally did not, and there is no evidence to suggest the existence of these officials in the town, although they were widespread elsewhere throughout the Empire, and their reputation would have been well known.

Effectively a kind of civil servant, exempt from military service and paid a fixed salary by the state, a lictor was usually not drawn from the most wealthy patrician class. Nonetheless he was always a freeborn citizen (as may be seen from the fact that he wore a toga) appointed as a personal bodyguard and attendant to some important magistrate, consul or governor. Indeed, the number of lictors was itself an indication of status: thus a consul might have a dozen lictors, a praetor a mere six, while the Emperor (at this period) was accorded twenty-four. (There were other kinds of lictors, too, at different periods, some representing different clans in the Curiate Assembly in Rome, and others who were attendants on official priests, but these do not concern us here.)

Such bodyguard lictors were generally less revered than feared. In addition to accompanying their master everywhere, even on a visit to the public baths, clearing a path for him through crowded streets and standing beside him when he made a speech, a lictor was entrusted with the punishment of criminals – usually a beating and occasionally death. (When Paul and Jesus, for example, were 'given to be flogged' it would have been the lictors who performed that task – and they were expert at it: flogging the victim to 'within a breath of death' but nonetheless carefully presenting him alive for whatever execution lay in store.) In short, a lictor was his master's official torturer and the heavy bundle of stout rods, bound round a sharpened axe, which he carried everywhere, was a symbol of that grim authority. (This bundle, called the *fasces*, was the symbol chosen by Mussolini in the twentieth century, giving rise to the word 'fascist' in the present day.)

So – like the tax-collectors, who were universally despised – a retired lictor was not much welcomed in good society, unless of course he had important sponsors who must be appeased, or was (as he might well be) an Imperial spy. This story hinges on this fact, and the dilemma it poses for the important citizens of the colonia.

Most inhabitants of Glevum, however, were not citizens at all. Many were freemen, born outside the walls, scratching a more or less precarious living from a trade. Hundreds more were slaves – what Aristotle once described as 'vocal tools'

– mere chattels of their masters, to be bought and sold, with no more rights or status than any other domestic animal. Some slaves led pitiable lives, but others were highly regarded by their owners, and might be treated well. Top-ranking slaves might even keep servants of their own – as the lictor's steward in the story hopes to do – though often they proved unusually cruel as masters, it appears. However, a slave in a kindly household, assured of warmth and shelter and enough to eat, might have a more enviable lot than many a poor freeman struggling to eke out an existence in a squalid hut.

The rest of the Romano-British background to this book has been derived from a variety of (sometimes contradictory) pictorial and written sources, as well as artifacts. However, although I have done my best to create an accurate picture, this remains a work of fiction, and there is no claim to total academic authenticity. Commodus and Pertinax are historically attested, as is the existence and basic geography of Glevum. The rest is the product of my imagination. (Gaul was of course the Roman province which is now largely France, although it is not certain that there was a change of Provincial governor there just prior to this date, as the text suggests.)

Relata refero. Ne Iupiter quidem omnibus placet. I only tell you what I heard. Jove himself can't please everybody.

PROLOGUE

The man sat at the table on the bench and carefully spread out one last sheet of bark-paper. He glanced around once more to check that he was quite alone, but of course he had already made quite sure of that: the servants had long ago been sent off for the night. 'Business matters to attend to,' he had said. 'Accounts to settle.' In a fashion it was true.

He moved the oil-lamp closer so that he could see, and stirred the mixture of lamp-black, vinegar and gum arabic which he had ready, waiting in the bowl. He fingered the handsome seal-ring beside him on the desk, but there would be no seal or sealing-wax on this – that would not be appropriate for what he had in mind. He smiled; not a pleasant smile. He dipped his iron-nibbed pen into the ink and began to write:

To Voluus, the ex-lictor of the Governor of the Gallic provinces. I hear you have been looking for properties to buy in preparation for a move from Gaul. So, you hope to settle in Glevum after all? I guessed that you would come here in the end. Did you think you would escape? Fool! I warned you once, my friend, that I do not forget. Set one foot in Glevum after this and I promise you that neither you, nor your treasure nor your family will be safe. You may not see me, but I know where you are – just as surely as you know who I am. He paused, and after a moment added with a scrawl, *Your secret enemy.*

He read it through again. Satisfied, he blew on it and scattered dust to dry the ink, then rolled it carefully into a tiny scroll, addressed it 'to Voluus', and tied it with a cord. Now, how should he proceed? One could not use one's own slaves for a task like this. Tomorrow he would find an urchin on the street and have the note delivered to the *mansio* – Glevum's official inn where Voluus had been staying for a day or two.

Better still, have it pushed in through a window-space, so that the messenger could not be caught and questioned afterwards. Of course, when the errand-boy came back to claim his fee, it would be wise to silence him, in any case. Nothing spectacular. A broken neck, perhaps. One more unclaimed body on the road – no one would even notice. Not this time, at least.

He was still smiling as he took his outer garment off, snuffed out the oil-lamp and – dressed only in his undertunic – lay down on the bed. A moment later he had fallen into dreamless sleep.

ONE

Voluus the ex-lictor was a newcomer to Glevum, recently retired from the Provincial court in Gaul, and I had never met him yet – though I could guess from his profession what kind of man he was. Glevum is a free republic within the Empire and we don't have lictors here, but he had boasted publicly of what his previous duties were: personal attendant, bodyguard and on-the-spot torturer and executioner for the outgoing Roman governor of Gaul.

People were already whispering that he could flog a criminal with such precision that the wretch was 'half a breath' from death, and yet present him living to be crucified – an example of commendable professional expertise, since to lose a prisoner by beating him too much was an official failure on the lictor's part.

Of course, Voluus was retired now, so perhaps was past his prime – though no doubt he was still strong. A man must have a certain vigour to carry a bunch of hefty five-foot rods, each thicker than my arm, especially when the bundle is bound round a heavy axe – yet that was the nature of the *fasces* which, as lictor, he would have borne in front of his master in public at all times. So perhaps he was not as old as I supposed. I couldn't find anyone who knew what age he was, though I'd spent the whole morning trying to find out.

I would have liked to know who I was dealing with, but it seemed that very few people in the town had actually encountered Voluus at all. He had yet to move into the expensive apartment which he had recently acquired and no one I asked had met him face-to-face. So far he'd merely paid one visit some time ago to inspect the area, staying at the mansio while he looked round to find a place that suited him. Then, having found one (and allegedly having paid the full asking price in gold), he'd left his steward behind to get the property prepared, while he himself went to back to Gaul to supervise the shipping of his things. Of course, it takes a long time for things to come from Gaul, but at last the move was under way. Of that, at least, there was no lack of witnesses. Half of Glevum had seen the carts arrive.

Wagon-loads of his possessions had been lurching into town every evening for more than a moon, as soon as wheeled traffic was permitted past the gates. Gossips spoke in hushed tones of what was on the carts – sack-loads of onyx vases and price-less works of art, or maybe it was Gallic silver coins and crates of jewellery: the rumours varied on the detail. Whatever form his fortune took, it was clearly sizeable and the new apartment (which had belonged to a tax-collector previously) was said to be palatial and beautifully equipped. One of my informants – a former customer – had been inside it once.

'Alabaster pillars and fine marble floors throughout,' he told me with a laugh. 'So it's no use you turning up there, my good citizen pavement-maker, offering your services to lay mosaics in his rooms. He would not hire a Provincial craftsman to do work for him anyway – he'd think it was beneath him, however good you are.' He looked at my face and added in alarm, 'Dear gods, Libertus, don't tell me that you really do intend to call! I've heard that Voluus has a wicked temper when he's roused and flies into a tantrum at the slightest of affronts. What will he think if you just turn up unasked? And he won't want your mosaics, anyhow. I should save yourself a journey, if that's what you're thinking of.'

But of course that was exactly what I was on my way to do.

Naturally the errand was not my idea. Left to myself I would keep well away from him – or any ex-lictor – especially after the warning I'd received. But when one's wealthy patron suggests an enterprise, it is not wise for a humble citizen to demur, particularly when the patron in question is Marcus Septimus Aurelius, rumoured to be related to the Emperor and certainly the most important magistrate in all Britannia. Besides, this was less of a suggestion and more of a command: Marcus had summoned me to his country house yesterday specifically on purpose to send me on this task.

At the time, I was not sorry to receive his messenger. It had been a bright, cold spring morning – the Ides of March, in fact – which was how my patron knew that I would be at home, in my little roundhouse in the woods, and not in the mosaic workshop here in the colonia. (The fifteenth day of every month is seen as *nefas*, or ill-starred, but the *Ides Martii* is easily the worst. Since the assassination of the first Emperor, it has been deemed one of the most unlucky dates in the calendar, so much so that all courts and legal business cease, the theatres close and even a humble mosaic-maker like myself might reasonably shut up his shop and stay quietly at home.) I had been mentally planning a pleasant morning watching cabbage grow.

However, my wife, Gwellia, who like myself was born a Celt with scant belief in Roman auguries, had decided that – however unlucky the day – she had a task for me. The thatched roof of the little round dye-house that we'd built had sprung a small leak in the winter rains, she said, and this was the perfect opportunity for repairing it.

My pleas that it was an inauspicious date to begin an enterprise impressed her not at all. Anyway, she reminded me, the Emperor had recently renamed all the months in honour of himself, so this was now the Ides of Aurelius – and surely there could be no special curse on that? So when my patron's messenger arrived it was to find me on a home-made ladder, fixing bundles of new reeds in place, while my three slaves tied more bunches and passed them up to me, with Gwellia supervising proceedings from the ground.

When I heard that I was wanted I actually smiled. A summons to my patron could not be ignored (even my wife could hardly gainsay that!) so I scrambled down gratefully and dusted off my hands. 'Maximus!' I said briskly. 'Bring me some water so I can rinse my hands and face.'

The boy – who, despite his name, was easily the smallest of my slaves – grinned up with evident relief and hastened off to get the bowl. Gwellia glared at me.

'I suppose that you will want him to accompany you, now?' she said. 'You'll claim it won't be proper to arrive without a slave?'

I nodded. 'Well, it is expected that I'll have an escort, as I am a citizen!' I said placatingly. 'And Marcus did give me that red-headed pair of slaves. I shan't take both of them, only Maximus. He is not adept at bunching reeds, in any case. I'll leave you young Minimus and the kitchen slave to help. They will be more use. And look who's walking this way from the house next door!' I gestured to the path that led through my enclosure to the rear, where my adopted son was hurrying towards us down the hill. 'It's Junio. I'm sure he'll lend a hand. I taught him years ago to thatch a roof, so I can safely leave the rest of it to him.'

Gwellia looked doubtful, but Junio was delighted to be asked. He had been my slave for many years until I freed him and adopted him, and the fact that he was now a citizen himself had given him no false ideas of dignity. Indeed, he had seen me working on the roof and come on purpose to see if he could help, and he seemed positively flattered to be put in charge, so I left him to it. I quickly rinsed my face and hands, and (with Maximus's help) changed my dusty tunic and put my toga on. Then – accompanied by the returning messenger – I set off with my servant to see His Excellence.

I was glad to be relieved of thatching, which was cold and tiring work, and was gleefully expecting to be welcomed to the house and provided with some delicious dates or cheese and wine. However, when we reached the villa, it was not to be. Marcus was in the garden with his wife and child, I was told, and having left my slave sitting snugly in the servants' waiting room, I was led out to the draughty courtyard garden at the back. The day was beginning to look ill-starred after all.

Marcus was sitting in an alcove near the apple trees, wrapped in his warmest cloak, watching fondly as his young son pushed a leather horse on wheels. When he saw me, however, his demeanour changed. He motioned his family to leave us two alone and extended a vague, ringed hand for me to kiss.

I knelt and made obeisance, as I always did, though the paving stones were chilly on my ageing knees. 'Your servant, Excellence!' I murmured, to the ring. And added, as he permitted me to rise, 'That son of yours will make a fine cavalry officer some day.' I gestured towards where the boy was toddling indoors, accompanied by his mother and the nursery slave.

But flattery, even of Marcellinus, won no smile today. My patron indicated a low stool where the nursery slave had sat and, almost before I'd squatted down on it, he was speaking urgently. 'Libertus, I have need of your advice. Voluus the lictor. You have heard of him?'

'Indeed so, Excellence.' I was taken by surprise. 'He has been the talk of the whole town.' Marcus said nothing, so after a moment I added hopefully, 'He has bought a grand apartment, so I understand. The one that wealthy tax-collector used to have. Very close to where you have your own?'

My patron, like every magistrate, had a residence in town – owning a property of a certain size is a prerequisite of many civic posts. Marcus's was large and in a sought-after spot – the whole of the first floor over a wine-shop near the forum – though he rarely used the place, as far as I could see, perhaps because the floors above it swarmed with poorer tenants, with their noise and smell. Of course, the distance to the town was not an obstacle. Unlike humbler folk like me, Marcus didn't have to walk the weary miles there and back: there would always be a gig or litter, or at least a horse, to carry him each way.

'His flat is a lot further from the forum than my own. And I hear he paid a great deal for the privilege!' Marcus snorted. 'But he's still to be virtually my neighbour in the town. A lictor, indeed. What are we coming to? You know he's holding a welcome banquet for himself? Half the town council boast that they're invited to his feast. I don't understand what the attraction is. He's not even a person of real patrician rank, only a freeborn citizen of Gaul. He must think himself important because his master was. Well, we've never felt the need for such officials here.'

'I believe your friend the Governor Pertinax had lictors, Excellence,' I ventured doubtfully. It was never wise to contradict my patron in this way, but if I failed to remind him of some salient point he was inclined to blame me afterwards.

However, I was relatively safe. All his irritation was for Voluus today. 'Pertinax? Of course he had lictors – eight of them, in fact, the whole time that he was governor of Britannia. But for ceremonial purposes alone – to accompany him in

public and to guard his house. Of course it is different now
he's been promoted to the Prefecture of Rome – in the capital
he has to have them all the time, even when he goes out to
the baths – but while he was here, he didn't have men in fancy
uniform dancing attendance everywhere he went, let alone
waving their rods and axes in everybody's face, just to
symbolize their powers of punishment. Certainly I never felt
the urge to make a show like that!'

I stared at him. I hadn't thought of it, but of course if anyone
was entitled to have lictors locally, it was His Excellence.
Quite junior magistrates in other places had them, so I'd heard,
simply as a token that they held *imperium*, which meant officially the right to read omens in the birds, but in practice the
power to summon soldiery. However, Marcus, despite his rank,
had nothing of the kind, even when travelling outside of the
town. His escort was more generally composed of hulking
men in tunics, armed with clubs and swords, which might not
have the pomp of a lictorial guard, but was just as effective
at expressing power and possibly better as protection on the
local roads. Bears and wolves are not impressed by ceremonial
symbols of success. I ventured to murmur something of the
kind.

That amused him. He very nearly smiled. 'Indeed. But I
did not bring you here to talk about my guard. The problem
which disturbs me is this Voluus. If he were simply an ex-lictor,
that would be one thing. One could just ignore him as a self-
advertising citizen of no especial high-born rank. But this man
clearly is immensely rich – and he has invited half of Glevum
to his welcome feast. The question is, should I attend or not?'

I gave an inward sigh. If my patron was just fretting about
whether to accept it seemed a trivial matter and I was keen
to get inside. I did not have the benefit of a woollen cloak,
and this brisk March wind chilled me to my bones. 'What
about the other important citizens? What are they going to
do?' I asked in a bright tone.

Marcus looked down his Roman nose at me. 'The other
magistrates and councillors will take their lead from me,' he
said, with some impatience. 'Several of them have sent to ask
what I intend to do.'

Naturally! I should have worked that out myself. I tried to make amends. 'Then surely you may follow your own impulses on this? If he has no status does it matter if he's rich? Simple wealth is not the sole criterion of rank. The tax-collector who lived in that apartment till last year was never quite accepted in polite society, though he got to be immensely wealthy in the end. Surely it is more a question of where the money's from?'

Marcus beamed at me. 'Exactly, my old friend. Where does Voluus get his fortune from? A lictor gets a reasonable salary, of course, but the amount is fixed. It is a respectable amount, but nothing that would give him riches on the scale he seems to have.'

I shifted on my stool. 'Perhaps he inherited from a relative?'

Marcus shook his head. 'I can't discover links with any major family. It's hardly likely either. No member of a really rich patrician tribe would take a lictor's post. The position was originally intended for the plebs, and even now is generally reserved for simple freemen citizens – though there are a few exceptions in the Senate, I'm aware, with people representing different clans in Rome. But Voluus was never one of those. He was simply a guard and torturer for a Provincial governor.'

He seemed genuinely to want solutions, so I cast about for some. 'People might have paid him to reduce their punishment, perhaps?' I said, and knew by my patron's sigh that this was foolishness. 'Or his master may have given him some sort of parting gift?'

'Both those things are more than likely true – but cart-loads of treasure? Come, Libertus, we are talking of huge sums! He's rumoured to be nearly as wealthy as I am myself. So how does that occur? I suspect that he has important friends somewhere – who either left him lots of money for some service in the past, or are paying him handsomely to hush up what he knows.' He looked hard at me. 'He could even be a spy who serves the Emperor.'

That was a thought more chilling than the day. 'You think so?' I said.

Marcus nodded. 'And that is just the point. If he does turn

out to have influence at court, it might be most imprudent to insult the man. And that's where you come in.'

'Me, Excellence?' Matters had taken an unpleasant turn. I was so startled that I almost jumped up from my perch. 'But what could it possibly have to do with me? I have not been invited to the feast.'

'Of course not, Libertus.' He was jovial now. 'You're not a councillor. Your own fault, of course, since you evaded my attempts to have you voted on to the *curia*, as I hoped to do last year. But that turns out to be very fortunate. Voluus will have never so much as heard your name, so that means that you can do this and he won't suspect the link.'

'Do what, exactly, Excellence?' I was beginning to think that the Ides of March were every bit as nefas as they were said to be.

'I want you to call at this apartment he has bought, and offer to lay a pavement there before he comes. I hear that the steward is already living there, making arrangements before his master arrives. I'll write a letter recommending you. That way you can get into the house and see if you can find out where Voluus got his wealth. The steward is obviously in his confidence.'

I goggled at him. 'Excellence! Rumour says the lictor will be here himself within a day or two.' At that time I hadn't heard about the marble floors, of course, so I just said lamely, 'How could I make a pavement in so short a time?'

He waved the objection loftily away. 'Oh, I know you have those pattern samples ready-made and fixed on linen backing to show your customers. You can use one of those. Offer to do the ante-room or something of the kind, a small one you could finish in a day or two. I realize that it's very likely they will turn you down, but if you have my letter they will have to let you in and that will give you the opportunity to talk to the steward. He's the one responsible for seeing that the lictor's treasure – when it comes – is taken off the cart, so he'll know exactly what it is and what it's worth. He may even have witnessed how it was acquired and what favours it is – or was – intended to repay. If so,' he smiled, 'I'm sure you'll manage to get it out of him. I know you, Libertus – you are skilled at

things like that. I am quite certain I can rely on you. Come!'
He got to his feet and began to lead the way back to the villa
door, motioning me to follow.

I rose stiffly to my feet. At least I had the prospect of going
inside where it was warm – all the main rooms in the villa
had a hypocaust – but all the same . . . I hurried after him.
'Excellence . . .' I stammered, still hoping to dissuade him
from this wild idea.

He had reached the atrium by now and held up his hand to
silence me. 'I have the letter on a writing-tablet, ready scratched
and sealed. I'll have my page-boy fetch it and you can take
it now. Then you can call there tomorrow – in the morning,
preferably – and report to me by dark. If you have other clients
I fear they'll have to wait. I need to have results as soon as
possible.' He gestured to a servant who was lurking by the
door. 'Bring this citizen the writing-tablet which is on my
desk.'

The slave-boy hurried to obey and Marcus turned, smiling,
to me.

'Well, now that is settled I won't keep you any more. I'll
send your slave to you and you can go. We are expecting
house guests later on – the chief Decurion from Corinium and
his wife – and I've no doubt you have other projects to fill a
day like this. Come to me tomorrow evening and tell me what
you've learnt, and then I can decide what I should do about
this feast.'

At least when I got home they had done the dye-house roof
– but the prospect of this errand clouded the rest of the day.

However, there was no arguing with Marcus, so this morning
I'd spent hours asking questions round the town – though to
not much effect (apart from my brief conversation with my
informant about the quality of decoration in the lictor's flat)
– and now I was hurrying to get there before noon. Judging
by the shadows there was little time before the midday trumpet
sounded, but at last I found the place. There was a row of
coppersmiths along the lower floors and I hastened to the side
entrance which would take me up the stairs.

I was dressed in just a tunic and a cloak against the rain
– a toga was hardly fitting for an interview like this and besides

would have made me too conspicuous – so my presence roused scant interest as I went inside. Lots of folk in tunics came and went round here – the whole top floor was crammed with little one-roomed flats, and the stairwell was noisy and crowded at every time of day. The whole area smelt strongly of unwashed humanity and echoed with the sounds of commerce from the street – in particular the hammering of the coppersmiths.

There were disadvantages to being dressed for trade. No one made way for me. Two girls with water-bottles on their heads blocked my path as they went giggling to the public fountain in the square. A bunch of children darted through my legs, carrying what looked like handfuls of kindling for a fire and there was a haze of smoke, although on the upper floors no brazier or cooking was officially allowed – there were no kitchen areas or chimney-vents up there, and some of the cramped apartments had no window-space. However, if there was conflagration it was not my affair. Perhaps the strong smell of greasy cooking really came from the hot-food *thermopolium* down the street, where the soup was dreadful but was cheap and warm.

A bent old woman struggled past me carrying a sack (half-rotting vegetables from the smell of it) and was sworn at by a group of fellows playing dice-games in the gloom. They glanced up as I stepped over them on to the landing space. The noises from below were almost deafening, but I was about to shout and ask them if this was the lictor's place when the apartment door in front of me burst open suddenly and a man in steward's uniform came out.

He was a stout man with a balding head and a protruding gut, but he had shoulders like a wrestler under the dark red tunic, and he was looking none too pleased. 'You!' he hollered, raising his voice above the din.

I was surprised to realize that this was addressed to me. I edged towards him.

'I saw you from the window-space as you were coming in,' he said, when I was close enough to hear. 'Have you brought a message?'

'I do bring a letter,' I blurted, wondering how he knew.

'Well, thank the gods for that. You'd better come inside.'

He stood back to let me enter and closed the heavy door again. The hammering and shouting was a great deal fainter now and someone had been burning scented oils to mask the smells. 'Well?' he said impatiently, 'what message do you bring?'

I looked around the room. It was a stately ante-room and all the rumours about marble floors were clearly true. I felt myself turn pale. 'His Excellence, my patron Marcus Septimus Aurelius, instructed me to call. He has sent a message recommending me.' I handed the writing-tablet to the steward as I spoke.

The man nodded gravely as he undid the seal. 'I have heard of him. The senior local magistrate. It is kind of him to send. How did he hear the news?'

'News?' I was naturally mystified. 'He thought your master might require a pavement – that is all. He merely wished to help. But I see that you . . .' The man was scowling and I was already attempting a retreat.

'A pavement?' The steward sounded quite incredulous. 'We don't need a pavement; we need help to find the thieves!'

'Thieves?' I could see that he regretted blurting out the word, so I urged gently, 'You had better tell me. I can pass the message on. That way at least you have reported it.'

The steward looked furious, but at last he shrugged. 'I've already reported it to the local garrison. I thought you'd come from there. But I suppose it is no secret and I might as well tell you, in case the patron that you speak of may be able to assist. The last of my master's carts has failed to arrive. The one on which he's placed his greatest treasures, too. It was due to come last evening but there was no sign of it. We thought it was delayed. But word has just reached us, not half an hour ago, that the vehicle has been discovered on the road outside the town, with the driver hacked to pieces and all the contents gone.'

'Great Jupiter!' I muttered. 'Was there not a guard?'

'Four of them, armed and mounted – all now lying dead. The horses have been disembowelled, too.' He gave a bitter laugh. 'So it is a matter for Great Jupiter indeed. We shall have need of Jupiter when Voluus hears of this.' He glanced at the writing-tablet in his hand and thrust it back at me. 'So you go and tell your patron that if he really wants to help he won't send me stupid pavement-makers, desperate for work; he will send me someone to help us find the thieves. A contingent of the local soldiery, perhaps, or a few of the town watch. Presumably he has sufficient authority for that?'

TWO

I t was clear that he expected me to go. Presumably he intended that I'd hurry off and report to my patron straight away. But I could not return to Marcus without at least a small attempt to fulfil the task he had given me. Besides, the steward had deliberately insulted both of us and I was not going to let him get away with that. I was only in a tunic and a woollen cloak, and I suppose that physically I look every inch a Celt, so the steward could not know that I was a Roman citizen. Describing me as a 'stupid pavement-maker desperate for work' was merely impolite. But disparaging my patron was a different thing – and might even be a trap. If this really was a house of Imperial spies, as Marcus seemed to think, any failure to defend my patron's name (as any protégé is duty-bound to do) might someday reach his ears.

So I said slowly, and with what dignity I could muster, 'You doubt that Marcus has authority? Then you don't know my master.'

The round face flushed beneath the swarthy skin. 'And you clearly don't know mine. He will make more trouble for this colonia than you can dream of, pavement-maker. He will have it howled throughout the Empire that he was robbed in Glevum before he even came. And he will demand the full rigour of the law. There will be crucifixions here before this business ends – you tell your patron that.' He pulled the door open and motioned me to leave.

But I had seen the fear behind the blustering. I did not move a thumb-span. 'And you will be lucky if you're not one of them?' I said, loudly enough for anyone on the stairs outside to hear. I knew it was a risk – the steward might have given me a push or called for other servants to remove me bodily, but we both were in full view and I was gambling that he would not wish to make a public scene. Gossip in Glevum spreads quicker than a fire, and the dice players on the staircase had already stopped to stare.

I saw them nudge each other and the steward saw them, too. He flashed an angry look at me and shut the door again – with me still inside the ante-room.

'Now, look here, pavement-maker.' He muscled up to me. 'What are you playing at? Deliberately talking so half the town can hear!'

I looked at him. 'Nothing I said would mean a thing to anyone out there.'

That was likely to be true, as he must have realized, but he wasn't mollified. He hissed into my face, 'Just wait until Voluus arrives and hears of this. They may not have understood what you were saying, but I did. You were suggesting that I might be to blame.'

I stood my ground. 'I did nothing of the sort. I did not say you were to blame – I said that you would be lucky to escape this with your life. You think so, too – I can see it in your face. I was once a slave myself and I know what it's like. When the owner is away and there is trouble in the house, don't the masters always blame the steward first?'

The florid face was ashen all at once. 'You think so?'

I had clearly got past his defences now. The haughtiness had gone. If I could find a way to rattle him again, I might persuade him to confide in me. I said matter-of-factly, 'But of course. Who else would know the details of the cart – what was on it and when it would arrive? Somebody must have planned to seize it on the road. That cart in particular – out of all the rest – when in fact it carried the most valuable load? You can't believe that was coincidence? And it had to be someone in the area, who had already found a place to hide the loot – someone with sufficient natural authority to enlist a group of thieves, and sufficient money to buy their loyalty. I imagine you have saved a good deal from your *pecunium*. If you were Voluus, who would you suspect?'

He leaned on one of the alabaster pillars as if he needed its support and stared goggle-eyed at me. 'But he must see that that would be preposterous! I have hardly set foot outside of this apartment since we came.' He was pressing his hands together under his gold-edged sleeves, so hard that his knuckles showed white against his dark red tunic cloth, but all at once he lifted his bald head defiantly. 'There are two other slaves here who are witnesses to that.'

'And will Voluus believe them?' I saw him flinch as if I'd flicked him with a whip. 'Will they even tell the truth? Do they have cause to love you?'

He lifted his linked hands to the slave-chain round his neck, but he could not hide the nervous bobbing of his throat. 'I don't suppose they do. My master bought them just before he left again for Gaul and instructed me to lick them into shape. I suppose I might have been a bit severe with them from time to time.' He spread his hands despairingly and looked into my face. 'But you don't think . . . ?'

I simply raised my eyebrows and pursed my lips a bit. 'Voluus is a professional torturer – or he was. I don't imagine that he'll simply ask them politely what they know. Under those circumstances, who knows what they might say?'

The steward was staring at the middle distance now. 'I saw him asking questions of a page-boy once, accused of stealing a *denarius*. The boy insisted he was innocent, but after half an hour . . .' He broke off, shuddering. A little bead of sweat was running down his brow and he was obliged to mop it with his sleeve. 'You're right. He would have confessed to anything.'

'So you see what I mean. I imagine he admitted to the theft – although stealing from one's master is a capital offence.'

He nodded dolefuly.

'And did he really take the money?'

An uncomfortable pause. 'Who can say? He was executed for it; that is all I know.' From his manner I guessed I'd touched a nerve.

I pressed the point a bit. 'And Voluus no doubt felt that justice had been done?'

He moved away and began to fiddle with a pretty quartz vase on a plinth nearby – though it had been placed to perfection as it was. There was a long moment before he answered me. 'Voluus was delighted with himself for forcing a confession, as one might expect from a man in his position. He had me fetch the entire household to watch the questioning – I suppose as a sort of dreadful warning to the rest of us.'

I came up behind him to say, briskly but not unkindly, 'Look, whatever-your-name is, I don't wish to pry . . .'

He turned and met my eyes. His own were dull with strain. 'My master calls me Calvinus,' he said.

I tried not to smile. The name means 'Baldy' and it suited him, but the fact that he had vouchsafed it at all was an indication that I won his confidence. 'Well, Calvinus, if your master is the sort of man you say he is, you can surely see what this unfortunate event could mean for you? Losing the cart and everything it held. You have my sympathy.'

He left the quartz vase roughly balanced in its place and turned to me with a gesture of despair. 'I wrote and told him not to move it on the Ides! But he took no notice – just replied that it would be cheaper then, since the roads were quieter and he would not have to hire the escort for so long. And now look what has happened! And – no doubt you're right – he'll blame it all on me. So what am I to do? I've sent a message to the guard-house, as I say, though I doubt that will help. The wretches who did this will have disappeared into the forest long ago. But what else is there, except to run away?' He gave a bitter laugh. 'Though from what you've said, I'm tempted to wonder about that.'

'And risk certain execution if they catch up with you?'

'You don't have to warn me about that, pavement-maker. Since I have served the lictor, I don't know how many fugitive slaves I have seen condemned to death. They always give the maximum penalty for runaways in Gaul. The courts round here are no different, I suppose?' He watched me shake my head. 'So all I can do is wait here till my master comes and hope that Jove affords me some kind of miracle. Like the thieves confessing of their own accord, though I don't imagine there is much chance of that.'

I shook my head. 'I think His Excellence my patron is your only hope. He has great authority in Glevum – as I said before – and could certainly call upon the garrison to help. If he can find the people who really stole the goods, then you would be spared any . . . questioning, did you call it? . . . when Voluus arrives. Indeed, you might even earn your master's gratitude. I am due to call on Marcus later today. So hadn't you better tell me everything you know?'

Calvinus looked around as if the walls were listening and, after a moment, moved into a corner of the ante-room, gesturing me to follow. 'What else is it that you need to understand?' he murmured grudgingly. 'I can't tell you very much. We lost a confounded treasure-cart, that's all.'

'Do you know what was on it?'

'Not in detail. I'll see the manifest when it arrives. Statues, gold and silverware, and jewellery, I think. Part of his new wife's dowry. I didn't see it packed.'

'Voluus is to marry?' That was a surprise.

'He's already done so, townsman. Shortly before he came to Britannia last time. Doubtless one of the reasons he hurried back to Gaul. And I understand there's now a child as well. He'll be delighted. He has no other family to carry on the line and he told me on his wedding day that if she didn't turn out to be fertile he'd look for a divorce. Though I'm not so sure of that. Pretty young lady, from what I saw of her.'

'A young lady?' I was even more surprised. I had been imagining some wealthy widow with a large estate.

'Well, not so very young. Rising twenty, so I understand.' For the first time in this interview he actually grinned. His teeth were stained and crooked, and the effect was less a smile than a hideous grimace. 'A good deal younger than Voluus, of course. He is over forty and as ugly as a goat. I don't know that she was really eager for the match, but her family were concerned that she would never find a groom. She was 'betrothed' before, at least in her own mind, to some auxiliary cavalryman in the army, I believe. Antoninus . . . Anteolus . . . ? Something of the kind. Most unsuitable. Not even a proper citizen until he earned the rank on discharge, and being a soldier he couldn't legally be married until then – although she swore that she would wait. Well, of course her family refused to sanction that, but fortunately the fellow was posted overseas and died of wounds soon afterwards, so that disposed of that. Her brother was very anxious to find someone else for her while she was still remotely of marriageable age.'

'Her brother?' I echoed. That was a surprise. 'Doesn't her father have the *potestas* over her?'

The bald man shook his head. 'Her father died a little while ago and her brother's been her guardian ever since, I understand, though I'm not sure that he relished the responsibility. She was a late child, and the only girl besides – and very much the father's favourite, judging by the portion which she inherited. But of course her eldest brother had to bring her up – in his own household and at his own expense. Not an easy task, it seems, as she was spirited.'

'Was she indeed? And Voluus didn't mind?' I was surprised again. A Roman wife is expected to be obedient.

Calvinus shook his head. 'Voluus was keen enough to marry her. She's attractive, as I said – but even more attractive was the dowry that she brought. I didn't oversee the packing of that cart, but I know that it carried most of her inheritance. The loss will infuriate my master even more, of course.'

I sent up a mental prayer of thanks to all the gods there were. Here was something to tell Marcus, anyway. Calvinus had answered several questions that I could not ask outright and it had been much easier than I had any right to hope. 'So that is where the lictor got his wealth?' I murmured, satisfied.

The steward looked at me as though the moon had turned my wits. 'Of course not, pavement-maker. Voluus obviously had considerable wealth before he ever wed even if, as lictor, it wasn't evident. Why else do you suppose Alcanta's brother was so keen? In fact . . .' He got no further. Someone was thundering up the stairs outside, shaking the floorboards, and the quartz vase, which obviously had not been securely placed, toppled from its plinth and smashed into a dozen fragments on the floor. The crash was deafening.

Calvinus moved towards it, but before he reached the spot the inner door flew open and a pair of slaves appeared: a skinny boy – scarcely out of childhood, by the look of him – and a plump wench, a little older, with plaited auburn hair. Both wore short tunics of a matching blue. They looked from the steward to the broken bits of quartz. Their consternation was almost palpable.

'Don't beat him, Calvinus, he put it safe, I swear . . .' The girl began to beg, half-sheltering the lad behind her as she spoke.

You could almost see temptation cross the steward's mind. It would be very easy for him to shift the blame and punish the slave-boy for the breakage which he had caused himself. I did not wish to be a party to anything like that.

'I am your witness to the fact that this was not the slave-boy's fault,' I said. 'It was an accident – occasioned by someone outside on the stairs, running so roughly so that he rocked the floor.'

The two young servants looked at me with gratitude, but Calvinus frowned. 'Does that give you two freedom to come bursting in when you had orders to remain elsewhere?'

He was still looking dangerous and the boy broke in. 'Forgive us, Calvinus . . .' he muttered abjectly. 'Of course we did not mean to interrupt. We heard a crash and we hurried here to see what might have caused it and if it was our fault. We did not realize that you still had a visitor.'

'A visitor?' The steward shot a sideways look at me. 'This man is hardly that. He is simply a pavement-maker who was good enough to call. But our business is concluded and he is about to leave. Brianus, you may show him to the door. Pronta, fetch a broom and tidy up this mess and find another vase to take its place. You will find some in the boxes we unpacked yesterday.' He turned to me and gave a little bow. 'Thank you for your visit, townsman. I shall expect to hear – and please thank your patron for me in advance.'

'This way, sir.' The slave-boy sidled past me and held the door ajar. And this time there was nothing I could do but leave.

THREE

I t was raining heavily as I wove my way back down the crowded stairs and hurried back towards my workshop in the swampy northern suburb just outside the walls. But I could not dismiss that meeting with the steward from my mind. The more I thought about it, the more I started wondering if those two younger slaves, Brianus and Pronta, actually knew about the fatal robbery from their master's cart. As soon as they appeared Calvinus had seemed oddly anxious to get rid of me and he'd scrupulously avoided any mention of the theft while they were in the room.

I shook the water from my eyes. No doubt I was making mysteries where there were none. Wasn't it only natural that he'd wanted me to leave, given the topic of our conversation a moment earlier? Openly discussing his master's private life – and with a stranger, too – was not acceptable behaviour for a slave of any kind, especially a senior steward in a trusted role. No doubt he was afraid that I'd say something indiscreet in front of the young slaves. One did not have to wonder how Voluus would react if, by any chance, he came to learn of our exchange.

Would the others have betrayed him to their master, then, if I had given them the opportunity? It was more than possible: Calvinus ran that household on fear, not loyalty. Clearly he was convinced that they were spying all the time: he'd taken good care to move out of their potential earshot while we talked. Well, I thought, he need have no fear of me. The last thing that I wanted was for Voluus to learn that I'd been impertinently asking questions of his senior slave: the lictor was powerful enough to make life difficult, even for a citizen tradesman like myself. As to what he'd do to a member of his staff . . . !

No wonder that Calvinus had taken fright and hustled me away. It was simply unfortunate that it had happened when it did – just when he'd seemed about to tell me something more about where Voluus got his wealth! As it was I had very little to report to Marcus on the subject when I saw him later on.

However, there was no help for it and it was too late now. Besides, there was a mosaic waiting to be finished in my shop. Marcus might think that my customers would wait, but I knew otherwise. The present commission was for a wealthy councillor, who would certainly expect his pavement to be laid on time, or I'd find myself subject to a heavy financial penalty. The man was famous for imposing them, if any contract was not scrupulously met. I pulled my hood more firmly round my ears and turned my attention to struggling on against the rain.

It required attention, too, since I had passed the northern gate and was into the sprawling suburb where I plied my trade. The roadways were not paved Roman ones like those within the town: here they were rutted, and treacherous with mud. Even when keeping to the pavements at the side I was forced to pick my way with care. If I slipped and broke a leg I could be there for hours – I was almost the only person on the streets.

Businesses were open – you could smell the tannery and there was cheerful sawing and hammering from the carpenter's – but there were virtually no pedestrians about. Even the keepers of the little shops, who generally looked out across their open counters to the street, had retreated to the gloomy rooms within and had either half-closed the shutters to keep out the rain, or had moved their goods indoors entirely, so only the hanging signs gave any clue as to what might be on sale. There were, in any case, no customers today. Only a straggling donkey-cart squelched by, with its drenched driver huddled down behind the reins, and a solitary vendor with a tray of sorry pies, sheltered in a doorway against the driving rain.

I would be glad to be inside myself, beside a warming fire – and was cheered to realize that it would not be long: I was almost at my destination now. I could already see the stockpiles of ready-sorted stone glistening wetly just outside my door. I clutched my cloak around my soaking knees and began to hurry the final block or two, just as my son Junio came darting

out of doors, holding a leather apron like a hood above his
head. He didn't look in my direction, simply bent down by
each heap and hastily collected several colours in a bag. No
doubt he needed extra pieces to complete the little pavement
that we were working on.

He raised his head and saw me, waved and scuttled back
inside. I was about to hasten after him when a soft tug on my
clothing made me whirl around. With the insistent patter of
the rain and the squelching of my feet, I had not heard anyone
approach, but I found a small, drenched, hooded figure standing
at my heels.

'Citizen pavement-maker,' this apparition said, its voice so
tentative that it was almost whispering. When I didn't answer,
it added nervously, 'You are a citizen, I think? That is what
they told me in the m-m-market-place. I would not wish to
show you disrespect.' The speaker pushed the cape back from
his face and I recognized the skinny boy from Voluus's
apartment.

'Brianus?' I said doubtfully. I hadn't noticed the stammer
earlier.

'You r-recall my name?' The thin cheeks flushed with
pleasure.

I nodded. 'But of course. I saw you only half an hour ago.'
I frowned. 'What brings you over here? Did Calvinus send
you?'

He nodded. He was a pathetic little figure – even younger
than I'd thought – and his legs beneath the cape were thinner
than a stork's. Hardly more than ten or twelve years old, I
guessed. He looked up at me speechlessly, from somewhere
in the region of my chest.

Naturally the steward must have sent him, I thought; otherwise the boy would not have dared to leave the house. 'How
did he discover where to look for me?'

The boy looked terrified, but he managed to reply. 'He told
me to ask around in the m-m-market-place and find out where
you l-l-lived.'

'But you managed to hurry fast enough to catch me on the
way?'

Another nod. 'I have a m-m-message for you.' Rain was

streaming down his face unchecked and his fairish hair was plastered to his head.

'Come into my workshop and give it to me there,' I suggested, with a smile. 'Perhaps we could let you dry off by the fire.'

'Oh, I c-c-couldn't do that, citizen. That would take too long. Calvinus will . . .' He stopped in confusion, and trailed off helplessly.

'Flog you?' I finished.

He didn't answer but I saw that I was right.

'Very well then, give me the message if you must,' I said. 'But be very quick. I'm getting soaked out here.'

'It's quite a short m-m-message and I have learned it off by heart.' He took a deep breath and went on – quite loudly and in a peculiarly artificial tone, as though he were a herald at the basilica: '"J-j-just after you left, we had a messenger to s-s-say that master reached B-B-Britannia a day or two ago, together with his wife and slaves and the r-r-remainder of his goods. He has found a ship's c-c-captain who will bring them round by sea, and they should be here in less than half a m-m-moon. He himself has taken horse, and sends word that he's already on his w-w-way."' He raised his streaming face to me again and added in a more normal tone of voice, 'That was the m-m-message. And I'm to add that, "the m-m-master doesn't know what happened yet, and this m-m-makes things urgent." Calvinus says that you will understand.'

I nodded. It was becoming obvious that my surmise was right and Calvinus had not told the other slaves about the theft. 'I understand,' I said. In the circumstances, I rather wished that I did not. What did the steward expect that I could do?

'Is there a reply, ci-ci-citizen?' It was not a stammer, I realized suddenly. The boy was shivering.

I looked down at him and felt a wave of sympathy. The lad was undernourished and soaked through to the skin and too afraid of punishment to come and dry himself – as any other slave would certainly have done – at once. I made a quick decision. 'Indeed there is an answer, but I will have to write it down. Come to my workshop and I will see to it.'

If he saw through my little ruse he gave no sign of it. He

bowed. 'In that c-c-case, citizen, you had b-b-better lead
the way.' I had forgotten that he did not really know where
we were going. I hurried the few remaining paces to where the
workshop was. The street door was half-open, and I motioned
him inside, but Brianus was too timid to precede a citizen so
in the end I led the way myself – through the front area where
the counter was, round the partition wall, and so into the inner
room beyond. A fug of smoky warmth enveloped us.

I looked gratefully around the room. A cheerful fire was
burning in the chimney-place and gangly Minimus – the second
of my little red-haired slaves – was warming something in a
small pan over it, while Junio was busy with a pattern on the
floor. It was a pleasant scene of humble industry and there
was a welcome smell of oatcakes, pies and newly spiced hot
mead.

Minimus saw me first. 'Master!' he cried, scrambling to his
feet. 'Come in and dry yourself.' He hurried over to take my
cloak from me. 'We saw you coming. What kept you so long
outside in the rain?'

I indicated Brianus, who was hanging back against the wall.
'This slave has been sent after me from Voluus's residence
with an urgent message,' I replied. 'He's awaiting my reply.
In the meantime, take his cloak. He's dripping on the floor.'
I winked at Junio, who had sat back on his heels and was
watching this exchange with amusement on his face.

He saw the wink, nodded, and went back to his work –
saying over his shoulder, 'See to it, Minimus. Hang it on that
nail there on the chimney-piece. We don't want water falling
on the tiles.'

Brianus looked doubtful but he slipped his garment off and
allowed Minimus to hang it, with mine, above the fire, where
it began to give off wisps of steam and odours of wet wool.

My own slave turned to me. 'Master, won't you take refreshment first? I am just preparing some of your favourite drink.
The young master sent me out especially to get the mead. And
we've left you a portion of hot pie and some of the oatcakes
that the mistress made for us. You must be hungry – you have
not eaten anything for hours. Or were you given something
at the lictor's residence?' He looked enquiringly at Brianus.

I shook my head. I'd had nothing since I left the roundhouse at first light. 'I would be glad to eat. But I'll do that in a moment, when I have dealt with this. First, can you find a writing-tablet from the upper room?' I indicated the steep ladder that led up to the attics in the roof.

Minimus looked startled. 'But master,' he began, 'you already have one. It's hanging at your belt . . .'

'That one belongs to Marcus, not to me,' I told him firmly, removing it and putting it aside. 'I cannot use my patron's writing-block. But I'm sure there's one upstairs that I once rescued from a midden-heap. I think the hinge is missing, but we can tie it shut. I'm sure you can find a stylus – or something that will do – and there's a pot of wax somewhere that I can use to seal the ribbon with.'

Minimus was still havering at the ladder's foot. I rarely sent him up into the upper room. The area had been damaged in a fire and, being draughty, leaky and unlit, was mostly used for storage nowadays, and then only of items which we rarely used. Before I married Gwellia those rooms had been my home but, unlike most of my tradesman neighbours hereabouts, I no longer lived above the shop – I had moved to my cosy roundhouse in the woods. It made for a walk of several hours a day, but I'd got used to that.

I turned to find Brianus goggling at me, clearly astonished that my slave would question my orders and not act at once. It made me speak a little sharply as I said to Minimus, 'Now do as I request, and quickly, too!'

'Can I take a candle?' I realized that Minimus was genuinely alarmed. He did not like the ladder – not since I once found a dead body lying at its foot – and was not used to being sent upstairs where there were certainly spiders hiding in the gloom, and very likely rats.

'Take one of those by all means,' I said more cheerfully, indicating the bunch of tallow tapers that I kept hanging on the wall. 'But you'll hardly need a light. I'm almost sure the writing-tablet's in the first box that you see, just beside the opening where the ladder comes. You could find it in the daylight that comes in from the roof.'

Minimus was still looking unconvinced but he took a taper

and lit it at the fire, then – holding it above his head like someone entering a house of ghosts – began to climb the rungs. There was a moment's thumping when he reached the top, and then he reappeared, brandishing the writing-block triumphantly. He blew out the candle, held it in his teeth, and came quickly backwards down the ladder, keeping his balance with his one free hand.

He handed me the writing-tablet and removed the homemade taper from his mouth with a grimace (it was made of goose tallow and no doubt tasted foul). 'I hope this is what you wanted, master?' he said. 'It was the only one that I could see but the wax is so old and fragile that it might be hard to use. And I found a stylus with it, though that's seen better days as well.' He produced the metal scratch-pen from inside his tunic folds.

'That will do very nicely,' I told him, with a smile. 'Though you are right about the wax. It has got damaged in the damp. We shall have to let it warm up for a minute by the fire. In the meantime, this young slave and I will do the same.' Minimus was about to speak again but my look silenced him. 'So I'll have a little of that food and warm drink while I wait. And you can give a crust of oatcake and some watered mead to this young fellow here – I want him to run the whole way home to take my letter back, and he looks as if he needs a little sustenance.'

Brianus, who had almost stopped shivering by now and had been watching us wide-eyed, began to make a protest but I waved his words aside.

'Brianus, I give the orders in this house, and I am instructing you to have a drink and half an oatcake. Is that understood? I don't want you fainting with cold and hunger in the town when you are carrying my confidential correspondence through the streets – anyone might get their hands on it. Now do as you are told while I compose this note.'

It was the second time that I had spoken sharply and Minimus looked abashed. I do not often speak so brusquely to slaves, and he looked chagrined as he went about his tasks. I've never had a meal served to me with more promptitude and I was soon clutching a warm and welcome cup of mead. I took a sip

of it. 'The boy will be embarrassed to eat in here with me –
which is no more than proper, since I'm the master here – so
Minimus, you can show him into the outer room.'

Brianus stammered, blushing. 'Citizen pavement-maker, you
are very good . . .'

I held a hand up to prevent him saying any more. 'On second
thoughts, Minimus, you'd better stay with him – make sure
he doesn't take fright and run away.'

Minimus looked astonished but he said nothing more. He
did as he was told and hustled Brianus away, round the partition, with his humble snack.

FOUR

J unio had been working in silence all this time but when the slaves had gone he scrambled to his feet and came to stand beside me. 'You guessed that the slave-boy would decline to eat unless you actually commanded him?' he murmured, too softly for the lads in the outer room to hear.

I nodded, my mouth too full of oatcake to reply. But it was true. I'd had the same problem with my wife when we were first reunited after years apart – she had been so long in servitude that she was unwilling to eat anything in my presence. Of course she always shared my table now, and very often the slave-boys ate in the same room as well, especially in the shop. I took a sip of mead. 'Besides,' I said, 'I want to gain his confidence. Bringing him to the workshop was only an excuse. I want to find out what – if anything – he knows about his master, Voluus.'

'You did not succeed in discovering anything while you were at the apartment?'

'On the contrary,' I said, 'there is alarming news. But not exactly what I set out to learn.' I told him briefly about the missing cart and what I had learned about the lictor's wealthy bride.

Junio whistled softly. 'Dear Jupiter! A murdered escort and a robbery. There's certain to be a lot of trouble, then. I hope it didn't happen anywhere near us. I would not care to be a suspect with a lictor in the case and no doubt suspicion will fall on everyone within a dozen miles.'

I hadn't thought of that – it was not a pleasant idea. 'I'm going to see Marcus later on tonight and I'll ask him to get the local garrison to look into it and try to find out who was responsible. It may have been just brigands who struck a lucky cart – but there hasn't been any banditry on that road for several moons, and I find it difficult to credit that it was merely chance.'

Junio frowned. 'More likely someone who knew the value of what was on the cart. Could it be the steward, do you think?'

'I didn't think so, from his manner. He seemed really shocked, though it had clearly occurred to him he might be held to blame. And now he's just had word that his master is only days away.'

'Dear Mercury! I should not care to be the steward, in that case. Or is this Voluus not the savage man that we are inclined to think?'

'It seems he's even worse.' I told him the story of the tortured page. 'But that's one of the things I wanted to check with Brianus. And the two of them have met. I understand the lictor personally bought him at the slave-market.'

Junio grinned. 'Well, if you meant to gain the slave-boy's confidence, you've certainly done that. I rather suspect he'd walk on burning coals for you. You should have seen him eyeing that little piece of cake. You'd think he hadn't seen a proper meal in days.'

'It's possible he hasn't,' I said soberly. 'I think the steward at the house mistreats him dreadfully – though there can't be any shortage of nutrition in the house.'

My adopted son gave my arm a gentle squeeze. 'Not everyone has masters as kindly as my own.'

That was an unexpected compliment – he had been my servant before I set him free – but it was not the sort of thing he often said. The moment might have been embarrassing, but he turned away and began to search for something on the shelf. 'You will want that pot of sealing-wax. I know I've seen it here. You had it when you were sealing that bill for the councillor the other day. Ah, here it is.' He brought down the little jar and bent down to set it on the trivet by the fire, where it would soften in the heat.

I had eaten every crumb of cake by now so I turned my attention to the writing-block. I did not often use a folding wax-tablet of this kind – most of our calculations are simply chalked on slates – but I had used such things before. I opened it out flat. The wax had melted slightly, as I'd hoped it would, and though it was badly crazed it was just usable. I smoothed out the surface as best I could, erasing the words that had been scratched on it before and, picking up the stylus, inscribed a message of my own.

Junio was still standing at my shoulder as I wrote and he read the words aloud. '"I have received your urgent message and will report developments to my patron as soon as possible. I have chosen not to send a verbal message with your slave, because I am not certain how much he should know, but I will call on you again tomorrow and let you know what Marcus says."'

He grinned. 'That is clever, Father. Giving a reason why you had to send a written note, though in fact you just wanted to get the boy in here. I know your little ways.'

'As I said, I want to find out what he knows.'

'Nothing to do with feeling sorry for the lad?'

I made a mock-rueful face. 'I'm sorry that my motives are so obvious.'

'All the same, what makes you think he'll talk to you, however much he wants to please? You can see that he's been trained in the old-fashioned Roman way: where a slave should never speak until he is spoken to, and preferably not then. He'll be far too shy and awestruck to tell you anything.'

It was my turn to grin. 'Why do you think I sent him off with Minimus?' I gestured with my head towards the outer room from where a murmuring of voices could be heard. 'A slave will often prattle to a slave. That's what I'm hoping for. But enough of that – I think they're coming now.'

Junio nodded and went back to his work, while Minimus ushered our visitor back into the room. A little food and warmth had clearly done Brianus good – there was a touch more colour in the sallow cheeks and he seemed a lot less nervous than he was before, although he still hung back against the wall.

I did not confuse him by addressing him direct, but busied myself with tying the cords around the writing-block and securing them with a little dab of heated wax. I don't have a fancy seal-ring, like patricians do, but I do possess a seal – a piece of wood with a raised iron pattern set into the end. I gestured to Brianus that he should pass me that, and – rather shyly – he stepped up to comply, while I winked at Minimus, who was sulking slightly at being overlooked.

I took the seal and pressed it on the wax across the knotted cords, so that the writing-block was securely closed despite the faulty hinge, then chalked the word 'Calvinus' on the outside of the frame. 'It is not elegant, but it will have to do,' I said. I looked up to find Voluus's slave-boy gazing at me as though I were some sort of conjurer. It occurred to me that writing might be a mystery to him: not every slave-boy in Roman households learns to read. 'Here you are!' I held it out to him. 'Make sure the steward gets it as soon as possible. Now take your cloak – I think it is a little drier now – and my slave will show you to the door.'

Brianus took the tablet and bowed himself away. A moment later we heard Minimus ushering him out.

Junio raised an eyebrow at me as he looked up from the floor. 'So much for your questioning of the boy,' he said. 'You treated him so gently, you haven't got any information out of him at all.' He frowned at a piece of pattern that did not seem to fit.

'That depends,' I told him, wiping the seal-block clean and returning the lid to the pot of sealing-wax, 'on what he might have said to Minimus.' I looked up as the boy in question came back into the room. 'And here he is. Let's ask him.'

Minimus looked from Junio to me with obvious concern. 'Have I offended, master? I didn't like to ask while Brianus was here, but you seem annoyed with me. Is it because I did not climb the ladder straight away? Or is there something that I've not done well enough? If it is about the preparation of the mead . . .'

I cut him off. 'The mead was excellent. Almost as good as Junio used to make. And you are quite mistaken, I am not annoyed at all – unless it's with myself, for failing to find out what my patron hoped to learn.'

'If my father spoke sharply,' Junio put in, 'it was for the benefit of that unfortunate young slave.' He took a piece of coloured stone and tried it in the space, first one way and then the other, before rejecting it. 'Brianus is not used to kindnesses, I think – and would not have accepted our warmth and succour otherwise.'

'Oh!' Minimus looked visibly relieved. He turned to me. 'Well, you may be right. I know that he was terrified the whole time he was here – he could not believe you'd given him a part of your own meal, but he was dreading what might happen when he gets home again. Apparently his master's left a steward in the house who beats him savagely for almost anything. Poor thing! You should have seen his back!'

'You did, I take it?' I enquired. I tried to exchange a 'told-you-so' glance with Junio but he pretended to be busy with his coloured stones.

Minimus, though, was nodding. 'He pulled down his tunic neck so that I could see. He's covered all over with blue bruises and red weals.' He glanced up sheepishly at me. 'He told me I didn't know how fortunate I was to have an owner as compassionate as you.'

'Because of a piece of oatcake and a sip or two of wine?' I laughed. 'What is special about that? Any other household would have done the same. No one sends a visiting slave away – especially the slave of a wealthy man like Voluus – without giving him something warming on a day like this.' I could see that Junio was really struggling, so I went back to join him at the mosaic as I spoke – though he'd obviously been making a good job of it so far. There was just that piece of pattern . . . I set to work on it. 'In fact, I felt quite sorry for sending you outside – it is much warmer in this inner room and he was soaked right through.'

'It wasn't only the food and drink that he was grateful for,' Minimus went on, handing me the *tesserae* that I gestured to. 'He says you saved him from a flogging earlier. Something about a vase which tumbled off its plinth? And you put in a word to say it was an accident and not his fault at all?'

'I had forgotten about that,' I said, sliding a fragment snugly into place.

'Brianus was especially impressed,' my slave said eagerly, 'not just that you spoke up on his behalf, but also that the steward took your word for it and did not even punish him when you were gone.'

'That was not entirely my doing,' I replied. I sat back on my haunches to view my handiwork. I was content with it. The space that I had left could now be filled in easily. 'There was another servant there and she defended him as well.'

'That would be Pronta – he told me about her,' Minimus

agreed. 'She does her best for him. The steward rather
fancies owning her himself, so she does not get beaten like
Brianus does. She does try to protect him, but it doesn't
always work. Sometimes her attempts to shield him only
make things worse.'

'The steward hopes to own her? I am surprised at that.' I
clambered to my feet and dusted off my hands. 'Surely she
is Voluus's slave?'

Minimus wrinked his freckled nose at me. 'Apparently the
lictor's bringing slaves with him from Gaul, including a whole
retinue belonging to the wife, so it's probable the girl will not
be needed after that. The steward thinks his master will agree
to pass her on – though at a price, of course. Apparently it's
commonplace in Gaul for the senior slaves of very wealthy
men to have servants of their own.'

'Not only in Gaul,' I told him. 'It happens here sometimes.
It's seen as a sign of status for the master, I believe.'

Minimus nodded. 'That's exactly what Brianus said, so he's
sure his owner will agree to let Calvinus have the girl. But
the boy's afraid the steward might try to buy him, too, and
then his life would be a total misery. He says it's possible.
The steward gets a small allowance from his master every
month and has been saving up for years.'

'But won't he want that money to buy his freedom with?'
Junio said, putting the last few pieces of the pattern into place.
'Isn't that more important than acquiring slaves?'

Minimus looked from Junio to me and back again. 'Oh,
Calvinus has negotiated for his freedom several times,' he
said, bursting with importance at knowing all of this. 'But
Voluus keeps demanding a more and more inflated sum,
claiming that it's the current market-price for any steward of
such experience.'

'And then he pretends it is a compliment, no doubt,' I said.
It seemed that – as well as being an expert with the lash –
Voluus had methods of being more cunningly unkind. 'But he
does allow the steward a small pecunium?'

Minimus nodded. 'And permits him to keep gratuities! But
then he fines the steward for all the breakages – like that pot
this morning – which makes it very difficult for Calvinus to

amass enough to buy himself free. But a basic slave – particularly a girl – is only a fraction of that price, so the steward could afford that as an alternative – it would give him status and she would be obliged to serve his needs, in any way he chose. He might even find enough to buy Brianus as well – though he would have to pay his master for their food and keep. The boy is sure that Calvinus is saving for something of the kind – he says they have been kept short of food and light for days, because the steward has been keeping money back out of what the lictor left to run the household with.'

Which explained why the slave-boy was so underfed, I thought. I said aloud, 'So Brianus will be relieved to know his master's on his way.'

Junio had completed the pattern by this time and, scrambling to his feet, he came to join me by the fire, rubbing his hands together to get more warmth in them. 'How will that assist? I heard that Voluus was famously severe and had a dreadful temper when aroused, though I don't know if it's true.'

'Brianus says he does,' Minimus put in. 'He witnessed it himself.'

'Well?' I murmured, to encourage him.

Minimus needed no more urging. He plunged into his story like a chariot horse let loose. 'When they were staying at the *mansio* – the official inn – there was a message for Voluus which he didn't like. He was having a meal with some patrician at the time – arranging to buy some land outside the town – but he did not seem to care that there were witnesses. He was so angry that he took a broken table leg and started hitting things. Turned an oil-lamp over, which almost set the place alight.'

'Dear Mercury,' I murmured. Fire is an ever-present threat and greatly to be feared. No wonder rumours of the lictor's temper had been rife around the town.

'And that is not the end of it,' the red-haired slave went on. 'He turned on the attendant and started beating him. There was quite a rumpus and he had to be restrained – or at least dissuaded – by his dinner-guest. Otherwise he might have killed the mansio slave, who had done nothing to offend him except bring the message in. They almost called the guard. Are you surprised that Brianus is scared?'

This was a story which I had not heard before – surprising, given the speed at which rumour spreads around Glevum. It would be something to tell Marcus when I called on him. Supposing it was true! 'Brianus saw it happen? You are quite sure of that?'

Minimus was clearly thrilled at knowing something we did not. 'Of course Voluus paid the mansio handsomely to hush it up, and the man that he was talking to – who was the only one to see the contents of the note – was sworn to silence, too, on pain of the valuable contract falling through. But Brianus was there – outside the door waiting to be called on – and he saw and heard it all. He was absolutely terrified and I am not surprised. He was saved from any ill-treatment at the time, because Voluus set off for Gaul again that very day – but I don't think Brianus is looking forward to his coming back.'

'All the same,' I said, trying to sound judicious, 'there may be advantages to having his master in the house. Calvinus will have to feed him better from now on, for one thing. A half-starved slave is no use to anyone. Besides, soon there will be a mistress in the house, and that sometimes leads to lighter punishments.'

Junio looked doubtful. 'That won't help if the steward buys Brianus for his own,' he pointed out. 'He will still have power to . . .' But he got no further. We were interrupted by a rapping at the door.

FIVE

I had half-expected to find that it was Brianus outside – it would not have surprised me if he had found some excuse to scurry back to us – but in fact it was the servant of the wealthy customer who had commissioned the mosaic that we'd been working on. I did not recognize the man, but I knew the uniform: the crimson cloak could only mean this was a senior slave. I knew what that meant – or I thought I did.

Florens, the town councillor, was an important man and if he had sent his prized servant out in all this rain, just to check on progress, it could only be because he thought the work would not be done in time for his impending marriage. He was preparing to impose that penalty – just as I had feared!

He had not left me a shadow of excuse. He'd done his best to facilitate the work: his servants had already prepared the site for it – a shady corner of the garden at his country house, which had been dug and cleared and provided with a roof, ready to become the summer dining-room. Even the weather could not be argued as much reason for delay. So I was relieved that we had an almost-finished article to show.

I was already talking as I ushered the visitor inside and showed him the prefabricated work. 'As you can see, we have made this section here. It's upside down on that thin skim of plaster, which is easily removed, so now we can attach it to a firmer backing piece which will keep the tesserae in place. Then we can slide the whole thing on to a carrying board and leave it there to dry while we come out and put the final touches to the place where it's to go.' I knew that I was gushing but I could not help myself. 'We should be out with you tomorrow or the next day – if it's fine – to smooth out the rubble and start putting down cement.' He was still frowning so I essayed a little smile. 'I assure you that it will be ready before the wedding day.'

The servant waved my eager explanations to one side. 'I'm sure that my master is expecting nothing less! But that is not why he has sent me here. You have heard about the pillaging of Voluus's cart?' His manner and the question were extremely brusque.

I gaped at him. 'Who told you about that?' Behind me I heard Junio's sharp intake of breath and young Minimus was standing as if turned to stone.

'My master heard it at the garrison.' The visitor gave me a look of ill-disguised disdain. 'And clearly you have heard about it, too – though not from there, I think. Of course it was unlikely to remain a secret long – a bloodstained cart found standing in the road with a dismembered driver and a slaughtered guard is certain to attract attention in the end. And naturally the contents of the cart have gone – as I'm sure that you are aware, since you visited the lictor's new apartment earlier.'

I suppose that I really should not have been surprised. I knew how quickly rumours in this town could spread – I had been warning people of this very fact myself – but I stood there boggling. Not so much that news of the robbery had spread, but that anybody should have noticed me! Who could have done so, except perhaps the people that I passed through on the stairs? And why was that of interest anyway?

Florens's servant misinterpreted the pause. 'Don't bother to deny it. You were seen to come and go, and I have reason to believe that you had scarcely left the flat before a slave-boy from the household was sent here after you.'

I shook my head. The question of denial had not crossed my mind. 'I do not contest that I visited the house. Surely there is nothing noteworthy in that?'

'Beyond the fact that you are the only person from the town to call at the new apartment and be allowed inside?' He was already taking off his cloak, and – uninvited and with as much assurance as if he were a councillor himself – handing it to an astonished Minimus to hold. 'Though perhaps you were expected? It is quite evident, since Voluus is not here, that your business was with the steward of the house.'

'My business was not with anyone in particular. I called at

the apartment to enquire if Voluus wanted a mosaic made –
though obviously that meant that I spoke to Calvinus. My
patron was good enough to send a note with me, recommending
my services.' I was uneasy now. There was something in his
manner which disturbed me very much. 'Though who might
have noticed me, I cannot understand. A trademan's movements
are hardly of much concern to anyone.'

The servant almost smiled. As he moved, his scarlet tunic
gave off wafts of perfumed oils. 'Perhaps you should not be
too confident about that, citizen. Several people are prepared
to swear they saw you there, immediately after the robbery
was known. What is more, it seems that you were welcomed
in – though previous would-be visitors had all been turned
away.' He had stripped off his leather mittens – a winter luxury
which was presumably a sign of household rank – and began
to tap them rhythmically against his open palm. 'You are said
to be a solver of mysteries, I think, so – if you were in my
place – would you not think that very interesting? And also
that this steward, whom you claim you have never met before
today, is none the less a person whom you can call by name?'

'But . . .' I protested.

A gesture cut me off. 'And would you not be more interested
still in the extraordinary fact that, immediately after a second
message reached the house, this same Calvinus thought it fit
to send a courier to you? If you did not know him, why should
he do that? My master and some of his fellow councillors
would be interested to know.'

It had taken me some moments to realize his drift, but all
at once I understood what this was leading to. 'You can't mean
that your master thinks I am involved in this?' I was too startled even to expostulate. 'I did not even know the cart was on
its way. What's more, I've never met the lictor in my life.'

'Then why were you asking questions of éveryone today
– including questions about the treasure on the carts?'

I spread my hands in a gesture of despair. 'I was attempting
to find out what sort of man he was, that's all.' I was tempted
to tell him the other part of it – that I was only doing it on
Marcus's behalf – but decided that discretion was the wiser
choice.

The servant's smile was disbelieving and disagreeable. 'Indeed? And does enquiry about his valuable possessions tell you that? You can't pretend, for instance, that there is any doubt about whether he could afford your services – not when he has taken an apartment on that scale! Which brings us to another suggestive circumstance. You had not, by your own admission, ever called there before. Yet there you are today – the very day on which the theft occurred.'

'Surely it's more likely that the cart was set upon last night and not discovered until daylight came?' I said, then devoutly wished I'd held my tongue. I could imagine how our visitor would construe my foolish words.

I was right. He raised an eyebrow. 'You might be a better judge of that than I!'

'That is merely a guess that anyone might make. We know that there are active bandits in those woods. At least I assume it was in that area,' I burbled, 'since I understand the cart was coming from the south.'

'Exactly so! And don't you live in that direction, too?' He smiled his knowing smile. 'But then, of course, this was not just a robbery: there are several savage murders to be considered, too – all of them no doubt committed, as you rightly say, under cover of darkness and discovered after dawn. Though very few people ever travel after dusk. Amazing that you seem to know so much about it, citizen.'

'It was merely guesswork . . .' I was beginning to protest.

'Naturally! But suggestive, don't you think? Especially in the light of all the other things I've pointed out. Of course this may all be mere coincidence but Florens and some of the other councillors would like to talk to you and have you explain it, if you are able to.'

I glanced at my son and servant who were standing by, as appalled as I was by this development. I murmured, 'They want to see me now? But I have work to finish here and I am due to report to my patron in just an hour or two . . .' I trailed off in dismay.

In my attempts to justify myself I was in danger of implicating Marcus Septimus as well. Indeed, as I realized with a sinking of the heart, this was possibly the purpose of this whole interview. Marcus, like any wealthy magistrate, has powerful enemies who would be delighted to see him humbled and brought before the courts: it had actually happened once before.

Perhaps I had unwittingly given a new pretext. As it was, I had already admitted that I was carrying a letter from my patron when I called at the flat. That clearly suggested that I was there on his behalf, and it was difficult to see how that could be disproved, because it was the truth. So if I were accused of involvement in the crime, he would seem guilty of complicity at least. I sincerely wished that I hadn't mentioned him.

But it was far too late to keep him out of this. The servant smiled. 'Of course, we know you are the protégé of Marcus Septimus,' he said. 'And we are aware that His Excellence is an important man. That is why my master has sent me here to ask you politely if you'll accompany me. At once, if possible. He is waiting for us at the curia. However, if you are reluctant to comply with this request, I could go back and summon the town guard and have you formally arrested – as we would have done with anybody else who could not claim such exalted patronage.'

Junio stepped forward to speak in my defence. 'Now look here, serving-man, I don't know who you are . . .'

I raised my hand to silence him. It is never wise to make unnecessary enemies – especially the servants of a magistrate. 'It is all right, Junio. This man is merely doing what he was sent to do. Of course I will go with him. There must be some mistake. My patron knows what I was doing at the lictor's house and no doubt he will speak up in my defence. The sooner I get this sorted out, the sooner we get home.'

Junio looked doubtful. 'Well, Father, if you're certain I will say no more. Though if you wish I will go with you to the curia.'

Florens's servant gave him a disdainful look. 'You're lucky that you've not been asked to come in any case. We know of your close association with this pavement-maker here, and therefore it is likely that you are involved in this yourself, though at present no one is accusing you. But there are many ways of finding out the truth – as you may discover, to your cost.'

It was my turn to leap to Junio's defence. 'Are you presuming to make veiled threats against my son? Be careful what you say. He is a citizen.'

A shrug of the shoulders, but my words had hit their mark. A sudden alarm had flashed up in the eyes and his manner was less haughty and hostile as he said hastily, 'I am not threatening anyone at all! Especially not a citizen; I know the law. I thought he was merely a manumitted slave. But I should not care to be in your sandals when the lictor gets here, either of you, I can tell you that.'

'Then, Father, I must certainly come with you to the curia,' Junio said. 'Minimus can shut up the shop and douse the fire and then come and meet us in the forum later on.'

Our visitor looked icily at him. 'And what about my master's pavement? I believe you said that there was work remaining to be done? Or would you rather he invoked the penalty?'

Junio looked at me, exasperation written in every lineament. 'What do you think, Father?'

There was only one thing I could possibly reply. 'There is not a great deal remaining to be done, but – since we are certainly not in receipt of stolen gold – we can't afford to risk the fine. You stay and finish that with Minimus, and then the pair of you can come and find me later on. You know where I shall be. In the meantime, I will do as I am asked and go and speak to Florens, though there is obviously nothing I can tell him which he does not know. Minimus, hand me down my cloak and give this servant his.'

Minimus is a timid person as a rule but I was amused to note that he took enormous care to wrap me in my cape and fuss around me making sure that I was dry – or as dry as possible in the circumstances – while he handed our visitor his wet wrap without a word and made no attempt at all to help him on with it.

'Very well,' I said, once the man had struggled into it. 'Let us go and see these councillors. You can lead the way.' And I followed him briskly out on to the street.

SIX

The rain was easing slightly by this time and people were beginning to come out on to the streets again. But my uniformed attendant, striding purposefully gate-ward in his splendid crimson cloak, looked sufficiently important for people to make way to let him pass, though their attitude was apt to change to a resentful one when they caught sight of me. Although escorted by this impressive slave, I was still in my tunic and damp workman's cape.

One old man in particular, who had struggled to one side, despite the heavy load of wood that he was carrying on his back, put down his burden and turned round to glare at me. 'And to think that I gave deference to him! Only a tradesman!' he muttered to the ancient woman at his side – deliberately just loud enough to make sure I could hear.

But his companion – who was probably his wife, since she was stooped under a load of kindling of her own – shook her head and whispered something in his ear. He looked alarmed and moved as far away as possible from me. Instead of glaring he gazed pointedly away, spat, then licked his finger and rubbed it on the skin behind his ear – the age-old ritual to ward off ill-luck.

Florens's servant noticed and gave a little smirk, while I felt myself turn redder than his cloak. It was obvious what the crone and her husband were so anxious to avoid. Dressed as I was, I did not look remotely like a Roman citizen, so it must have looked suspiciously as though I were being hustled into Glevum under loose arrest – no doubt to be accused of some unpleasant crime, and very likely thrown into the jail, there to await some painful punishment. The wood-sellers were afraid that my fate might somehow pass to them, and that my breath and shadow were contagious, like the plague.

Their comic superstition almost made me smile, but then I thought again. Perhaps their interpretation of my plight was nearer to the truth than I supposed. For some reason which I couldn't understand, I seemed to be suspected of collusion in this crime. But why? Was it simply because I had chanced to call on Calvinus today? That was unfortunate timing on my part, perhaps, but hardly more than that.

I couldn't possibly have known about the robbery until I reached the flat, I told myself, mentally marshalling arguments in my own defence. The message had only reached Calvinus a few minutes earlier, and there was no opportunity for the news to get to me.

That made me pause. Who could have known, in fact? I could see how Florens might have learned the news. He was at the garrison, by all accounts, and Calvinus had sent there for assistance as soon as he heard about the crime. But, if Florens was at the army headquarters at that time, how did he find out that I had visited the lictor's flat? There was no time for him to have set a watch on it.

Could it have been simple gossip which reached him after-wards – for example, from those gamblers on the stairs? I shook my head. Between the garrison and the curia, there was little opportunity for idle talk to reach his ears and no one would have made a point of going to find him to report the news. Unless . . . I felt myself turn cold. An awful thought had just occurred to me.

Suppose that Voluus had posted spies himself, to watch the place and guard his property while he was away? Such things were not unknown, especially if the resident house-slaves were not trusted very much. So had there been somebody watching the apartment all the time? Or, more unnerving still, was someone watching me? But why should they do that? Because I had been asking questions about the lictor and his treasure-carts, perhaps? I had, of course – and Florens knew it, from what his servant said.

Dear gods! In the light of subsequent events, that must seem peculiarly suspicious now. What is more, my reasons for those enquiries, though genuine enough, would sound woefully feeble and unlikely, I could see. What an unfortunate series of events! I would have to call on my patron to speak for me, after all! I only hoped that he already had business in the town today; if they had to send and fetch him from the villa to speak on my behalf, he would be imperially annoyed.

'Citizen? Are you planning to stay where you are all day? Remember they are waiting at the curia!' My escort's voice came sharply from somewhere ahead of me. I realized that I had been so lost in thought that I had paused, stock-still, and he was waiting in a doorway further down the street.

I paddled after him, my sandals squelching damply in the mud, and we walked on in silence to the northern gate. The sentry on duty watched us pass, openly astonished at this incongruous pair, and I felt his amused eyes upon us as we hurried through the archway and on into the town.

The forum, when we reached it, was filling up again after the passing storm – customers and people with business with the council or the courts were emerging from their shelter under temple porticos. Here, too, it had clearly been raining heavily: there were muddy puddles on the paving-stones outside the shops, and most of the bedraggled stalls now stood in little pools, although the live fish-market (a building with an open pond which did not mind the rain) seemed to be doing a substantial trade. The stone steps of the basilica were still slippery with wet, but there were already clusters of councillors and clerks standing in earnest conclave here and there, and an excited crowd was gathering below to hear the reading of a will. We wove our way amongst their babbling, up the flight of steps, and into the basilica itself.

Though I had often been to the basilica before, I had never seen the inner council room where committees of the curia – or town council – met. Like every other citizen, I knew exactly where it was: not in the main section of the building, which was given over to the great public assembly area, with its towering pillars, fine floors and enormous vaulted aisle, but in the centre of the range of rooms across the rear. All the same, I had never been inside, so I was curious to see it when my escort led me in.

It was a chamber between the central *aedes*, where the Imperial shrine was set, and the smaller offices of clerks and copy-scribes, and despite the musty smell of damp and candle-wax, it was much more spacious than I had supposed. It had a row of window-spaces high up on the wall, three tiers of wooden benches set on either side, and an imposing dais for the presiding magistrate. There was a large mosaic in the centre of the floor: an ambitious design of flowers and deities, though there was evidence – in places – of indifferent workmanship.

But there was no time for professional assessments of that kind. There were people in the room. Three members of the curia were sitting in a row beside the wall – all purple-stripers, naturally, indicating that they were men of rank – while Florens, whose toga bore the widest stripe of all, was standing on the dais, resting his elbows on a fine carved speaker's stand, with the expression of a man who has been kept waiting far too long.

He looked up and saw me. He said, without a smile, 'Ah, citizen Libertus, there you are at last. Thank you, Servilis, you may leave us now.' There was a moment while the messenger bowed himself away, then Florens turned to me. He was a plump and portly little man, with a fringe of wispy hair and faded pink-rimmed eyes. 'We've been expecting you.' He raised a podgy hand to indicate the other councillors. I was not sure if he intended me to sit as well – and to do so uninvited would be worse than impolite – so I bowed in their direction and remained standing where I was.

'Sit down, sit down, citizen,' the youngest of them said. 'This is just a friendly meeting, not a formal trial.'

Until that moment I had not imagined that it was, but suddenly I began to have real feelings of unease. This was constituted rather like a court, and it did not look friendly – despite what had been said. Florens was forbidding and his tone severe, and the other magistrates were looking just as grim. However, as I walked across to take my place – painfully aware of my heavy sandal-nails on that expensive floor – I noticed with relief that two of the others were people I had met: the tall, thin man was Gaius Flavius, while the fatter one with acne was Porteus Tertius, both occasional dinner guests at my patron's house.

I essayed a timid smile. Porteus ignored it and Gaius looked the other way. Nothing to be hoped for in that direction, it was clear. Matters were swiftly going from bad to worse. As a known protégé of Marcus's, I had expected a measure of respect – from them, in any case. I felt my hands going clammy with anxiety.

I edged myself on to the lowest bench. It would not do to rank myself beside the magistrates. In fact, I was so concerned with avoiding such a thing that I made my first mistake. Instead of sitting on the form in front of them, I sat down opposite, like a scholar taking a test in rhetoric – so I found myself facing a panel of judges, as it were.

'Well,' Florens linked his short, fat fingers on the desk in front of him, 'I'm sure you know why we have summoned you.'

'Something to do with my visit to Voluus, I understand from what your servant said – Servilis, as I now understand that he is called.' Despite my nervousness – or perhaps because of it – I was privately amused to learn the servant's name: it means 'lowly and submissive', despite that crimson cloak. No wonder he hadn't chosen to introduce himself.

'You regard that as amusing for some reason, citizen?' Florens's voice was icy.

Another error. I had not realized that I had smiled at all. Certainly I had not intended to. But all the councillors were scowling at me now, visibly disapproving of my apparent levity. I said quickly, 'Not amusing, councillor. I'm surprised, that's all. I do not understand why you have called me here. I am just a humble tradesman seeking work and I called at the apartment – as I told your slave – to see if Voluus required to have a pavement made.'

Porteus gave a disbelieving sneer and scrambled to his feet. 'And you expect us to believe that, citizen? In an apartment of that quality? You must have known it would have splendid floors!' He looked around as if for approbation from his peers.

I had begun to realize that I was genuinely pleading for my liberty, and I saw a chance to win a point or two. 'Of course I hadn't seen the inside of the flat; otherwise I would never have presumed. The floors, as you say, are already excellent.' I paused a moment to achieve the full effect before I added, in a puzzled tone, 'But I understood from Servilis that no one but myself had been allowed inside? Yet it seems that you have seen it, Porteus?'

Porteus turned pink beneath the acne on his cheeks, while the youngest councillor – the same one who had instructed me to sit – looked at him quizzically. 'He is quite right, Porteus. Unless he had visited he couldn't know about the floors. And nor could you. So how is that you speak about them with such confidence?'

I sensed a potential ally here and I looked at him with more interest than before. He was a youngish, untidy-looking man – in his thirties if I am any judge – with an energetic manner and a tow-coloured mop of tousled hair. His face was moody but intelligent and he wore his toga rather as I wore my own, as though it were a slight encumbrance. I noticed, for instance, that several times he hitched his shoulder-folds, as though they were in danger of cascading down in coils.

'I visited when the tax-collector owned the place,' Porteus mumbled rather sullenly. He was clearly embarrassed at admitting this to his associates (as I said before, tax-collectors are not usually accepted in good society). There was a murmur among the other councillors.

'Just a business matter,' he went on, reddening. 'Nothing of importance, but he invited me to dine . . .' He tailed off.

He must have known, as I did, what the others thought: that he had been prepared to feast with the taxman and to drink his wine, against the generally accepted rules of what was socially acceptable. Was this just greed for expensive food and wine, or had he been seeking favours when it came to paying dues?

Titus Flavius voiced the feeling in the room. 'Seeking a contribution, were you, Porteus? Still eager to be selected as Imperial priest and hoping to impress the people by funding public works?'

Porteus sat down, saying testily, 'Well, if I am, what has that to do with anything? We are not here to talk about my presence at a feast, we are here to ask this pavement-maker to explain himself – and I, for one, am not convinced by what he says. Of course he claims he's never visited the flat before today, but that is no proof that he hasn't. In fact, it is just what you'd expect a guilty man to say.'

'Guilty man?' I blurted out the words. This was sounding more and more as if I were on trial – and since this was a convocation of town magistrates, I might as well have been. 'But surely this was simply banditry!'

There was another little murmur in the room. Florens appeared to feel the need to exercise control. He rapped the dais sharply, so that all eyes turned to him, then he hooked his pudgy thumbs into his toga folds and looked around the room – exactly as though he were an advocate – seeking the gaze of every councillor in turn.

When he was assured that attention was on him, he said portentously, 'Banditry, citizen? That's what it was meant to look like, I am sure. But we are not convinced. I am inclined to concur with Porteus's view of this. Remember, fellow coun-cillors, what the witnesses declared. When this pavement-maker visited the lictor's flat, he didn't even reach the door before Calvinus came out to greet him. It's obvious he was expected before he even knocked.'

My heart sank further at this talk of 'witnesses'. This was more indication (if I needed it) that spies had been watching me throughout. I had entirely forgotten that the steward had not waited for my knock. That could look suspicious to unfriendly eyes. I said, 'Calvinus was awaiting someone, but it wasn't me. He told me he was expecting a messenger from the garrison.'

'And yet he immediately welcomed you inside?' Florens looked pityingly at me. 'Do you think perhaps you looked like such a messenger yourself? That Calvinus mistook you for a member of the guard, and that's why he let you in?'

That caused a titter among the councillors. It was a jibe, of course. Naturally I could never be mistaken for a member of the guard.

Porteus stood up to press the joke a little more. 'Of course, councillor Florens, one can see how the steward was confused. Our pavement-maker here looks much like a soldier to the casual eye – apart from the fact that he is far too old and wears a faded tunic and a workman's cloak, instead of an armoured breastplate, helmet, greaves and sword! Obviously an error that anyone could make.' He sat down again and looked around triumphantly, delighted to make me look ridiculous.

I said, with an attempt at dignity, 'Anyone can bring a message, councillor. And Calvinus was entitled to suppose that I'd brought an answer from the garrison, telling him what support he could expect from them, since he had sent requesting help.' I paused. 'I assume that such a message was eventually sent?' It had occurred to me, while I was speaking, that I hadn't heard of it.

It was obvious from the whispering that my words had touched a nerve. Even Florens looked discomfited. However, he was not nonplussed for long. After an instant he tapped the desk again and said in a peremptory, dismissive tone, 'What message the garrison commander may have sent is none of our affair. Our concern is you and what your business was with Calvinus today. You say you called to offer him a floor. I presume that he did not engage your services?'

I shook my head. 'Indeed not, councillor. He was so disturbed about the theft of the dowry treasures from his master's cart that I doubt he would have felt able to order pavements then, even if the household had needed such a thing . . .'

Porteus was on his feet again, seizing on my words before I'd finished them. 'So he did speak to you about what was on the cart? You admit as much? And yet you say you were a perfect stranger to the man?' He gazed around the room triumphantly. 'Florens, fellow councillors, I call on your good sense. Do you think it likely that Calvinus would confide his master's business to a man he'd never met? Isn't discretion the first duty of a steward anywhere?'

This was going badly. There were murmurs of assent.

'Well, citizen?' Florens indicated that it was my turn to speak.

I could hardly believe what was happening to me. Accused of arranging a violent robbery, and effectively found guilty before a trial was held! And all because of simple circumstance! I felt like shouting that they were a bunch of fools, but it was essential that I defend myself as much as possible and not inflame the councillors more than I could help.

So I controlled myself and simply pointed out that it was

natural – since he thought that I'd come in answer to his
request for help – for the steward to suppose that I already
knew about the theft. I was about to add that he had been a
good deal more discreet in front of the other servants in the
house, when some god of self-preservation whispered in my
ear that this would only make things worse. I stopped, aware
that there were already mutterings.

Florens held up his hand for silence in the room and,
gesturing to a reluctant Porteus to resume his seat, he said,
'Which brings us to another matter, citizen. You were not
engaged to lay this pavement, you have told us that. Thus, by
your own admission, you should have had no further business
with the lictor's house. So why did Calvinus send his servant
after you, as soon as he had the message that Voluus had
reached Britannia and was already on his way? What possible
concern can that have been of yours?'

Clever trap on clever trap! I shook my head despairingly.
'I'd promised him that I would get my patron to investigate
the theft. Calvinus just sent to tell me that there was not much
time to find the answer before the lictor came. Obviously he'll
be here in just a day or two.' It did not sound persuasive, even
to myself.

Even tow-headed Titus Flavius was looking unconvinced.
'Oh, come, Libertus,' he said, with the heartiness of a nurse-
maid chivvying her charge. 'You would do better to admit the
truth. You told Calvinus he'd be lucky to escape detection as
one of the plotters. Don't bother to deny it – you were
overheard.'

For a moment I was genuinely mystified. Then I remembered
that I had indeed said something about his being 'one of them'
– deliberately loudly, too, on purpose so that the people on
the stairs would hear – when I wanted to stop Calvinus from
sending me away. Another of this day's terrible mistakes!
However, I knew it would be hopeless to explain.

Titus Flavius was already speaking anyway. 'I see that you
do not deny it, citizen. So what was that about, if not the
robbery? And if it was about the robbery, how did you know
of it?' He paused, but I was still silent – at a loss for words
– and after a moment he added urgently, 'Libertus, I am trying

to do my best for you, but I cannot save you if you will not save yourself. This is no moment for keeping silent for your patron's sake. I know you have a reputation for unmasking criminals. I am myself inclined to think that there was indeed a plot, and you and Marcus had discovered it and were trying to extort money from Calvinus because you knew he was involved. If so, you would do better to admit it to this company. Blackmail is a dishonourable thing, but at least it would absolve you from complicity in this crime.'

Clearly Titus only meant to help, but his suggestion left me even more nonplussed. I bowed towards him, saying with respect, 'Councillor Titus, I am flattered and grateful for your confidence in me. But I fear it is misplaced. I genuinely know nothing whatever of all this: until I spoke to Calvinus today I did not know the special treasure-cart was even on its way – far less when and how it was expected here. As for the murders and the theft, I had not heard so much as a whisper about either of those things until he mentioned them. I certainly have no theory as to who committed them.'

Porteus was on his feet again, his face so pink the acne showed like little pits of white. 'Don't listen to the man. Of course he knew about the cart – though he tries to deflect suspicion from himself by feigning ignorance. Why else would he be pointedly asking questions in the town today, very specifically about Voluus's wealth and what he was bringing with him out of Gaul? That did not happen by mere coincidence. If Libertus did not carry out this robbery himself – and I grant you that he probably did not – then I say he helped at least to organize the raid. It required armed men and horses and probably a vehicle to remove the treasure too, which means his patron, Marcus Septimus, was almost certainly involved as well. Marcus assuredly knew all about the lictor's carts. Weren't we, as councillors, all discussing them and the amount of treasure they contained – here on the steps of this very basilica, just the day before the Ides?'

Titus Flavius gave a barking laugh. 'I know that you were, Porteus, because you were boasting of the lucrative deal you made with the lictor while he was here before! How much was it that Voluus promised you for that piece of land of yours?

Hundreds of denarii – twice what it is worth. It's clear why
you might have an interest in the safe arrival of the lictor's
wealth. But why should you suppose that Marcus Septimus is
involved? He is immensely rich. What interest could he have
in raiding Voluus's cart?' He shook his head. 'Much more
likely to be that steward, I should think, bribing accomplices
and seeking to get rich at the expense of a master who was
not kind to him. He would not be the first.'

Porteus snorted. 'And where would Calvinus hide the
treasure? It isn't in the apartment! I tell you, Marcus had a
hand in this. You've just heard that he sent a letter to the
steward there, and ordered this pavement-maker to deliver it.
As for his being wealthy, that's no argument! Who would not
be interested in wagon-loads of gold, however rich they are?
And who can hide treasure more easily than a man of wealth?
In Marcus's villa a few more gold coins and jewels would
scarcely raise remark!'

'But Calvinus . . . ?' Florens interrupted, with a frown.

Porteus held up a restraining hand. 'I agree that Calvinus
played a part in this: most likely he told the ambush where to
strike and when. But he doesn't have the money to buy arms
to mount a raid, and he doesn't have the goods that were taken
from the cart. I've had the apartment searched most thoroughly
and there is nothing there that wasn't on the earlier manifests,
beyond a few gold coins beneath the steward's bed. I say that
we should seize Libertus and search his patron's homes – both
the town apartment and the country house. And the pavement-
maker's own roundhouse, too. That is near the villa, so I
understand, and would make a splendid temporary hiding
place.'

SEVEN

I was struck with horror at this new development. The idea of them rummaging through my roundhouse was ominous enough – likely to cause damage and terrify my wife – though I was merely a private citizen. But offering to search Marcus's property as well? That was an indication of how serious things were. This affair was escalating like a dreadful dream.

I was so shocked and startled that I could hardly speak, but at last I managed to collect myself. I said with such calm dignity as I could conjure up, 'Gentleman, you are completely wrong. I'm certain that my patron had no part in this. He's famously honest: look at his record as a magistrate – he has never taken bribes or altered the course of justice to protect the powerful. He will be as shocked as I am when he learns about this crime. He always says that robbery on the highway is bad for all of us – it gives the colonia a bad name for trade. As for his personally conniving at the theft, I am amazed that you could imagine such a thing. Certainly, I swear that he never plotted anything with me.'

This time it was Gaius who shuffled to his feet. I could see he was embarrassed because he would not meet my glance. He was as old as he was skinny and his voice was tremulous. 'Citizen, your loyalty to your patron is commendable. But – and it pains me to say this, as I have always held Marcus Septimus in very high regard – I fear that I must contradict your evidence.' At last he raised his rheumy eyes to look at me. 'You say that he didn't plot anything with you. Do you deny that you were with him yesterday, in private conference, a little before noon?'

I could hardly argue, since it was the truth and others knew it – Maximus, for one. I didn't want him questioned by the local torturers. 'That is no secret. Marcus summoned me to attend him at his country house,' I said.

'Exactly, citizen. And what did he want to talk to you about?'
Gaius waited a moment while I debated what to say, then
pressed the point again. 'Wasn't it precisely about Voluus and
his wealth?'

'Don't try to deny it!' Porteus said, with an unpleasant
smile. 'You are too careless, citizen. You were overheard on
this occasion too! Tell him, Gaius.'

Gaius looked even more uncomfortable but he said, 'I lament
this, Libertus, but what Porteus says is true. I sent my page-
boy on an errand to the villa yesterday, consulting Marcus on
a point of etiquette, but when he arrived it was to be told that
His Excellency was already occupied with a visitor – yourself
– on a matter of importance and could not be disturbed.'

'I have agreed that I was there,' I protested. 'That does not
prove that we were plotting robberies.'

'You were talking about Voluus and his treasure – and how
you could inveigle yourself into the lictor's house and talk to
the steward about what he'd done with it.' Porteus was bobbing
in his seat impatiently.

'We were talking about nothing of the kind. I was merely . . .'

Porteus leapt up to interrupt and point an accusing forefinger
at me. 'The page-boy – who is a professional courier, trained
to learn a message off by heart at a single hearing – heard
everything you said and reported it to Gaius, verbatim, afterwards. So don't try to tell us otherwise.'

'He was deliberately listening in to us?' I was indignant,
but my mind was racing, too, trying to recall exactly what we
might have said.

'He didn't come and spy deliberately, of course,' Gaius said
apologetically. 'It was an accident.'

Privately, despite the old man's mildness, I rather doubted
this. Spying on other men of power is what everybody does:
Marcus has a dozen people in his pay – other people's servants
who report to him about their master's households and who
came and went, and why. Very likely Gaius had private spies
as well and this eavesdropping was perfectly intentional – what
else would explain the careful reporting afterwards? However,
I could hardly voice that thought aloud.

Gaius spread his bony hands, appealing to his fellow

councillors. 'My page had already loitered in the servant's
waiting room, hoping to speak to Marcus when he was available, but in the end it was taking far too long. He tried to find
a slave and explain that he was now obliged to leave, but he
couldn't find one in the public rooms, so he went out to the
courtyard garden at the back.' He turned to Florens. 'In case
you are not familiar with the house, that leads out through a
gateway to the outer court, where the stores and servants'
living-quarters are, and thence to the rear entrance on the
farm-lane at the back, where he thought at least he'd find a
gatekeeper.'

It was a common pattern for a country house, of course,
and Florens nodded. 'I understand. Go on.'

'Well,' Gaius resumed, a little plaintively, 'on his way across
the courtyard garden towards the inner gate, he heard people
talking in an arbour to one side . . .'

'And sneaked up behind them to listen to their words?' I
said angrily. Yet another piece of foolishness, I realized
instantly. By saying that I'd half-admitted guilt.

Gauis turned reproachful eyes on me. 'Of course he had no
inkling that it was His Excellence. He imagined that the master
would be inside the house – in conference in his study, as you
would expect – so, supposing that the speakers must be merely
slaves, he skirted round and went to talk to them. But as he
drew nearer he realized it was indeed the voice of Marcus
talking to his guest. Once he'd discovered that, he backed
away, of course, but not before he'd had time to overhear.'

'Then he must know that we were not talking about robbing
anyone,' I said.

'On the contrary. As Porteus has said, my slave is skilled
at learning messages by rote. And since these words were
rather startling, even an amateur could have remembered them.
I made a careful note.' Slowly, Gaius took a writing-tablet
from his belt, undid the binding and held it up for me to see.
'My fellow councillors have already heard this, citizen, but I
will repeat it for your benefit. These are the very words of
Marcus Septimus. "If you have my letter they will have to let
you in and that will give you the opportunity to talk to the
steward. He's the one responsible for seeing that the lictor's

treasure – when it comes – is taken off the cart, so he knows exactly what it is and what it's worth. He may even have witnessed how it was acquired and what favours it is – or was – intended to repay. In any case I'm sure you'll manage to get it out of him. I know you, Libertus, you are skilled at things like that. I am quite certain I can rely on you." There you are, citizen, you may read it for yourself.'

I shook my head. There was no point in reading it. I recognized the words. Of course I could try denying everything – it would be my word against the messenger's – but I dismissed the thought. Marcus might thoughtlessly confirm what he had said – in which case my denial would make bad matters worse: lying to the authorities is a significant offence. At the very least, I'd have lost my reputation as an honest man – which, admittedly, did not appear to count for much among these councillors.

Gaius was shaking his thinning locks at me. 'What can that conversation mean, citizen pavement-maker, except that you and Marcus already knew about the theft?'

'But how could we possibly have known about it in advance? We had that conversation shortly before noon, and the robbery did not take place till after dark!'

'Did it, citizen?' Porteus was standing up again, his pock-marked face wreathed in an ugly smile. 'Thank you for that information. I am sure that the garrison will be pleased to know. That, as these other councillors are aware, was the commander's guess, but since all the occupants of the cart were dead and the road was unfrequented, there was no proof what time the raid took place. And thank you also for the confirmation that Gaius's courier was correct in his account.'

Too late, I realized what I'd admitted to. 'I did have that conversation with my patron,' I said desperately, 'but it did not mean what you have twisted it to mean. It is true that he was interested in where Voluus got his wealth, but that was simply in order to decide whether or not it would be wise to accept the invitation to his feast. His Excellence thought the steward would have information on the point. That is all I was attempting to find out. Ask my patron. Ask Calvinus himself.'

'Oh, we intend to ask your patron, believe me, citizen.' Porteus's manner was nastier than before. 'And we are already asking Calvinus. He is a prisoner at the jail, being questioned as we speak. Of course they cannot interrogate him to the full – not until his master gets here anyway – but I have no doubt that in the end he'll tell us everything.' He sat down noisily.

I blanched. I could guess the methods Porteus had in mind – and no doubt Calvinus, as the steward of a professional torturer, had an even clearer picture of what might lie in store. Poor Calvinus! I did not especially like the man, but he had done nothing that I knew of to deserve a fate like that.

'But there isn't anything to tell,' I murmured hopelessly, though that would not help the steward, when it came to it. Like the page-boy that Voluus once accused of theft, he might well end up confessing falsehoods just to make the beatings stop. And one thing was becoming very clear to me: if I was not careful, I would be the next. Highway robbery is a capital offence and, though as a citizen I'd be protected from the worst and (unlike Calvinus) was in little danger of being cruci-fied, all the same this preposterous affair might prove to be extremely serious.

I had been worried about getting home betimes, but if this went badly I might never see my home again. Nor indeed my wife! I could find myself in exile for the remainder of my days, deprived of 'water and fire' throughout the Empire – and that was if the magistrates were fairly lenient. I did not care to dwell on what might happen otherwise.

Florens was speaking. 'We have already questioned Calvinus about you. It was the first thing we asked him. He says you threatened him.'

'Threatened him?' I was incredulous.

He made a tutting nose. 'Citizen,' he said impatiently. 'We've been through this before. You told him privately that he'd be held to blame, and publicly that he'd be lucky to escape. People on the stairwell will testify to that. And they will also swear that you had some kind of fight – though Calvinus is still persisting in denying it. What were you doing, citizen? Arguing over how to divide up the spoils?'

'Fight?' I was turning into Echo, doomed – like the nymph – to repeating everything.

'We are told that when you went back into the flat, there

was some sort of altercation, ending in a crash. We have at least a dozen witnesses to that.' Florens twisted his pudgy fingers as he spoke.

It was astonishing how unrelated facts could be interpreted. I said dully, 'A vase was shaken from its stand by someone running up the stairs. Nothing to do with any robbery. Look in the midden pile outside the house, and no doubt you'll find the shards.'

'A valuable vase?' Porteus looked around triumphantly. 'No doubt taken from the treasure-cart.'

I sighed. 'I assure you it was not. Ask the messenger who brought the news about the theft. He must have noticed it – it was a most distinctive piece and it was in place when he was there, so clearly it could not have been stolen from the cart. I did not arrive until after he had left – your own witnesses will testify to that – and anyway, there wasn't any fight. Hearing a crash is no proof of anything.'

Titus Flavius spoke up in my defence – or what he obviously took to be in my defence. 'The citizen is right. Even if there had been a scuffle in the flat, that does not suggest collusion in the robbery. Quite the contrary. Like everything else that we have heard today, it would point not to this man and his patron having taken part in any raid, but to their having learned that the steward was involved, and were now attempting to blackmail him in consequence. In that case, would you not expect a heated argument?'

The rest of the councillors were on their feet by now, and talking all at once. Florens gained silence by tapping on the bench. 'One person at a time. I can't hear all of you. Porteus, you were the first, I think.'

Porteus had turned blotchy and his ears were red. 'Titus is talking nonsense. This man and his patron were begetters of the crime. You heard the words yourself from Gaius's messenger. Calvinus was to be responsible for unloading the treasure from the cart, and this man was sent to "get it out of him". Libertus clearly went to claim their portion of the stolen goods – though evidently he did not succeed in taking any away. Perhaps Calvinus thought to cheat them too, since we know the treasure has been hidden somewhere else.' He turned to me. 'But we shall find it, citizen, you can be sure of that. And we will be the ones to instigate the search, not your precious patron, as you clearly hoped. You have already told us – haven't you, you wretch? – that you actually promised Calvinus that Marcus would take charge of investigating this. It isn't difficult to see the reason why! So that the theft would be attributed to brigands in the woods – as you yourself were ready to suggest – or some other conclusion favourable to yourselves?'

He might have gone on ranting in this way, but Florens raised his hand. 'Enough Porteus, we know what you believe. You've made it clear you wish to bring this matter to the courts and I'm inclined – reluctantly enough – to think there is suffi-cient evidence to support a case. Titus, you have a different view of things, I know. And Gaius . . . ?'

Gaius looked as though he wished that Jove would strike him dumb. His bony face was whiter than a newly-fullered sheet. 'Marcus Septimus has been a friend to me. I wish that I could believe this pavement-maker here . . .' he began, his voice more tremulous than ever now.

'But you can't believe him, and I'm not surprised,' Porteus interrupted, with a triumphant smirk. 'You have the evidence of your courier-slave – you were the one who confided it to me!'

That was one mystery solved, at any rate. Now I knew how Gaius had come to be involved in this 'friendly meeting' so much against his will. But there was scarcely time for me to frame the thought, for Florens said briskly, 'That makes us three to one in favour of taking this man into custody.'

'I agreed to further questioning, that's all. Not to have him thrown into the jail.' Gaius was stubborn in his plaintive way.

This forlorn attempt to soften things was briskly waved away. 'Then I'll have him committed to the garrison instead. They'll keep a watch on him till Voluus gets here. That should be within a day or two.' Florens turned his still unsmiling face to me. 'Libertus, I must ask you to accompany me. My guards will form an escort.'

And that was that. The old wood-seller and his ancient wife had been right in shunning me. I'd come in here a citizen, of my own free will, but I was leaving as a prisoner.

EIGHT

There was no doubt of my status as we left the curia – though I was not in bonds. Florens did not have lictors as he might have done in Rome, but he had the next best thing – a band of burly attendants all bearing clubs and arms. They were not even dressed in household livery but variously attired in different shades of brown, which matched their bronzed faces and their muscled arms, and they smelt overpoweringly of damp wool and sweat.

I was hustled between them as we went back down the steps and through the forum, where the rain had stopped. The crowd that had gathered for the reading of the will parted like butter to allow us through, though some of the urchins who always gather near the market stalls (more in the hope of finding a dropped coin than the expectation of earning anything) began to follow after me with mocking taunts and jeers.

As soon as we had got out on to the street again the company dispersed. The other councillors made polite farewells to Florens and – accompanied by their own attendants – went their separate ways. I thereby lost whatever faint support I had. There was one advantage to their departure though: it saved me the humiliation of a whole procession of purple-striped magistrates escorting me towards the garrison.

Florens on his own was eye-catching enough in his patrician toga, which he had now topped with an elaborate fur-trimmed cloak, dyed (of course) in expensive blue – thus making a striking contrast with Servilis, who walked in perfumed crimson, half a pace behind, while the motley guards propelled me after them. The councillor strode at a smart rate for such a pudgy man, and I was soon reduced to a state of breathlessness. I tried to pause beneath an arch to catch my breath again, but as soon as I attempted to slacken pace at all I found the grip of hairy hands upon my arms and heavy cudgels threatening my legs.

We took a route across the cloth-market. The streets were busy now and full of townspeople, but most of the cobbled pavements were still pooled with wet, so we were not hampered by the displays of merchandise – rugs, cloth and leather goods – which generally spilled out of all the little shops. Pedestrians are usually forced to slow and pick their way through these, so that the crafty traders can accost them as they pass – ('Special price for you, citizen, highest quality'). However, there was none of that today and we made swift progress through the area.

Only when we reached the guard-house at the southern gate did Florens slacken pace. He strode straight up to the sentry on guard and was peremptory. 'I am a senior member of the curia. I have business with the commander of the garrison. Have a message sent to tell him I am here. He is expecting me. I'm bringing in this pri . . .' He looked at me, and broke off in mid-word, 'I mean "citizen", of course, to him for questioning.'

The sentry gave him a jaundiced glance. 'Name, citizen?' he said. To a councillor, it was almost insolent.

Florens had turned pink, but he gave his name in full and the soldier nodded. 'Very well. You there, orderly!' He gestured to an off-duty soldier just inside the wall, who was lounging against the corner of the barrack-room, idly burnishing his helmet with a pumice-stone.

The young man jammed his headpiece on at once and came hurrying across and the sentry solemnly gave him the message to pass on – though the fellow must have heard what Florens said, in any case. The sentry watched him scurry off and then turned back to us.

'Until there is an answer, I'm afraid you'll have to wait,' he said, as though the resplendent councillor was a common citizen. 'You could come inside the compound and sit down over there.' He gestured to the guard-room just within the gates.

Florens attempted to retain his dignity. 'That would be convenient. I don't imagine the commander will keep me waiting long.' He moved as if to go in through the gate.

The sentry raised a casual arm to block his path. 'One thing,

though! I'm sorry, councillor – they'll have to stay outside.'
He nodded towards the armed brutes who were guarding me.
'We don't let anybody come in here with weapons, I'm afraid.'
He grinned, showing a set of neatly pointed teeth. 'Except
ourselves, of course.'

Florens looked furious at this, but there was little he could
say in argument. This barrack area was the property of the
Roman troops and the Glevum town council had no jurisdic-
tion here. 'But what about guarding . . .' He broke off and
waved a pudgy hand at me.

The sentry showed his pointed teeth again. 'You can keep
that attendant in household uniform.' He jerked his chin
towards Servilis as he spoke. 'There's nothing against that.
He can keep watch on the pri . . . I mean, citizen . . . for you.'
He sniggered a little at his private jest. 'Not that he is likely
to get away in there. The place is full of soldiers at this time
of day.'

It was. The inner courtyard was crammed with soldiery.
Half of the unit was preparing for some training exercise,
apparently a route-march carrying full kit. Such an event was
not unusual. You often saw a marching column somewhere on
the road – a spectacle designed not just to keep the soldiers
fit, but to remind inhabitants of who their masters were. Florens
paused, clearly flurried by this activity, and a plump centurion
came hurrying across.

He addressed himself to Florens, ignoring me. 'Excuse me,
citizen, we can't have you all out here. Perhaps if you, patrician, would like to come inside? One of the orderlies will find
some wine for you . . . ?' and he hustled the councillor away
to the lower office of the guard-house tower. I glimpsed them
through the window-space a moment afterwards, Florens
comfortably ensconced upon a bench, while an orderly stood
beside him offering a tray.

Servilis and I had no such luxury; we were obliged to huddle
up against a wall where a chill wind etched itself into our
bones. There was nothing to do but watch the route-march
forming up. The century (which, like all others, was composed
of eighty men and not the hundred which you might expect)
had by this time ranged itself in ranks and now the musicians

and standard-bearers took their place in front. There was a moment's shuffling, a barked command – then all at once the very walls appeared to shake with sound, as trumpets and shell-horns blared out the signal-call and a thousand hobnails rang on the cobbled stones.

The soldiers marched away, the standard swaying high. The court felt oddly silent after they had gone. The grey stones echoed the bleakness of my mood. As if on cue, it began to rain again.

Servilis looked resentfully at me. 'This is all your doing, pavement-maker . . .' he began, but he was interrupted by the plump centurion bustling over from the tower.

'Now then, you two, if you would like to follow me. The garrison commander will see you straightaway. The councillor is with him and they're ready for you now.'

I glanced towards the guard-room window in surprise, but obviously Florens was no longer there. I had been so busy watching the departure of the troops, and so consumed with my own wretched thoughts, that I had not seen him go.

The centurion used his baton to point the way for me, making it clear he wanted me to walk in front where he and Servilis could keep an eye on me. I already knew the way to the commander's room – so off we went, through the cool dark of the guard-room, where candles flickered in sconces on the wall, and through towards the steep stone staircase at the rear.

A youngish officer, perhaps an *octio*, was seated at the table in the guard-room as we passed, busily working with an abacus and scratching something on a piece of bark. He looked up as we went past. 'Ah, there you are, Centurion Emelius. I should be quick if I were you. The commander does not like to be kept waiting, as you know.' And he turned his attention back to his accounts.

I was more than willing to meet the commandant. I had met him several times before and had found him to be both sensible and intelligent, so there was hope I could persuade him of my innocence. I climbed the staircase as quickly as I could, even without the soldier's baton flapping at my heels. Servilis was still grumbling as he toiled up after us.

The centurion rapped sharply on the door of the commander's room and was answered by a shouted instruction to come in.

The commandant was exactly as I'd remembered him: tall, rangy and athletic, with a weather-beaten face, and armour so gleaming you could see the room reflected in the scales, right down to the objects on the table top: oil-lamps, ink-pot, seals and scattered scrolls. Apart from a lamp-stand, the commander's desk and stool and the shadowy statue of a god set in a wall-niche at the rear, there was no other furniture to see. The commanding officer had ascetic tastes.

The room, which smelt of lamp-oil and pomade, and the beeswax which had obviously been used to shine the desk, seemed more austere today, against the flamboyance of Florens and his slave.

'Centurion Emelius reporting, Worthiness. In the name of His Imperial Divinity, the Emperor . . .' The plump centurion was launched on the lengthy list of honorific titles which Commodus had assumed, and which was required by army protocol as the proper preamble to addressing a senior officer.

The commander (for the first time in my acquaintance with him) stood and heard him out, presumably because the councillor was there – Marcus was not the only one to fear Imperial spies. Servilis, meanwhile, had abandoned me and gone to stand behind his owner with a smirk.

The centurion completed the formalities at last. 'I have brought the prisoner Libertus as you requested, sir,' he finished breathlessly.

The commander raised an eyebrow laconically at me. 'Well, pavement-maker. So we meet again. And in connection with more deaths and robberies, I hear? This member of the curia has explained the facts to me and requests that I should keep you here for questioning. He wants me to put your patron under guard as well, and thinks he has sufficient evidence to bring a formal charge against you both in court.'

Florens was looking exceptionally smug. 'I want this matter settled before Voluus arrives. Libertus may in the end be glad of that himself. I did not meet the lictor personally last year, when I went to Gaul, but I did meet his household – and I warn you, citizen, he is a man who demands the fiercest penalties. He will doubtless hold the town responsible if this is not resolved.'

The commander shook his head. 'Given that, Libertus, what am I to do? It almost seems that troubles follow you about. I'm beginning to think it would be sensible to do as he proposes and to lock you up – if only for the safety of the rest of us.'

I hoped this was ironic but I could not be sure. My chances of getting home to Gwellia tonight were looking very slim. Florens – urged on by Porteus, no doubt – was obviously intent on having me kept at the garrison in chains, in order to bring me securely to trial. It is the responsibility of the man who brings a charge to ensure that the accused appears in court on the appointed day; otherwise there can be no trial at all. Obviously, that can often prove difficult to do. However, if I were already in Roman custody it would be easy to compel me to appear before the magistrates.

That was clearly what Florens had in mind. He gave a mirthless smile. 'Then I will leave him in your hands.'

'Thank you, councillor. This man will show you out.' He nodded to the plump centurion who snapped to work and held the door ajar.

Florens gave me a mocking bow as he passed close to me. 'Then farewell, Libertus. I doubt we'll meet again, unless it is officially in court. I've told the commander everything that points to your involvement in all this – including your excuses and explanations for today, although I don't believe that he's much impressed with them. However, he is willing to let you plead your cause. If you fail to convince him of your innocence, he has agreed to summon your patron in for questioning as well – and in any case, I'm sending my escort to search both your properties. Come, Servilis. Your grateful servant, commandant!' And still accompanied by his crimson slave, he bowed himself away.

There was a little silence after they had gone. After a moment I said daringly – since it was not my place to be first to speak – 'I swear I had nothing to do with stealing from the cart. Nor Marcus either.'

'I'm tempted to believe you,' the commander said, sitting

slowly on his stool and looking up at me. 'Though the evidence against you is looking rather black.'

'But surely,' I said, 'we know that there are rebel bandits in the wood, and they mount raids on passing carts from time to time. It would not have been difficult for them to learn that there was gold – it seems to have been common knowledge in the town. Isn't it more likely that they carried out the theft?'

The commander ran both hands through his thinning hair. 'That might seem the obvious solution, certainly – if it were not for what happened before Voluus left the town last time.'

I felt a sudden sinking feeling in my guts. 'And what was that?'

'I'm surprised you haven't heard. He had a letter threatening that he would be robbed and killed if he attempted to move to Glevum. They found it when he'd left. It wasn't signed or sealed of course – just a scribbled scroll left anonymously at the mansio. It was done so fast they did not even catch the messenger.'

I remembered Brianus's story of his master's outburst at the military inn. That had been in answer to a message he'd received. I managed not to nod. I said, rather shakily, 'That does not sound like the way the rebels operate, it's true. And I suppose a lictor does make enemies.'

'Voluus clearly thought so. He was evidently so worried by the threat that it appears he paid . . .' he hesitated, and obviously decided against mentioning the name '. . . someone to keep watch on his apartment day and night while he was gone.'

I did nod this time. That explained how I came to be observed. 'I see. He was obviously alarmed. So you are taking this threatening message seriously?'

He looked at me gravely. 'Very seriously indeed. And whoever made the threat is serious as well. There is not only this robbery to take into account. There has been murder, too – and of a citizen.'

'Not the lictor?' I wondered if there was something I had not heard about.

'Not the lictor, but a Roman citizen all the same. He was with the cart.'

'One of the mounted escort? I'd assumed that they were all

slaves, either owned by Voluus or hired from somebody to guard the cart for him.'

'I believe they were. I understand that there were slave-discs discovered round their necks. Of course those deaths are most unfortunate, but obviously the killing of a citizen is of more immediate concern. He seems to have been the driver of the cart. I'll show you what was brought here by the traveller who happened on the scene and brought us word of it.' He stooped and picked up a bloodied bundle from the floor beside his desk, and slowly unwrapped it so that I could see.

'Dear gods,' I murmured. I was looking at a handsome travelling cape – or the remains of one. It was not difficult to see what had occurred – it was slashed in several places and each hole was drenched in blood. 'Someone was clearly savagely attacked. But how can you be certain it was a citizen?'

'Several reasons, citizen. That cloak was wrapped around the driver's hacked remains. It is clearly not the sort of garment a common slave would wear. And the man who found him recovered this from round his waist.' From a drawer in the table he produced a *balteus*, a handsome military belt, distinguished by the silver chasing on the front and the holster for a dagger on one side. 'Most veterans choose to keep these when they leave the force, though the studded apron is – naturally – removed. Perhaps we are lucky that the finder brought it in. If it were not so clearly a military thing, he might have tried to sell it for the silver it contains.'

'So the driver was almost certainly a veteran, you think?' The commandant's concern was making sense to me. 'Retired cavalry, do you suppose?' Most soldiers simply married when they left the force and used their accumulated pay to buy a piece of land, but those in the mounted units – having spent a life with horses – sometimes chose to carry on, purchasing an animal and a cart which they could ply for hire and so make an honest living for their remaining years.

The commander nodded as he put the things away. 'Exactly so. We think he was an auxiliary from this very garrison: one of the Gallic contingent that was here before I came. One of my officers thinks he recognizes the pattern of the belt. This

kind of silver chasing is distinctive, as you see – typical of
the kind those Gallic horsemen wear.'

I drew a sharp breath inwards. 'So you think the dead man
was, at one time, stationed here?' No wonder he was interested
in pursuing this. 'And that's why you think he was a Roman
citizen! Even if he was not born into the rank, he would have
gained his diploma on retirement, of course.'

'That is the assumption that I am working on. It looks as
if he served until retirement age.' He ran the fingers through
his hair again, and because he was closer to me now, I caught
the faint whiff of horseradish and spice – the most famous
cure for baldness in the world. In any other circumstances it
would have made me grin. I had not expected the commandant
to be vain.

He took my silence for disagreement with his argument. He
sat down to face me, leaning forward as he pressed the point.
'Look, Libertus, he could hardly be a private driver if he were
not discharged, and the body – or what is left of it – appears
to be unmarked. No mention of any ancient scars, as you'd
expect if he was wounded and invalided out.' He looked
thoughtful for a moment. 'Though I suppose there might have
been damage to an arm. I understand that both were missing
when the corpse was found.'

'What's happened to the body?' I demanded suddenly, earning
myself a disapproving glare: it was not my place to be putting
questions here. I added, by way of half-apology, 'I ask because
I feel it should be checked again. Whoever found it might not
have looked for things like that. It is enough to find a mutilated
corpse without stopping to examine it for signs of ancient
wounds. And of course there might be other clues as well.'

The commander put his veined hands on the desk in front
of him. 'I believe there's a detachment of my men out at the
site of the attack. They were going to move the bodies – there
are five or six of them – and bring them back to Glevum to
be buried here. I had not considered travelling to see the place
myself, but you rouse my interest.' He looked at me wryly.
'Would you care to come? I understand you are an expert in
this kind of thing. Marcus Septimus is always telling me as
much.'

I was so astounded that I could only mutter, 'Me? Accompany you? But Florens has demanded . . . ?'

The lean face softened to what might have been a smile. 'Oh, don't misunderstand me, citizen. I don't mean to set you free. The law obliges me to keep you under guard. And you will have to answer questions as we go along. However, I would be glad to have your views. Officially, we'll regard it as cooperation on your part, and I can quote that in your favour if you come to court.'

I had really expected that I'd be dragged away in chains, so I could hardly believe my good fortune as he shouted a command and the plump centurion, Emelius, came hurrying in again.

My elation vanished very quickly, though, as the commander said, 'Take this man away and shut him in a cell until I send for him. When you have done that, see that some transport is arranged for me, with the fastest horses that we have available. Something substantial, not a military gig – I intend to see this crime scene for myself, and I'm taking the prisoner with me when I go.'

You could see the question forming on Emelius's face, though he was too well-trained to say anything aloud.

'It's perfectly in order. He has agreed to help us with the crime. I'm not releasing him, he will be under guard. In fact, I can't think of a better person to guard him than yourself, so I am relieving you of duties here and you'll accompany us. I shall want a mounted escort, too, of course. Half a dozen horsemen should suffice. Report to the officer of the day and tell him what I've said.' He turned back to the documents on his desk again and picked up an iron-tipped pen. 'Well, man, what are you waiting for? You have your orders. See that they're obeyed.'

The centurion, who was still looking very much bemused, came to a smart salute and then marched – a careful military march – across to me. Before I realized what was happening he had seized me by the arm and twisted it cruelly up behind my back. Thus pinioned and unbalanced I could not resist as he propelled me expertly towards the door.

He was about to thrust me through it when the commander called him back. 'One more thing, officer!'

I relaxed, hoping that this heralded relief from my discomfort, but I was disappointed.

'While you are about it bring me a report from the officer of the day, saying who has been deployed to bring those bodies in. That is all – dismissed.'

Another swift salute and then I found myself being bundled headlong down the stairs again, through the guard-room – under the startled stare of the man with the accounts – and out into the court. I scarcely had time to recognize that it was raining hard again before the centurion had propelled me round the corner of the tower, unbolted the door of a small and airless cell, pushed me unceremoniously into it and slammed the door again.

NINE

I fell on my knees in an inch of stinking straw and, even as I did so, I heard the bolt slide to. I tried to look about, but there was no window in the room so it was too dark to make out anything at all and the thickness of the door was muffling all sound – even the patter of the rain could not be heard. A feeling of helpless terror flooded over me.

I had heard – all of us had heard – the story of the thief who had been kept for days in a darkened cell like this, with only a flask of water and a loaf of bread, and who had been found crazed and screaming when they unlocked the door. I fought my rising panic and tried to gain control. I knew from my quick glimpse as I tumbled in that I was the only human occupant, so I edged myself gingerly into a squatting pose and was pleased to find there was no scuttling of rats. My exploring hands discovered several iron rings set into the wall and a sort of rough stone trough in the centre of the floor, with something slimy in the base of it – presumably used for feeding the chained-up prisoners. The smell was overwhelming: rotting straw and damp and – most of all – the stench of human fear.

Including mine, no doubt. I tried to tell myself that I would not be here for long, although . . . I gave myself a shake. I would not think like that. I forced myself to think of something else – wondering if Calvinus the steward was being held somewhere like this, and what his fastidious nature would have made of it.

I found a relatively dryish spot and eased my aching thighs by sitting down on it, though there was little comfort in the change. The chill of the stones soon reached me through my tunic and my cape, which in any case was damp. Damp? And getting damper? A trickle of rain was seeping in from underneath the door – somewhere there must be some sort of gap, through which air and light could also pass. My eager fingers traced the moisture to the place – a tiny crack above one corner of the sill. There was the faintest suspicion of a draught and by concentrating very hard indeed I could make out a line of glimmer from beyond. It was a small thing, but it gave me comfort all the same.

Time had no meaning in this environment. Already it seemed that I'd been shut in here for hours. Gwellia would be frantic when I did not appear, and there was no way now of getting any messages to her. It seemed impossible that only a short while ago I had been a free man walking through the town with nothing to threaten my life and liberty, and no more than a contract for a pavement on my mind. And now . . . ! I tried to still my fears by thinking through the facts.

I was still convinced that bandits would prove to be to blame. Only the threats to Voluus suggested otherwise – though that explained the reason for there being watchers at his flat. To whom were they reporting while Voluus was away? It must have been someone. The garrison, perhaps? Or maybe it was to Florens or – more likely – Porteus, since he had some sort of business dealings with the lictor regarding tracts of land. Voluus must have taken him into his confidence. And then when the threatened raid had taken place the trail led back to me.

I shook my head. Why had the lictor chosen Glevum, anyway? It seemed a strange decision after years in Gaul. I could understand a wish to move away from where he'd served – a lifetime of inflicting punishment does not earn one friends, and once the governor of the province had retired back to Rome there was no longer his protection to be relied upon. But why to Glevum? Why Britannia at all? This northern province with its cold, wet winters and so far away from Rome seemed an unlikely choice for someone who had no ties to it. There must be a reason, but I could not think of one.

My musings were interrupted by the opening of the door and a ray of sudden daylight so bright it dazzled me. I was still sitting, hunched up on the straw and blinking stupidly, when someone grasped my elbows and levered me upright. Firm hands pulled me gently out into the court and then, amazingly, begin to dust me down.

'Citizen, I can't apologize enough!' I realized that it was the plump centurion, his face now scarlet and his voice concerned. 'Nobody told me you were a citizen! I trust you have not taken any serious harm?' He was pulling damp straws from my dishevelled cape. 'Come into the guard-room and I'll see you get some wine and perhaps a bowl of water so your slave can rinse your feet.'

I gazed around and realized who my saviours were. My heart gave an idiotic leap of hope. Junio and Minimus were standing in the guard-room, staring out at me. My son, I saw, was looking furious. 'So, am I to be freed?' I murmured foolishly.

Emelius shook his head. 'I'm afraid not, citizen. It's simply that I put you in the common cell instead of taking proper care of you. I can only beg you to pardon my mistake. It was an honest one. I knew that purple-striper was a citizen, of course, but I didn't realize what treatment you were entitled to, until members of your household informed me of your rank.' He swallowed visibly. 'I hope you were not planning to file a complaint.' His distress – in the circumstances – was almost laughable.

I did not permit myself even the vestige of a smile. Having a legal hold, however faint, on the centurion might well prove to my advantage later on. I tried to look like an affronted man of dignity – instead of an ex-slave who was relieved to be outside in the clean rain. 'I have not yet decided,' I told him loftily. 'But I would be glad to receive the little comforts you suggest. And I believe that I'm entitled to confer with the members of my household who I see are here.'

The centurion nodded. I knew what he supposed. It is not uncommon for a prisoner (provided that he is not charged with an offence against the state) to pay his captors to bring him extra comforts in his cell, like food and drink and something warm to wear. If he does not have sufficient wherewithal for that, a coin might at least persuade the jailors to permit his household to bring things in for him. Emelius no doubt surmised that I was going to ask Junio for some little luxury, or for money with which to pay the guard! Perhaps it would be wise. However, that was not what I'd been thinking of. I wanted to have someone go back to my wife and let her know what was happening to me.

'Your son and slave are waiting in the guard-house now,' my captor said. 'Come in and speak to them.' He was already opening the door and ushering me inside.

The soldier with the abacus had finished his accounts and was now carefully sprinkling the bark-paper with sand to dry the ink. He was doing it so slowly that I was almost sure he was protracting the job deliberately in order to stay and listen in. He'd obviously heard about the incident, though I suspected – from the expression on his face – that he was not so much concerned that I'd been locked in the wrong cell as he was keen to know if this meant trouble for the plump centurion.

However, he did not have the chance to satisfy his curiosity. The centurion was already ordering him away with instructions to have wine and water brought for me. I, meanwhile, was waved on to the stool on which the octio had been sitting up till then.

Junio had already risen from the bench beside the wall. 'Father!' he cried. 'What have they done to you? Your face and hands are filthy, and your cloak as well.'

I looked down at myself and saw that he was right. I hadn't realized what a spectacle I made. I flapped a muddied hand at the still-clinging straws. 'They haven't hurt me. I'm dirty, that is all.'

Junio was clearly not convinced by this. 'If they have harmed you, tell me instantly. I'll see that Marcus takes the matter up with the Provincial governor.' He saw me shake my head and went on urgently. 'I am sorry that it took so long for us to get to you. We went to the curia, where we thought you were, but we couldn't find you. One of the street-urchins told us you'd been marched away.'

'You've finished the pavement, then?' I asked him.

That earned a bitter smile. 'Only you would worry about a thing like that! Certainly we have completed it. But whether you wish us to deliver it – now that Florens has done this awful thing to you – that's quite another thing. On what possible pretext has he brought you here and had you treated in this appalling way?'

I quickly outlined what the situation was.

'So it's the fact that Voluus received a written threat which really caused the problem?' Junio said. 'That's clearly the letter that Brianus was talking about. I wonder if he could tell us any more? I'll see if I can find him when I leave.'

'I wanted you to tell your adoptive mother where I am and warn her that I might not be coming home tonight.' That was the least of it, as Junio well knew. If things went ill for me, I might not be coming home at all, but there was no point in worrying Gwellia with that – for now, at any rate.

He inclined his head to show he understood. 'If there is nothing more that we can do to ease your plight, I think I'll go and see if I can talk to Brianus. Minimus can take your message to the roundhouse straight away and I will follow when I've finished with the lictor's slave.' He turned to me. 'I'll look in again here before I leave the town, and make sure that at least they're still treating you aright. If I learn anything from Brianus, of course, I'll tell you then. Come, Minimus. Take leave of my father and then take that message to your mistress as fast as possible.'

Minimus came to kneel a moment at my feet. It wasn't a gesture I expected from my slaves and I found it rather touching, especially as he whispered as he kissed my hand, 'Don't lose heart, master. We will get you out of here.'

Then he and Junio left the room – just as the octio came in with the wine, followed by a skinny domestic orderly carrying a basin of clean water and a towel.

It felt wonderfully normal to rinse my face and hands, and to have the freedom to take my muddy sandals off and wash my grimy feet, though I was still uncomfortably aware of Emelius and the octio watching every move.

My ablutions took a little time and I didn't hurry them. I have become so spoiled in recent years that I am not accustomed to doing this without a slave, and the orderly did not offer to assist except to hand me the towel afterwards. However, after my confinement in that airless cell it felt like luxury merely to be clean – and besides, the chill had clearly been taken off the water for my benefit.

When I'd finished, I was almost looking forward to my

drink. Watered Roman wine is not my favourite beverage –
especially not the rough kind which the army use – but today
it seemed a symbol of respect. However, I did not get a chance
to so much as sample it, for no sooner had the octio lifted up
the jug to pour me a beakerful, than a stout soldier in burnished
scale armour and military boots came bustling in and told us
brusquely that our transport was outside.

TEN

'Ready and waiting,' this apparition said. 'And the message has been sent up to the commander too and he is on his way – so I hope that we've managed to get him what he wants.'

I looked at Emelius, surprised, 'Was that so difficult? I thought the army had lots of carts at its command.'

The plump centurion shrugged. 'It's all a question of the type of vehicle. The commander asked for something that would hold all three of us – I think you heard him saying so to me – and there will have to be a driver, too, of course: I am no use in that capacity. The army expects the cavalry to ride and the rest of us to march: it doesn't have many carriages to transport passengers. And he specified fast horses, so we couldn't use an ox-cart, though we do have lots of those, for transporting food and all that sort of thing. But I gather something suitable was found?'

The reporting soldier looked extremely smug. 'We didn't have anything available ourselves – except for the commander's gig, which carries two at best – so I've requisitioned a carriage from the hiring-stables just outside the walls.'

'And who is driving it?'

'I demanded one of theirs. The stable-owner wasn't very pleased, but I quoted the regulations about *angaria* – "the army has first call on private transport at any time and civilian owners must cooperate, by order of the Emperor" – and there was nothing he could do. So he's got this carriage waiting at the gate. Our own escort is armed and mounted and ready to depart. I hope all this is satisfactory.' He waited for the centurion to nod, then went on silkily, 'If so, perhaps you'd mention this to your superiors? I'm hoping for promotion to be in charge of stores.'

Emelius waved this loftily aside. 'Later, perhaps. There is no time now for anything like that. The commander is likely

to be there ahead of us and he does not like to be delayed.
Come, citizen prisoner, I'm afraid your wine will have to wait.'
So saying, he took the half-full beaker from the octio's hand,
put it on the table and marched me from the room.

Heads turned to watch us as we crossed the court and left the
military enclosure, then past the sentry and through the public
gate that led out of the town. The carriage and the horsemen
were assembled there, as promised, and the commander, too. He
was talking to the leader of the escort-party as we approached,
but he looked up, saw us and signalled with a wave that we were
to precede him into the vehicle.

The carriage was of a kind that one often sees for hire: a
two-horse vehicle with a driver's seat in front and a covered
compartment for the passengers, complete with leather
curtains at the side to keep the dust at bay. The driver was
already sitting in his place, a picture of resentment, studiously
looking the other way and making no attempt to help. He had
not even provided any temporary step, although the sill was
high, so I must have looked remarkably undignified as I
hoisted myself in.

Emelius gestured me to take the central seat, then scrambled
up himself, puffing and clanking his armour as he came, though
the garrison commander – with the assistance of a military
slave – managed to mount the other side with grace.

He fastened back the leather curtain, so that he could see
(after the recent rains there was no chance of dust), then
signalled to the horsemen and they trotted on ahead, while we
lurched into motion and jolted after them. We had no sooner
started, though, than I expected we would have to stop again
– for as we pulled away a plump figure in a patrician toga
came hustling through the gate, calling after us and waving
something in his hand. Our driver must have seen him because
he slowed the cart, but the commander briskly banged the
floor and told him to drive on, leaving the purple-striper
standing helpless in the road.

As soon as we were safely on our way and had cleared the
outskirts of the town, the escort wheeled and cantered back
to take up close formation round the coach: one pair to the
side of us, another to the rear, and the last two continuing as

outriders in front. This might have been for the commander's safety, I suppose, but it underlined the fact that I was under heavy guard.

It was an uncomfortable journey, as such trips always are: though this carriage had the luxury of being hung on leather straps, and as we were on the military road there were no huge bumps and potholes to bounce us from our seats. However, we were travelling as fast as possible and the constant rattling over cobbled stones still set up a vibration in your skull which seemed in danger of loosening your teeth. I pitied Voluus and his party who must have suffered this, and worse, for days and days on end while they were travelling through Gaul to reach the coast.

There was a leather loop provided on the frame and the commander was holding grimly on to it. 'I wonder what Porteus wanted . . . He seemed to be in haste . . . Nothing to your advantage, I imagine, citizen?'

So it was Porteus at the gatehouse, and the commander knew that he was there! I dared not ask for reasons, so I shook my head. 'Perhaps he's found another witness to swear that I was visiting Voluus today. Anything to prove that I'm involved in stealing from that cart. He obviously believes I'm guilty, although I don't know why – or why he is so exercised about this theft, in any case. People are set upon by brigands every month or two.'

The commander smiled. 'Porteus has a lively interest in Voluus's affairs.'

'I heard . . .' I broke off as one wheel struck a cobble and pitched us in the air. 'I heard he'd sold the lictor a parcel of his land.'

The commander nodded. 'Voluus was looking for a place to build a villa on, and Porteus sold him some land. He's been boasting ever since that he's got a hefty price for it.'

'Titus Flavius was teasing him about it in the curia, saying that he wanted gold to bribe his way to being Imperial Servir – though if he is planning to finance public works to win the vote, it does seem odd of him to sell the land. You'd think he'd need continued income from whatever crops he grew. Or was it not successful?'

'It was for several years. Porteus owned a forest on the western hills . . . good stands of oak and pinewood . . . and was doing very well. He was shipping timber everywhere and making a small fortune out of it. But last year there was a devastating fire . . . he tends to blame the rebels, though other people say it was the hand of Jove.'

'Meaning that it was struck by lightning?' I asked, trying hard to sound intelligent, though it wasn't easy when your teeth were rattling.

A nod. 'Perhaps it really was the work of Jupiter. In any case it almost ruined him. More than half the trees were burnt to ashes in the blaze, and his store of cut timber was destroyed as well . . . But Porteus had already spent his profits for the year. He was glad to –' He broke off as the carriage noticeably slowed, and he leaned out to look. 'We seem to be stopping. I wonder why?'

Even from my seat it wasn't difficult to see. We had caught up with the route march from the garrison. This was obviously a nuisance but I resigned myself to wait – the army always has priority. Non-military traffic simply has to yield.

However, there were benefits to having the garrison commander in the coach. He beckoned to the escort-rider next to him and murmured a command. The fellow cantered off, and shortly afterwards we heard a shouted order from far in front of us. There was a synchronized scuffling of scores of sandal-soles, and suddenly the single column of soldiers divided into two, leaving a central passage down the midst of them. The marchers halted – still in unison – and drew up in neat ranks, lining the route on either side to let us through, while the march officer and signifer both tendered a salute.

There was momentary silence (from us, in any case) as the carriage gathered speed and the tooth-loosening jolting recommenced. Emelius had taken off his helmet when we stopped – it had twice earlier hit the ceiling of the coach, endangering the distinctive sideways plume. He was now holding it between his knees, which gave me even less room than before.

I clutched the seat with both hands to hold myself upright and avoid bruising from the armour on either side of me. This news about Porteus's financial problems was causing me to think. Here was someone who knew the treasure-cart was due and had both some indication of what it might contain, and a lively motive for appropriating it! Was it possible that accusing me was just a bluff, and he had been the one to steal the lictor's gold himself?

It was no doubt a ludicrous idea, and I dismissed it instantly, but I was hoping the commander would finish his account. However, he was staring at the passing countryside, watching the land-slaves and farmers struggling with the mud, and the pigs and chickens straggling by the road. I could see that shortly we'd be in the wooded area where the cart was found, and then perhaps I'd never hear the rest.

'You were talking about Porteus,' I prompted finally. 'He found himself in trouble with his creditors? Because he had no timber for the market-place?' I was trying to see how this might be relevant. 'I suppose that no one local would buy the forest after that. People would no doubt say that it was cursed.'

The commander turned slowly back to me. 'Exactly so! So when Voluus wrote to him and offered a good price – saying that he wished to build a villa on the site – naturally Porteus struck a bargain instantly.'

'But did the lictor know about the fire?' The law puts responsibility on the purchaser to ensure that what he buys is fit for use.

'He went so far as to joke about it, I believe, saying that it saved the labour of clearing off the ground. Porteus was thrilled. He was boasting about it in the curia. He got his slaves to take away the ash and level the whole area to put the building on. Voluus was to pay him when his goods arrived from Gaul.' He smiled. 'You can see why Porteus is anxious to discover where they went.'

It was no use nodding; my head was already being jiggled firmly up and down. I said, 'I can see his problem when the treasure disappeared – but not why he should think of blaming me!'

'Perhaps you are the first solution which presents itself? You must admit that circumstances seem to point to you. And he has an even greater problem than you think: he also has a daughter to be wed – plain as a gladiator's sword and about as feminine – and he has promised a handsome dowry to the prospective groom.'

'So he doubly needs the money?' I gripped the seat still tighter as we jolted round a bend.

'He even tried to earn some,' the commander said, 'when he learned about the threat to Voluus. It seems he made a second contract with the man, undertaking that – for another promised fee – he would post some slaves and keep a watch on the apartment night and day while the lictor was away. Voluus did not wholly trust his steward, it appears, and the slaves reported back to Porteus constantly. I don't have to tell you what they said today – what they told Florens pointed straight to you.'

We had moved into the outskirts of the forest now and even the military road was suffering from the recent storms. Branches had fallen from the older trees and here and there the road-stone had been washed away. 'But what does Florens have to do with it?' I said, still trying to brace myself against the lurching of the cart.

The commandant allowed himself a little smile. 'Who do you suppose is the prospective groom?'

That was a surprise, though I should have thought of it. I knew that Florens wanted that pavement to be laid in honour of his forthcoming marriage to some second wife. What I had not guessed was who the bride would be – I had imagined some wealthy dowager, 'dutiful and suitable', as the saying was.

The centurion was obviously equally amazed. I had forgotten that he was listening to all this. 'Florens? Dear Mercury!' he gasped. 'But he's half as old as Rome! That girl can't be fifteen!'

The commander raised an eyebrow and said reprovingly, 'I don't remember giving you permission to converse! Kindly do not speak until you're spoken to. But enough of that – it seems that we have arrived.'

He was right. The carriage was grumbling to a halt. One of the mounted escort slid gently from his horse and came across to us.

'We've reached our destination, sir. The fatigue-party is here and removing bodies now – or they were until we ordered them to stop. Do you wish to come and see? It isn't very pleasant, as you will understand.'

For answer the commander put one hand on the cart and vaulted down, making it look easy, like the athlete that he was. The escort-rider offered me his arm and helped me to the ground, while Emelius came lumbering after us, stuffing his helmet back on to his head, his baton and sword-case clanking against his armour as he ran. Then – looking sheepish – he pulled his dagger out and made a half-pretence of guarding me with it.

I turned away to look around the scene. The outrider was right. The sight which greeted us was not a pleasant one. The ground was littered with the arms and legs and bodies of the dead – strewn across the edges of the road and scattered in the rough grass and bushes of the forest-edge. I even saw one limb, still dangling a shoe, which evidently had been tossed into a tree. Half-dismembered horses added to the scene. It seemed that there were bloodstains everywhere. The damp forest air was heavy with the smell of it.

The army dead-cart was parked over to one side, one or two parts of corpses already loaded on, and its crew of soldiers were standing next to it, obviously having been interrupted in their work. The garrison commander looked them up and down. 'Who seems to be in charge here?' he demanded.

'Me, commander. Sesquipularius Auxiliary Brunus at your service, sir.' A swarthy senior soldier in a knee-length woollen cloak, sweat-stained leather tunic and a chain-mail jerkin stepped forward and performed a smart salute. I realized that I'd met the man before. I'd nicknamed him 'Scowler', though he wasn't scowling now. He was treating the commander to an obsequious smile. 'Hard to believe there were only five of them.' He gestured to the human pieces lying on his cart. 'Of course some idiot has half-dismembered several horses, too. And have you seen the state of that?'

He pointed. In the midst of this carnage stood another cart – this one half-lurched into a nearby ditch. Slumped across the titled driver's seat was the limbless torso of a man. It was dressed in just a tunic – or what remained of one – and it told the same tale that the cloak had done: the savage, bloodstained slashes could be seen from here.

'Merciful Mars!' I heard the centurion's muttered oath. He had been standing close beside me – apparently in case I tried to make a run for it. 'In my life I've seen some gruesome scenes – on a battlefield you expect such things. But so many corpses on a public road . . . !' He made a helpless gesture with his muscle-armoured arm, incidentally lowering the dagger as he spoke.

I turned to the commander, but he was staring at the beasts with a peculiar expression on his face. I realized that the slaughter of the horses had affected him – perhaps more than the killing of the driver and the slaves. It was vaguely shocking, though I recollected he'd been a member of the cavalry himself.

He cleared his throat and said, quite gruffly, 'Poor brutes – what had they ever done to anyone! But, Libertus, there was something that you wished to say to me?'

'That seems to be the driver of the coach – or what is left of him. The owner of that belt and cloak you showed to me – and therefore your Roman citizen, I suppose?'

He looked then, and nodded. 'Hardly an inch of flesh that's not been slashed. Not much chance of finding ancient scars on that. Or of having him identified, as I had rather hoped, so that someone at his funeral could call his name aloud. All the same we must see that he is treated properly, in accordance with his rank.' He turned to Scowler. 'See that the driver's body is accorded due respect. Find something suitable with which to cover him.'

Scowler looked puzzled. A sesquipularius is a fairly junior rank, merely a one-and-a-half-pay petty officer – as such, he clearly did things by the rules and this unexpected order took him by surprise. 'But, sir, we don't have anything to cover bodies with. We never carry anything like that – usually we are only dealing with people who don't count, paupers who perished on the public road. We just sling them on the pile then tip them out in the communal pit and cover them with lime – along with those who died of plague or common criminals.'

The commander gave him an icy look. 'I see that you are

wearing a military cloak. That would do very well. And make
sure that you do not simply "sling this body on the pile" – to
use your charming phrase. We think he was a Roman citizen.
More than that, in fact – we have reason to believe that he
was once an auxiliary soldier like yourself. So bring him to
the garrison when you have finished here, before you dispose
of any of the rest. The army will see that he has a proper
burial.'

'Whatever you command, sir.' Scowler looked both
astounded and abashed. Then he recalled himself. He seized
the swagger stick that was hanging on his belt, thumped his
palm with it and turned to his outfit with the scowl I'd seen
before. 'Come on, you lazy good-for-nothing sons of whores!'
he roared. 'You there, on the end. You heard the commander.
Let us have your cloak. Put it round that body over there and
leave it till the last. We'll put that one on separately when we
have loaded all the rest. And try to find the arms and legs that
go with it. Well, don't stand there gawping. You have your
orders, what are you waiting for? Move! Before I use this
baton on your backs!'

ELEVEN

The men moved off grumbling and Scowler strutted self-importantly across to supervise. The soldier that he had singled out, muttering imprecations when his superior could not see, stripped off his cloak and wrapped the driver's corpse in it, while the others began collecting dismembered parts, apparently to see if they belonged – rather as I'd fitted tiles into the pavement earlier. They were so dispassionate about the task, it made this an oddly gruesome exercise to watch.

The commander clearly thought so. He turned to me again. 'Well, citizen, I'm very glad we came, if only to get a first-hand view of these events and ensure that the driver's body gets a proper burial. But now it seems there's little more we can do. It is quite clear what happened. I see that I was wrong and you were right. This must have been the work of brigands, after all. Nothing to do with any threats that Voluus received.'

I looked around me at the carnage on the ground. There was something niggling in the corner of my mind – some detail that I could not quite identify – which made me feel this was not exactly what it seemed. Perhaps it was that feeling of disquiet which prompted me to ask, 'What makes you so positive of that?'

He looked at me, surprised. 'Well, surely, citizen, it is obvious. This is no casual assault and robbery. It would take a band of well-armed people to overcome that guard – swords and axes by the look of it – and who but rebels carry weaponry like that? No law-abiding citizen could lay their hands on them – far less use them to such horrible effect.'

I wished I were as certain as he was about that. It was true that civilians are forbidden to carry sharpened weapons in a public place – that law had been in force since the first nefas Ides of March. However, even the humblest landowner has hatchets and large knives on his estate, if only for chopping timber and butchering the stock – I even own such implements myself. But obviously I did not volunteer that fact. Instead I said inanely, 'This was clearly not a law-abiding man. And almost everybody carries blades from time to time – if only knives when they are going to dine.'

Emelius, who had his own dagger half-pointed at my ribs again, laughed scornfully. 'It would take more than dining-knives to make a scene like this! And it was not one man – it was a band of them. What is more . . .' He seemed to feel the commander's icy glare. 'With your permission, sir!'

His superior nodded. 'Go on, centurion.'

'It must have been a well-commanded band and very used to stealth.' He shot a look at me. 'I've been in a few ambushes and I can tell you that. No one else could have crept up on this lot unobserved, not even in the night, let alone while they were wide awake and travelling along.'

The commander glanced at me. 'Go on,' he said again.

Emelius, encouraged, was happy to rush on. (The name means 'eager' and it clearly suited him.) 'These guards would have been watching for attack – that's what they were here for – and most of them were obviously armed. Some of those bodies still have cudgels hanging from their belts. Not even time to heft them, by the look of it.'

'Well said, centurion!' the commandant approved. 'That seems to confirm my views beyond all doubt.' He turned enquiringly to me. 'I think we can report back to the curia that there was a rebel ambush on the cart, and the guards were taken by surprise and overwhelmed. Perhaps it's not surprising that such a thing occurred – the news that there was treasure on the way was common gossip, I believe. It would not have been difficult for it to reach the bandits' ears. This might have been avoided – with sufficient care.'

It was very tempting simply to agree and thus deflect suspicion from Marcus and myself. After all, this was the conclusion that I'd been urging up till now. But I was still uneasy – though I could not say why. It was perverse, I knew, but some demon of honesty obliged me to reply, 'Yet if this were the work of rebels, why not take the weapons, too? And why kill the horses,

which could be of use to them – or at least sold for profit at
the market-place?'

I moved towards the nearest creature as I spoke – a stocky
animal, clearly one of the horses which had pulled the cart. It
had been cruelly disembowelled, the tail and head removed, and
it had bled disgustingly. The commander seemed unwilling to
approach, but the centurion followed me, still affecting to keep
me under guard but at the same time taking a closer look himself.
He was obviously emboldened by the commander's earlier praise
and was now anxious to offer his opinions about everything.

'Perhaps the rebels didn't have the time to deal with the
horses when they took the treasure from the cart,' he ventured.
'They would have had to hide whatever they removed, and
quickly, too, I suppose.'

'Then why should raiders – who presumably are simply
after gold – stop to chop the bodies up and scatter them about?'
I countered.

The commander smiled at me indulgently. 'Questions,
always questions, citizen! But there is an answer this time. It
has been known for rebels to mutilate a corpse – especially
those of Roman soldiers, when they can – though the army
does not advertise the fact. It happened to a couple from this
very garrison not two years ago. It was just before I came,
under the previous commander of the fort: the two men ran
into a rebel ambush on the road and when the army found the
hacked-about remains they couldn't have identified the bodies
of their own if they hadn't known who they were looking for.
But as for severed heads – that's quite another thing. You don't
need me to tell you that – if there are Druids in the rebellious
ranks – the victims' heads are always seized, and taken as
trophies to the sacred grove. Everyone knows that.'

I nodded. I had seen such groves myself, hung with the
grisly offerings of the severed heads of foes. I looked down
at the mutilated animal again. 'Heads, I will grant you. And
perhaps the human mutilation is what you say it is – a gesture
of defiance against the Empire. But why the animals?'

He winced. 'For the same reasons, wouldn't you suppose?'

I shook my head. 'At such a risk? Take that horse for
instance: it clearly died there, where it lies – you can still see

the hoof prints in the mud, and the pool of blood and trampled grasses where it fell – but most of the hacking must have happened after death. All that dismemberment would have taken quite some time. Why jeopardize your getaway by stopping to do that? You would suppose – whoever did it – that having made the raid, they'd want to disappear as soon as possible. This, after all, is a major public road and it could not be long before somebody arrived.'

The commander heard me out, then answered patiently, 'Yet I could ask a dozen questions of my own which point the other way. If this was not the work of local brigands, why attack the cart-load here? Why not attack it nearer to the port or somewhere where there is no garrison nearby?'

'Most of all, if this was personal revenge on Voluus, why not wait till he got to Glevum and murder him as well?' That was Emelius, proudly laying his idea before his senior officer, as a cat will bring a mouse. 'Once the lictor is established in the town, with only his own house-slaves for company, robbing and attacking him would be far easier. Imagine deliberately setting on a guard as strong as this!'

I half-expected that he would be rebuked, but the commander smiled. 'True again, centurion. Remind me to commend you for a bonus on the Nones.'

He took a step or two towards the nearest human corpse, which was lying in the long grass among the trees, and I followed suit to get a better view. This one still had its face and arms attached though both the legs were gone. The owner had hardly been a handsome man in life, but he was young and virile and very muscular. He had clearly been a slave – there was a brand on the shoulder and a slave-disc round the neck – but bizarrely the dead face appeared to wear a smile.

I stared down at the sorry spectacle. Hard to believe that only a day or so ago this fellow had been very much alive and in his prime. He had a dagger too, despite the law, still firmly in its sheath. By whom, and how, had he been set upon – so suddenly that he had not had time to draw the blade? It was just as the centurion had said: death seemed to have caught him entirely unaware.

I shook my head. 'I suppose that you and the centurion are

right. This must have been an ambush by an overwhelming force which made no noise at all on its approach and which caught all the riders – in one stroke – entirely off guard.' Even as I said it, it sounded improbable.

I looked around again. The fatigue-party had found what seemed to be the driver's arm, and were still foraging for the rest of him, retrieving bloody limbs to try against the stumps and, under Scowler's supervision, making a collection of assorted legs and feet. Grisly, certainly, but disquieting as well? There was something – I knew that there was something – right in front of me. What was it that I should be noticing?

There was one severed hand which lay not far away, and I went over to take a closer look at that. I did not pick it up, but crouched down on the grass, consciously attending to every detail. The centurion followed me across and this time the commander accompanied me, too.

'Found something of interest?' he said to me at last.

'I think perhaps I have. See it for yourself.' I turned the object over gingerly. 'There is a little staining from the mud but otherwise there are no marks on it. Look at it closely. What does it suggest to you?'

'The ring has not been looted,' the centurion said, pointing to a silver ring still on the finger. The promised bonus had redoubled his attempts to help. 'Though perhaps that's no surprise. Compared to other things, it was not valuable enough. Obviously they haven't even tried to pull it off.' He looked triumphant at his own cleverness.

The commander nodded. 'But look how relatively undamaged the hand is otherwise. I see what Libertus might be driving at. Even the fingernails are perfect and there's nothing under them, so it seems that the victim didn't even scratch or scrabble as he died.'

'Exactly! There's no sign that he tried to defend himself at all, even when the killer was right on top of him. No bruises, cuts or scratches on the flesh, except the one blow that lopped it from the arm – and the slight loss of blood that happened after death. Literally, it seems, he did not raise a hand to help himself.' I got back to my feet, rubbing my hands together to brush off the mud and grass. 'I wonder . . . ?'

The commander was looking searchingly at me. 'What is it you wonder?'

It was just a hazy notion, but I voiced it all the same. 'Possibly he thought his attacker was a friend? Maybe the whole escort thought something similar. Surely it must be something of the kind? How else would a band of people acting as a guard – and an armed guard at that – permit another group to come close enough to kill?'

He looked a little brighter. 'I suppose that's possible.'

'It would have to be a group that they were not surprised to see – a relief contingent, perhaps, which they'd been warned they might expect?'

'Which would bring us back to some sort of conspiracy from here.' The chiselled face relapsed into a frown. 'Oh, dear Mercury, let's hope that you are wrong and this is the work of simple rebels. It makes things so much easier to understand.' He moved aside to let two of the soldiers pass, dragging a headless, legless corpse between them to the pile. 'If you are right, this could be anyone. Anyone with a grudge against the lictor, anyway.'

'The person who wrote to threaten him, in fact?' I said, aware that I had previously argued just the opposite.

The commander made a doubtful face. 'In that case why not wait and kill Voluus himself? Everyone in Glevum knew he wasn't on the cart.' He caught my look and realized that he, too, was now refuting a position he'd once advanced himself. He turned away towards our carriage with an irritated shrug. 'It does not make any sense to me at all.'

Scowler was loitering a step or two away, and as soon as we moved off he gave a whistled signal to his men and one of the fatigue detachment immediately rushed in and carried off the severed hand that we'd been looking at.

I watched him toss it nonchalantly on to the pile of other parts. One of his colleagues had retrieved the limb from up the tree by now, and that was being tried for size against the driver's corpse – with some success, it seemed. The whole business was so casually brutal that it made the blood run cold.

Was that the whole idea? I asked myself. I was beginning

to rethink my attitude. Was this indeed the private vengeance threatened in advance? Or just the precursor? Was this conspicuous butchery designed to terrify – a kind of promise of what might happen next? That could explain why the bodies were so hacked about and left so conspicuously in a public place – because they were put there on purpose to be found! It would fit with a killer who sent a written threat.

Perhaps, indeed, the whole design was not to kill the lictor at the first attempt, but to make him suffer as his victims must have done: force him to lie awake at night, sweating with cold fear, waiting for the moment when his turn would come to die – yet never quite knowing when that moment was to be. I could imagine how that would be a very sweet revenge.

I turned to give the commander an outline of my thoughts, but he was already making his way towards the path again. He halted as I picked my way towards him, over the trampled bloodstained grasses (duly followed by my ever-present guard) then he gestured to the body pieces heaped up on the cart. 'Do you want to look at any more of these? Or have we learned everything there is to learn from them?'

'I ought to examine the driver, at any rate, I suppose.'

He nodded. 'Sesquipularius!' Scowler bustled up. 'Have one of your men unwrap this corpse again. This citizen and I would like to have a closer look at it.'

Scowler saluted and roared orders at the unfortunate owner of the cloak, who hurried over to do as he was told. When he had finished, Scowler turned to us. 'Ready for your inspection, gentlemen.'

In fact, there was not a great deal to inspect. A bloodless torso in a tunic slashed to shreds, each slash the gruesome centre of a fringe of blood – just like the cloak that I'd seen earlier – except that here one could see the livid wound beneath each savage gash. I lifted back the tunic to take a closer look. No sign of earlier scars. Such internal blood as had remained to him had by this time pooled towards his back, making it dark and mottled like an ugly bruise: the tunic blood-smeared where he'd been propped against the driving-seat. I turned my eyes away – then turned them back again.

That was it! The detail which had been escaping me! I said so to my companions. 'Why isn't there more blood?'

Scowler was astonished into a retort. 'Great Mars, citizen, have you not seen the cart? It's covered with bloodstains, and the grass is, too. Amphoraeful of it. Even after all the rain we've had. How much do you expect?'

I nodded slowly. 'You're quite right, of course. There is a huge amount of blood around. On this corpse, for instance. But it isn't in the places where it ought to be. Look at these stab wounds – there is blood all right, but only on the very edges of the cut. If this man had been knifed while he was still alive, the whole of his tunic would be drenched with blood.' I knelt and gently turned the garment back again. 'You see the stains are darker on the outside of the cloth. It's almost as if the killer dipped the knife in blood before they thrust it in – on purpose to make it look as if the man was stabbed to death.'

'But, citizen,' the centurion chimed in, 'you cannot doubt that he was! There are knife marks everywhere.'

I nodded. 'And almost none of them have bled. At least, not very much. And that can only mean one thing. It is not only the hacking of the limbs that took place after death – most of this stabbing was done afterwards as well. In fact, I can't find a single wound that bled as you'd expect. I think he was dead before the blows began.'

Scowler was earning his nickname again. 'But what about the cart? It's covered in the stuff. Where did all that come from, if it didn't come from him?'

I heard myself speaking as if in a dream. 'I wonder if that is why the animals were killed?'

The commander was frowning down at me, perplexed. 'What are you suggesting? That none of what we see is human blood at all?'

'There is no way of telling!' I rose stiffly to my feet. 'I was the one who first supposed this was a rebel raid, but I'm beginning to wonder if Porteus is right. I've a terrible suspicion that this whole affair is staged – rather like a spectacle in the theatre. Oh, there were savage murders, there's no doubt of that, and people have been hacked to pieces, as you see. But I'm not certain that it happened here at all.'

TWELVE

There was a moment's silence. Everyone looked shocked. Then Scowler laughed, a little doubtfully. 'Forgive me if I'm being impudent, citizen,' he said, 'but I think you're reading too much into all this lack of blood. Have you forgotten that it's been pouring half the day? Look at the driver's tunic – or the clothes on any of the corpses come to that – you can see that they are wet. Surely the stains you're talking of aren't there because they've simply washed away.'

I shook my head decisively. 'It would not account for why there's more blood on the outside of the cloth. Quite the opposite! And if he had bled to death here – as it was made to seem – the pools beside the roadway would be streaked with blood, and you can see they're not.' The man looked so chastened that I softened my remark. 'I know there's been an awful lot of rain, but here we are in the shelter of the trees. If it's not been wet enough to wash the bloodstains from the cart, how could it dispose of bloodstains on the inside of a cloth?'

'Of course!' The centurion chimed in – not so much in my support as to make some contribution, however limited. 'So, sesquipularius, what do you say to that? Or do you believe that Jove has favoured us with some kind of miracle?'

Scowler gave him a poisonous look but retreated, muttering.

Meanwhile, the commander was examining the cart. He came back looking thoughtful. 'I do believe the citizen is right. I don't think the driver was murdered where he sat. Though whether he had simply got down from his perch to help the others when they were attacked, and was mutilated with them, perhaps we'll never know. Certainly, like them, he has been dead some time.'

I nodded. 'Sometime late yesterday, I would estimate.'

'I agree,' Emelius put in, anxious as ever to be part of this. 'The bodies have gone stiff – I remember that happening on the battlefield, when we did not have time to move the dead for several hours. They get quite hard to bury when they do

not bend, and we sometimes left them for a day or so, till they
went limp again; but not too long, or they start to putrify. These
have not been dead long enough to smell.' He looked around,
as if alarmed by some unpleasant thought. 'Let us hope that
at least their spirits are peacefully at rest. This forest might be
haunted for ever, otherwise.'

The commander silenced him with a look. 'Of course we
know these bodies have been here some hours – they were first
discovered shortly after dawn. I wished we'd asked the finder
if they were stiff by then. It's possible they weren't. I was
inclined to think this happened after dark, but it might be that
I'm wrong. Few people travel in the forest after dusk – at least
not willingly – and there is no sign that they had torches with
them on the cart. This may all have taken place today.'

I cocked an eyebrow at him, more confident by now. 'You
don't believe my theory, then, that they were killed elsewhere?
While they were off-duty for the night and resting, possibly?
If, for instance, there was only one of them on watch, it
might explain how the others could be taken so wholly by
surprise.'

He did not seem impressed. 'But how would all this have
got here, if that were the case? The cart would need a driver,
wouldn't it? And you could hardly bring a pile of corpses
through the forest on the back of it . . .' He broke off thoughtfully. 'Though, come to think of it, I suppose you could if
you had already moved the treasure off the cart. Provided you
still had something to cover up the load – and no one stopped
to ask you what you were carrying.'

I said nothing. Better to let him think out these answers
for himself.

He looked around the clearing and I did the same. It was
still a scene of carnage, though less chaotic now. Only the
horses were still littering the ground, their disembowelled
bodies lay closest to the path, entrails protruding from each
sorry corpse, while their heads and legs and tails were scattered far and wide. Their blood was everywhere.

I turned to the commander. 'Could you – or I – be certain
that all this is human blood?' I gestured to where Scowler's
fatigue had piled the humans on the cart, and were in the act

of flinging in the heap of severed parts. 'Suppose those victims were already dead, and simply smeared with it?'

'I suppose it is remotely possible,' he murmured. 'Though, I can't believe it! It is simply too bizarre. Carving up dead bodies, then flinging them about to make it look as if there'd been a rebel raid! Killing those poor horses – which were valuable too – just to use their blood to add to the effect! Let me have another look at them.' He went over to examine the topmost body on the cart. I left him to it, and he soon returned, saying doubtfully, 'You honestly believe that that's what happened here?'

I nodded. 'I'm more and more convinced that it was something of the kind. Certainly this was not what it appeared to be.'

He sighed. 'I was going to give instructions to dig a pit and give the poor dumb creatures a decent burial, but you make me wonder. Do you want to look at them again?'

I shook my head. 'I don't believe there's much more to be gained by that.'

'I confess that is rather a relief. I'll have them start at once.' He summoned Scowler and murmured his instructions to the man, who went swaggering off to bully his fatigue. A moment later two of them were starting on the pit, each using the mattock which is standard kit and which had been waiting for them on their cart.

The commander watched as the first of the horses' legs were gathered up and brought, then turned away as if it hurt to look. 'Why would anyone do a thing like this?' He turned to me. 'Why take the trouble? What would be the point?'

I outlined my theory about scaring Voluus. 'I think it was intended to look like a rebel raid, and only the lictor would understand – or fear – that it was not.'

'And why not wait until he came himself?'

'I think the idea was to terrify, all of a piece with sending him that note. He would recognize this raid as further proof that he was under threat, and that the writer of that letter meant what he had said. But it would be hard to convince the authorities of that: they'd think the bandits were to blame for this.'

He made no answer and I glanced at him. His eyes were fixed on what was happening in the woods. The rest of the fatigue-party had finished loading up the cart and hastened over to assist with the digging of the pit. The commander said heavily, 'I think you might be right. Without you, we'd assume that this was rebel handiwork.' He gave a hollow laugh. 'And if some of the rebels happened to be caught, it would simply be assumed that they were holding out against the questioning and telling lies. It is even possible that one of them would break down under torture and "confess", and that would seal the matter finally.'

'Why should anyone confess if he is innocent?' the centurion chimed in. I had forgotten him. I was about to answer when he worked it out and reddened to his ears, realizing that he sounded like an innocent himself. 'Oh, hoping to make his own death a little easier, I suppose?'

'Perhaps you should ask the lictor that, when he arrives – it is a situation which I understand he's quite familiar with,' I said, remembering the story of the page. 'Unfortunately the method is not reliable. The victim cannot tell you what he does not know, so the contents of the treasure-cart, for instance, would be sought in vain, whatever imaginative answers he might have supplied.'

I glanced at the commander but he was still watching the progress of the pit, which was quite large by now. Roman soldiers are all trained to dig a ditch and they are remarkably efficient at such things.

Emelius (who had put away his dagger by this time and was looking at the ongoing work approvingly) murmured something about bandits deserving all they got – whether they were innocent of a given raid or not. 'Though I suppose that this is hypothetical; none of the rebels might be caught at all.'

I looked at him. 'I expect the killers hope they will, and that there'll be a special effort made to capture them. After such a violent raid – and on the public road – the authorities would be certain to retaliate.'

The commander nodded. 'You are quite right, of course. I was already planning to send for reinforcements to mount a hunt for rebels hereabouts.' He sighed. 'It would give me satisfaction to track the rebels down, capture as many of their leaders as we could, and make an exhibition of them at the games – have them whipped and feed them to the bears, perhaps. I am quite tempted to do that in any case – they have given us sufficient cause these last few years. But most of all I want to find the men responsible for this . . .' He gestured to where the men were picking up one disembowelled horse ready to fling it in the pit. He turned away abruptly. 'But you really think it was not the rebels, after all? In that case, I shall have to look elsewhere – starting with the person who sent Voluus that threat, I suppose?' He gave another sigh. 'I only wish I'd been there and could tell you who it was.'

He set off towards the carriage which had brought us here, with myself and Emelius pottering after him. Our driver had tethered his horses to a tree and was sitting forlornly under it himself, huddled in a woollen cape, his hood pulled firmly down around his ears. He saw us coming and struggled to his feet to heave the carriage round, while the escort – who had been detailed to stand up and down the road to make sure no idle travellers tried to pass – hurried over to retrieve their mounts.

We stood and watched all this activity. 'You really have no idea who sent the threatening note?' I said. 'I thought they found it at the mansio after Voluus had gone? What's happened to it now?'

The commander shook his head. 'I never saw it. I was busy with my duties when the lictor left, and this was really none of my affair. He was just a casual visitor, looking in Glevum for a place to live – albeit one who had his master's letter as an official pass.'

I understood exactly what he was implying and had not said aloud. Voluus was neither an army officer nor a patrician of important rank and did not merit the attention of someone who was both. 'So you had no cause to go and seek him out?'

'Exactly and, of course, he didn't ask for an audience with me. I only heard about the letter afterwards – and then only because it had occasioned such a scene. The officer-in-charge was contemplating asking him to leave! He didn't do so at the time – he told me that he was alarmed in case the lictor turned on him – but fortunately the problem solved itself. Before he'd assembled his objections and screwed his courage up to confront the man, Voluus announced that he was leaving anyway, and returning immediately to Gaul. Because he'd found the flat and land he'd wanted, one presumed.'

'Or perhaps was genuinely worried by the threat, and frightened off,' I said.

'I hadn't thought of that!' He made a musing sound. 'It obviously caused him real anxiety. After all, he hired Porteus's men to guard his home while he was gone.'

'Wouldn't Calvinus do that in any case?' I said.

'The lictor wrote to Porteus – in strictest confidence – that he sometimes doubted his steward's loyalty and thought it possible he could be bribed. Florens told me that. That's why he and Porteus had the fellow put under arrest immediately after they heard about the raid. And then they learned that Calvinus had sent a messenger to you! You can see how . . .' He broke off as the riders cantered into place. 'Ah, here is our escort. If you and the centurion would care to climb aboard I will give the orders to take us back to town.'

I did not instantly obey. I was feeling confident enough by now to say, politely and with proper diffidence, 'With your permission, commandant, I had been hoping you'd allow me to go home at least to assure my household that I'm safe, and perhaps collect a toga ready for the court? My roundhouse is not very far from here.'

He gave me the kind of look that he had given Emelius. 'Citizen, surely you're aware that such a thing is quite impossible? You were entrusted to my custody, charged with involvement in a crime of robbery and murder on the public road.'

'But surely, now you are convinced I had no part in this . . .'

He raised an eyebrow in the way I recognized. 'Libertus, I was fairly confident of that before we started out – do you suppose I favour many prisoners with my company on a journey out of town? But Florens delivered you to me, having accused you in accordance with the law, and in accordance with the law I must continue to hold you until you come before the courts or he decides that he'll withdraw the charge. I imagine that he'll do so – he's a reasonable man – when we can provide him with sufficient proof that you are innocent.'

'But surely . . .' I began again.

He stood back to indicate that I should get into the coach. 'When I say "proof" I'm talking about something tangible. Actual evidence – not simple theories, however plausible. But real proof, I fear, is something that we really do not have.'

THIRTEEN

I was astounded at this answer. Dumbfounded, in fact. I had come to look upon the commander as a sort of personal ally, so Jove might have thrown a thunderbolt at me with less effect. Really, of course, I should not have been surprised – I have seen the law in action many times before, and a charge against a man must stand until it is disproved or else withdrawn. I was still a prisoner of the garrison and to have imagined otherwise was presumptuous.

Emelius had got his dagger out again, now that my status was no longer in any kind of doubt, and was trying to urge me up on to the carriage-seat, but I was desperate. I ignored him and went on trying to convince the commandant.

'But Mightiness,' I pleaded, 'we do have evidence. I drew your attention to the nature of the stains, the lack of blood around the injuries and the likelihood that all these men were murdered somewhere else . . .'

The commander gave me the eyebrow-raise again. 'And I unwillingly accept that you are very likely right. But all that is not proof that you are innocent – as I'm sure your enemies would be quick to say. In fact, they're almost certain to maintain the opposite: that you know so much about it that you must have been involved.' I was about to interrupt him, but he raised his hand to silence me. 'I don't necessarily agree with them, but I'm obliged to take you back.' His mouth twitched in what might have been a smile. 'Though I'll see that this time you are held in a more comfortable place. Perhaps you would even care to dine with me in the *Praesidium* tonight – if my orderly can stretch my meal to two. It will be rather Spartan. I'm a soldier, after all.'

I nodded, too relieved and grateful for a moment to find words. A humble tradesman like myself, being invited to dine with the commander in his official house – there could not have been a clearer signal of his belief in me. I was aware of seeming graceless and I managed to blurt out, 'I would be truly honoured.'

He nodded, satisfied. 'Florens and Porteus will have you tried as soon as possible, they have told me that – by tomorrow if they can manage it, as with their influence I am sure they will. In the meantime, we will have to muster up what evidence we can.' I was encouraged by that pronoun, but he amended it. 'So it is up to you. Proving who did this would be the surest way. Otherwise, I hope you have a hundred witnesses to prove that you didn't leave your roundhouse after dusk last night until several hours after dawn.'

I winced. 'Only my family and slaves,' I said. 'And the last thing I want is for them to be involved.'

He understood. 'Of course. And in any case the support of your household does not count for much in law.'

That was true. It is supposed that slaves will always speak up in defence of the master of the house, irrespective of whether he is innocent or not. In fact, they are routinely tortured on those very grounds, before they are permitted to testify in court. The theory is that anguish will ensure they tell the truth. I did not want my servants to endure that. And Gwellia was a woman – against the word of councillors hers did not count at all.

'Their testimony might not be much help, in any case,' I added, 'because at first light this morning I was out of doors, on my way to Glevum to open up the shop.' Though – it suddenly occurred to me – that might be hard to prove. Not many people saw me doing it. It was raining and there was no one out that did not have to be.

There was a snigger from somewhere, hurriedly suppressed. I looked around, surprised. The escort all wore expressions of careful innocence, but I realized that they had been listening. I could judge by that reaction what the magistrate would think and the commander had already worked it out.

He gave me that laconic look again. 'Libertus, what in Jove's name am I to do with you? You're telling me now that you were on the road just when the treasure-cart was passing through – or certainly around the time that it was found? I'm bound to ask the question, which you'll be asked in court: how is it you did not see the vehicle yourself?'

'If I had travelled on the military road I suppose I would have done, but in fact I didn't go that way. I took the other route – there's an old Celtic cart-way that passes close beside my home. It goes to Glevum through the forest and I followed that.'

He frowned. 'I've heard all about that ancient track and how treacherous it is. And through the forest, too, where there are bears and wolves. Why choose to go that way?'

'With respect, commander, remember I'm on foot. I don't possess a cart or mule, and the old track, though steep and winding, cuts off several miles. Roots and ruts don't make much difference to pedestrians. I simply went the way I always go.'

'You will have witnesses, no doubt?'

I did have witnesses, in fact. Junio and Minimus had of course accompanied me, but I shook my head. 'No one that I want to implicate. And there is no one else that I could call upon. There was a small boy with a herd of goats and an old woman picking up kindling on the path, but no one I recognized. I didn't see their faces and would not know where to find them if I had. Otherwise, I don't remember seeing anyone.'

The commander shook his own head in mock-despair. 'We had better mount a hunt for those two, anyway. I'll send out a scout as soon as we get back. In the meantime, centurion, get this prisoner in the carriage.'

Emelius used his dagger to prick me gently in the rear. 'Are you getting in the carriage, citizen?'

I nodded and began to climb up to the seat. It was no easier than it had been before: there was still nothing obvious to use as a step.

I managed to lift one foot to the door-sill and tried to hoist myself aboard by grasping the frame in either hand and pulling with my arms. Unfortunately my sandals were muddy by this time and the foot slipped under me, leaving me half-lying on the floorboards of the coach with my bottom sticking in the air. I cursed inwardly, knowing that I presented quite a spectacle.

Someone clearly thought so. There was a mocking laugh as I made another effort and hauled myself into the carriage, scarlet with embarrassment. But it was not from the centurion, who was looking quite concerned, nor from any other of our party – perhaps they didn't dare: it was from a horseman who had just ridden up the road. He must have reached us just in time to witness my ignominious fall – like a comic acrobat performing at the games – and by the time that I had settled on the seat he was already reining in.

His back was towards me, but some things were evident. This was not a soldier but a private messenger, resplendent in a gorgeous scarlet hooded cloak. I wondered that the escort had permitted him to pass, until I saw that he was holding out a letter-scroll fastened with a seal – obviously a message for the commandant. There was a silence, broken only by the scrape and thump of Scowler's detachment filling in the pit.

That officer had already turned to meet the newcomer, and I saw that he was frowning disapprovingly – obviously irked at being thus detained. He was thudding one hand with his baton and seemed about to speak, but before he did so the rider had slipped nimbly from his horse. He fell to one knee on the forest road, at the same time holding out the scroll and shaking back his hood.

'A message from my master Florens and from his mightiness the councillor Porteus,' he said, tendering it to the commander as he spoke.

I knew the voice before I saw the face. 'Servilis!'

I was so surprised that I said the word aloud, sufficiently loudly for it to be heard. Everyone in the vicinity turned to stare at me. It was an appalling breach of etiquette, of course – interrupting a formal message in this way – and all the soldiers were aware of it. Emelius, who had followed me aboard, dug his elbow sharply in my ribs, while the commander paused in opening the seal and glared reprovingly.

Servilis turned his head to stare at me, contriving to look both condescending and appalled. He said, with more than a touch of mockery, 'Ah, citizen Libertus. I did not recognize you from the rear! However, I was told I'd find you here, though I'd understood that you were being kept in custody.'

'And so he is,' Emelius put in, leaning across me to brandish his dagger in the air.

Servilis dismissed him with a glance. 'Thank you, centurion. But I see the citizen has managed to persuade the garrison-commander of his so-called innocence, sufficiently to be given special privilege. However, Libertus, I fear I am the bringer of bad tidings, once again. My master managed to obtain the incriminating letter that you sent to Calvinus.' He gestured to the scroll. 'And he has had it copied for the commander here. He is keeping the original for evidence in court.'

The commander was reading the document by now. It had clearly been written out by some professional scribe: the scroll was made of vellum and the script – even from this distance – was bold and beautiful. The effect was to give my words a gravitas they did not have when scratched with a stylus on an ancient piece of wax. The seal, which was an elaborate one, presumably belonging to the councillor, also conspired to make the letter look significant – quite different from the fraying ribbon with which I had secured my little writing-block. I tried to remember what I'd written in the note.

I need not have bothered. The commander read it out. '"I have received your urgent message and will report developments to my patron as soon as possible. I have chosen not to send a verbal message with your slave, because I am not certain how much he should know, but I will call on you again tomorrow and let you know what Marcus says."' He cocked an eye at me. 'You wrote this, citizen?'

I nodded. I tried to explain the little ruse I'd used to question Brianus but the commander brushed my words aside.

'It does not matter why you wrote it, the fact remains you did.' His face was stony, though I swear there was a glimmer of amusement in his eyes. He turned to Servilis. 'Ride back and tell your master that you have delivered this. Thank him for his trouble and assure him that I will study it more fully when I return to town.'

Servilis shot me a triumphant glance. 'You see the implications, commandant, of course. This letter proves his patron was involved as well. I am to remind you that you promised that – if there was evidence enough – Marcus Septimus should be brought in for questioning at once.'

The commander nodded gravely. 'I am aware of what I undertook to do, and I assure you that the matter is in hand. Please give my message to the councillor – though I fear I cannot write it down for you, especially in such an impressive form as this.'

I felt myself breathe out, a long sigh of relief. The commandant was making it quite clear that he was not to be swayed merely by the magnificent appearance of the scroll. I could only hope that whoever was my judge proved to be equally unmoved.

Servilis was not aware of any irony. 'At your service, commandant,' he replied, obsequiousness dripping from him like the raindrops from his cloak. He bowed over the commander's proffered hand and got back to his feet. He turned to me, and made a mocking little bow. 'So farewell, citizen! Until we meet again – as I am sure we shall.'

I eyed him sourly as he went back to his horse. He vaulted on, with an unexpected ease which made me dislike him even more. Of course he was Florens's senior messenger, and clearly very adept on a horse. He was conscious of it, too, swerving round and preening like the peacock Marcus had once brought – briefly – back from Rome, which had strutted round the villa like an avian Emperor, until it was unfortunately taken by a fox.

I watched Servilis canter out of sight, wishing that something similar would befall him, too – a sort of vulpine nemesis – but nothing did, of course. He pressed the horse onwards and galloped out of sight.

The commander spoke briskly to the escort, then turned towards the coach, but he was prevented from getting into it by the arrival of Scowler, who came hurrying up and sketched a quick salute.

'In the name of His Imperial . . .'

The commander sighed. 'What it is, sesquipularius?'

'With your indulgence, sir, we have completed the loading of the cart and buried all the horses – what we could of them – so we have finished here. Permission to join your escort-party back to town?' He saw the expression which crossed his commander's face. 'Whoever killed this cohort must be somewhere quite nearby – at least supposing that the cart set off at dawn. We wouldn't care to have them intercept us on the way. Seeing how they treat their captives, if you catch my meaning, sir.' Another wheedling glance at the commander's face. 'Especially the hors . . .'

I cut him off. 'Of course!' I said aloud. 'If they did set off at dawn they must have spent the night not very far away. Voluus would not have them camping by the road with all his treasure on the cart. And even if this happened after dusk last night, it is still likely that they made a pause somewhere here-abouts, if only to refresh the horses and have a meal themselves. They would not use the mansio,' I was reasoning to myself. 'It was not a military convoy, and they wouldn't have a sealed commendation from the governor of Gaul, the way the lictor did – so they would have had to use a common inn.' I turned to the commander, who was still standing poised, with one hand on the vehicle. 'Would it be possible for us to . . .'

His turn to interrupt. 'You wish me to neglect my duties to the garrison and take you to visit every private doss-house in the vicinity?' he said. 'Citizen, you cannot possibly expect me to agree. There must be a dozen villages within an hour's ride.'

But for a moment he had contemplated the idea! 'I was thinking of the escort,' I amended hastily. 'They could travel fast. In fact, if two of them could go, they could do this twice as quickly as one man alone. Just swiftly check the local inns and then report to us.' He was still looking thoughtful, so I cast a final die. 'If there are costs involved, I'm sure my patron would be prepared to cover them.' I hoped that I sounded properly convinced, though I could not, of course, be certain that Marcus would do anything of the kind.

The commander shook his head. 'And supposing they discover where the party spent the night? What do you expect the escort-men to do? Ride to Glevum to inform us? And what would that achieve? There would be a hundred questions you would want to ask, I'm sure, so you would be asking next to go and see the place. There is no time for that, the day is drawing on – night falls quite quickly at this time of year – and anyway, I could hardly let you leave the fort again.'

'Then if Florens drags me before the court tomorrow, I shall simply have to hope I can persuade the magistrate to allow me extra time to find some witnesses.' I sat back in my uncom-fortable seat. 'Someone must have seen the escort on the road, so at least we could discover whether it set out at dawn today – or whether it was genuinely travelling in the dark.'

The commander gave me an exasperated glance. 'Oh, very well,' he said at last. 'You give me little choice.' He called the escort over. 'Two of you ride on towards the south. Go as quickly as you can to all the inns along the road – let us say within five miles or so of here. I can't agree to any more than that. Ask the owners if the lictor's cart paused there, or stayed there overnight, or whether they even saw it pass, and if so, when that was. Oh, and whether there were any other people passing through who might have seen it, too.' He turned to me. 'Is that right, citizen?'

'More than I deserve,' I mumbled gratefully.

He turned back to the horsemen. 'If you discover anything at all, ride back to us at once. Speed is everything.' He climbed into the carriage lightly, as he had done before. 'We will return to Glevum as fast as possible.' He turned to Scowler, who was still fidgeting nearby. 'Though the death-cart can come with us for mutual protection, as it were, and that is obviously not designed for speed. The sesquipularius, however, will travel in the back, to accompany the driver's corpse and begin a proper lamentation as the ritual demands. If this was a member of our garrison it is the least that we can do.'

Scowler looked rather less than pleased, but he had asked to join our party and he could not well object. He bowed his head and said, 'The commander is most gracious.'

His senior officer nodded and turned his attention to the escort once again. 'As soon as the shadows start to lengthen and it lightens in the west, the outriders turn their horses and start back again, no matter where they are, even if there is another inn in sight. Is that understood? I don't want anyone benighted on the road. Very well. Give orders to the drivers that we are ready to depart.'

The leader of the escort wheeled his horse round to obey. He shouted to his riders and two of them set off, while the others formed up loosely around the coach. Our driver, looking sulky, climbed back on to his seat and a moment later we were lurching off, with the death-cart taking up position at the rear.

FOURTEEN

I glanced sideways at the commander as we jogged along. I was feeling rather uncomfortable by now – and not only because of the motion of the carriage. Though he had sent his riders out at my behest, I was not at all certain that much would be achieved.

I squirmed a little on my seat. What I had really hoped, forlornly, was that I might be permitted to go with them myself. Sending mounted soldiers to ask questions in this way – even the questions that I wanted asked – was not likely to be much of a success. Many villagers and country folk round here still clung to Celtic ways – much more so than people in the towns – and were generally suspicious of Roman cavalry. I would have spoken to them in their native tongue, but I doubted that the horsemen would get much out of them, especially given the constraints of time and distance which had been placed on them.

I could understand the commander's reasoning, of course. He was thinking in military terms. A fully laden cart does not travel very quickly, at the best of times, and when the load is a really weighty one – like gold and marble statues, as this one had been – progress can be particularly slow. So as they would only have been travelling since dawn, five miles was probably a reasonable estimate.

Equally, if the attack had happened before dusk yesterday (as I was still personally inclined to believe), it was logical to suppose that they were aiming to reach Glevum before dark – no one willingly frequents the road at night without a torch – in which case they would almost certainly have made a rest-stop in the latish afternoon, if only to water the horses and buy some food themselves. Again, five miles was a likely radius.

But I had my doubts about the basis for that whole argument. I was still convinced that there had been two parts to this attack. If I was right in thinking that the treasure was removed along the way and the corpses loaded in its stead, the cart could have travelled a good deal faster and further than we were allowing for. Human bodies weigh a great deal less than gold.

The commander had turned in time to see my frown. He raised his brows at me. 'Something worries you?'

I shook my head. There was no point in confiding my misgivings to him. It was too late now to bring the horsemen back and I'd already given him an outline of my views. I still found my own theory thoroughly bizarre. Even given that someone wanted to frighten Voluus, who would kill a half a dozen men and carry their corpses stacked up on a cart, simply to strew them in the woods and make it look as though the rebels had attacked? It seemed such an elaborately unlikely thing to do.

'Libertus?' the commander prompted, breaking through my thoughts. 'I asked if something was concerning you?'

'Everything about this worries me,' I said, and made him smile. 'I have a hundred questions. But there is one you might know the answer to. What will happen to Calvinus now – since it seems unlikely, after all, that he was involved in this?'

The smile faded and he looked surprised. 'What makes you come to that conclusion, citizen?'

I stared at him. 'But surely . . . ?'

'Libertus, you are the one who convinced me that this whole affair was indeed a premeditated plot against the lictor, and not a simple accident of fate. That means that someone in his household must have been involved: somebody who knew about the cart, what it was carrying, when it would arrive and how big the mounted guard was going to be. Who else but the steward was in possession of those facts?'

I was about to comment wryly that half of Glevum could have made a guess, but the commander did not pause to let me speak.

'And you yourself suggested why the escort was off guard and how they could be so quickly overwhelmed: because they supposed their attackers to be friends or, at least, a pre-arranged relief. People, in any case, they were forewarned about and expected to encounter at that time and place. Who but a steward arranges things like that?'

There – it was true – he had a valid point. 'I can see the

force of what you say,' I answered carefully. 'But I would swear that when I met him, Calvinus was shocked – and not a little frightened – by the news he'd just received. Wasn't his first act to send to you for help?'

'And isn't that exactly what a guilty man would do, to divert suspicion from himself?' the commander countered. 'As for being tense and frightened – what else would you expect if a man had just connived the theft of half his master's fortune and the murder of that same master's – no doubt expensive – hired escorting slaves? It's hardly evidence that the steward's innocent.'

'Or proof that he is not!' I protested earnestly. I did not hold the steward in very much esteem – especially when I knew how he treated Brianus – but I could not let this accusation pass. The steward's fate was now bound up with my own. 'As for having information,' I went on, 'weren't there others, too, who might have known about the cart? People with equal motive and more opportunity? Porteus himself, for instance. We know that he is desperate for gold. Or Florens, possibly? He has a personal guard at his command – huge, well-armed brutes with muscles – who could have carried out an ambush of that kind, and with relish, too.' That was daring, given Florens's rank, but I felt that I could speak with some conviction on that point.

There was a silence broken only by the creaking of the carriage, the sound of the horses and the rumbling of the wheels and – very faintly – from somewhere in the rear, Scowler's half-hearted ululation of lament. The commander made no answer, so I tried again.

'Porteus, no doubt, has some sort of escort, too. And probably the writer of the threat to Voluus has something similar. Any band of heavy ruffians like that could have done what we have seen – especially if there was some question of reward.'

The commander still said nothing. He would not meet my eyes. All the same I felt that he was paying me the compliment of thinking carefully about my arguments.

'How could the steward muster such a force?' I urged. 'He could hardly have done this by himself. He would have had to hire people – and thereby run the risk that someone would betray him to the authorities, or to anyone prepared to pay them slightly more. Does that seem probable? And where would Calvinus get the money to do that anyway?'

The commander leaned back on the seat. He ran his fingers through his hair again, creating another little waft of horse-radish and spice, and then said – with finality, 'I agree he was unlikely to be in this alone. That was never what I intended to suggest. I think he just provided information to the lictor's enemies – doubtless for a fee. No doubt he has dreams – like every slave – of buying himself free.'

I nodded. 'I believe he does.'

He gave me that slow, laconic smile again. 'Well, there you are! I tell you, citizen, in cases such as this, nine times out of ten the servants prove to be involved – especially if the master is a brutal one and does not command his house-hold's sympath . . .' He broke off, leaned over and stared out at the road, from where a frantic clucking and squawking could be heard. 'And what, in Vulcan's name, is that cacophony?'

I could have made an educated guess, even without the escort-rider who arrived, saying urgently, 'I am very sorry, commandant, there is a short delay. My men are attempting to move the people on, but there's a donkey-cart ahead which has just overturned and spilt its crates of chickens everywhere. It will take a few moments to clear a passage through.'

The commander slapped his palm impatiently. 'This is ridiculous.' He had to raise his voice above the chickens' outraged squawks in order to be heard. '. . . Obliged to wait in line with common poultrymen!'

That was the least of it, of course – as he must have known. The roads were always crammed with wagons at this time of day: people wanted to reach Glevum before the gates were shut, but after the onset of official dusk – the time when civilian wheeled transport, forbidden during daylight hours, was permitted into town. We were sharing the roadway, not just with poultrymen, but with all kinds of cargoes from the neigh-bourhood: stones and barrels, wooden planks and nails, carpets, casks – anything too heavy to carry into town by hand. I even saw a ragged farmer on an empty cart – not bringing anything to town, but hoping, I surmised, to shovel up the stinking midden-heaps and carry them away for use as makeshift ferti- lizer on his fields. A strong smell wafting from the wagon-tray suggested that it had been used for this before.

The escort had succeeded in clearing us a route and we jolted into motion, past the upturned poultry-cart. I glimpsed the owner attempting to right it as we passed, surrounded by crates full of flapping hens. The frantic cackling faded as we lurched away.

Emelius grinned at me. 'Singing like that steward's doing, I shouldn't be surprised.' He saw my face, and added instantly, 'And no doubt he deserved it, as the commander says.'

His commander acknowledged the comment with a nod. 'I fear that he is right. Calvinus must have passed the informa- tion on. I can't see how it would reach the killer by any other means. Don't look so doubtful, citizen. I will wager he's admitted it by now. Remember that Voluus had suspicions about him anyway.'

'How do we know that?'

He looked at me, surprised. 'Florens assures me it is true. The lictor himself wrote to Porteus saying so – though that was not common knowledge, naturally enough.'

'But Porteus told Florens, who confided it to you.' I was too concerned to be properly polite.

No offence was taken, luckily. The lined face creased in an unexpected grin. 'Put like that it does not sound very confi- dential, I agree. But it has gone no further than the three of us. And now yourself, of course.'

'And Emelius,' I pointed out, knowing that I risked a serious reprimand.

The commander looked startled. He glanced across at the centurion, who turned his head away and affected to be looking at the countryside. His ears had turned an alarming shade of red. The commander raised his eyebrows at me with a shrug that said, as plainly as if he'd spoken it aloud, 'I hadn't thought of that.'

'I only mean to show you what is possible,' I said. 'For instance, that Porteus's household might have known as well. And Florens's servants, too. People talk too openly in front of slaves, you see. They think of them as almost furniture, and forget that these are people who have ears and eyes, and sometimes wagging tongues. One casual word from Porteus, overheard by slaves, could be spread around Glevum quicker than the plague.'

Both of the soldiers turned to frown at me.

'I learned that when I was a slave myself, and I always warn Marcus to be circumspect when there are servants standing by. Or – in your case, commander – junior officers.'

The commander harrumphed and sat back in his seat. 'In that case, citizen, we will talk no more until we are safely in the garrison. If you are to dine with me tonight, no doubt we will find an opportunity. I'll ask for information about what Calvinus has confessed.'

'Is it possible that I could speak to him myself, tonight? His evidence will be of great concern to me. Or perhaps tomorrow morning, if Florens and Porteus do not arrange to have him brought to trial as well.'

The commandant said brusquely, 'I imagine they'd prefer to wait until Voluus arrives and gives permission for proper questioning, as – under the circumstances – I've no doubt he will. And I can't release you from my custody to go and speak to him. I don't have to remind you, you are also facing trial.'

'Do you think they would delay the case against me, too? So there's a chance of me establishing some proper evidence?'

He shook his head. 'I doubt it very much. The steward may be called to witness against you, so I imagine they will want you summoned first, while he's still in a position to comply. In other times and places I could have heard this case myself, and ruled for an adjournment – but this is Glevum, and under modern laws you must be brought before a civil magistrate.' He lapsed into silence and gazed out at the passing countryside.

I rather wished I hadn't pointed out that he was in danger of being indiscreet, but there was no undoing it. I sat back in my own seat and said no more, but this talk about 'my hearing' made my blood run cold. I had refused, till now, to contemplate what that would entail – indeed, I had positively tried to blank it out. However, I was forced to think about it now.

If I could afford a bribe, or persuade Marcus to provide one on my behalf, I could have a well-bred lawyer, skilled in argument, to plead in my defence. I could wear sack-cloth and ashes – as many people did – to show how distraught I was, and to try to influence the court to pity me. If necessary, as a very last resort – which meant, if I were condemned to death, instead of merely to lifelong exile – I could even appeal to the Emperor himself, although from what I'd heard of Commodus that might not help me much.

Even another diversion on the road – this time a travelling magician, in a red and orange robe, with a parrot on his shoulder and a gibbering monkey on the cart – failed to divert my attention very long. I was rather like the monkey – about to be produced as a public spectacle – and like the parrot I would be obliged to talk.

It was not a happy prospect, taken all in all. Two important councillors were accusing me, circumstances seemed to point towards my guilt, and as the commander said, 'the court will decide on what is probable'. So if I were exiled, what would happen to my wife? I could not expect her to share the harshness of the flight. Perhaps I could find some way to start again so I could send for her – though that was fraught with danger, too. I wished I'd spent a little longer bidding her farewell – it was possible that we would never meet again.

I tried to remind myself that I was fortunate. I would enjoy a meal tonight, and have somewhere half-comfortable to sleep. Poor Calvinus would have neither of those things. I would be taken to a proper court, before a magistrate; Calvinus had no such luxury. A slave – even the chief steward of a very wealthy man – could not only be tortured to ensure he talked, but could expect only a brief hearing by some harassed clerk, often conducted in the open air in front of jeering mobs, whose opinions were sometimes allowed to sway the case: and punishment, if called for, would be immediate.

And I had probably, unwittingly, contributed to his fate. All the same, I would like to talk to him again.

I glanced at the commander, but he refused to look at me. He was staring at the wagons drawn up beside the road. Emelius, on my right-hand side, was doing just the same. We jogged in silence for what seemed like hours – still slowed by traffic making for the gates – and the light was almost fading by the time that Glevum came in sight.

My every bone was juddering from the vibration of the vehicle and my arms were aching with the effort of clinging to the seat – though mercifully the slower speed had made things easier. As we pulled up at the public arch that led into the town, I felt a wave of something like relief. Whatever awaited me at the garrison, I was going to be happy to get down from the carriage.

FIFTEEN

What was awaiting us was a flustered orderly. He was clearly bursting with a message of some kind, and could scarcely wait for the commander to dismount. As soon as he had done so the man sketched a salute and drew him aside to murmur urgently to him.

It must have been important. The commandant looked immediately grave and made a gesture to Emelius and me, indicating that we two should get down and go into the fort ahead of him. Scowler, meanwhile, had drawn up in his cart, and was arranging a detail to take the murdered driver's corpse inside.

'Get a move on, you lazy lumps of meat. This man was an ex-auxiliary officer and a citizen to boot. The army's going to give him a proper funeral, so treat him with respect. You, there on the end, take up the lament. The rest of you go and find a shutter so we can carry him.' The men got down grumbling and he added with a sneer, 'And look sharp about it – when we've finished here, we've got the others to dispose of before you can stand down.'

They would drive the other bodies to the common pit, of course, where with the rest of the day's haul of the unwanted dead – vagrants, paupers and common criminals – the butchered escort would be unceremoniously thrown in and covered up with lime.

The sentry standing on duty at the gate still had his eyes on us, and I was aware again of the sight I must present as I climbed down – very stiffly – from our own vehicle, with Emelius close behind. The centurion seemed conscious of the scrutiny as well, because he immediately snapped back into officious mode and marched me at dagger-point through the city arch and back into the courtyard of the garrison.

This time there was nobody in the yard as we approached, though a moment later the requisition man came running out, cramming his helmet back upon his head. He did not speak, but simply nodded and rushed on towards the gate.

'Obviously in a hurry to sign the transport off,' Emelius said. 'He must have seen us come. I expect the owners of the vehicle have been enquiring for it.'

I nodded. This was the busiest time of day for hiring firms, and although the carriers could not actually demand to have the carriage back, they were no doubt pointedly requesting its return as soon as possible.

The soldiers in the guard-room raised their eyes as we went by and watched us curiously through the window-space. I expected to be led back in there, but Emelius's dagger prodded me straight on, past the barracks and down the road towards the centre of the fort. He didn't pause until we reached the open area in the very heart of it, opposite the combat training field and the regimental shrine.

'That is where you are heading, citizen!' he gestured with his non-dagger-bearing hand.

Opposite the entrance to the drill-field was the praetorium itself, where the commander had his personal rooms and private offices. It was a well-proportioned building, long and low, more like a villa than an army residence, and arranged around three sides of a pleasant shaded court – in contrast to the rows of grimly rectangular stone-built barrack blocks elsewhere, which were the living quarters of the other ranks.

'Nice place,' I murmured to Emelius.

I meant the house, but he took me to be talking about the fort itself. He dropped his knife and said, as though he owned the establishment himself, 'Nothing to what it used to be. At one time it was twice as big as this – took up most of the area which is now the town, right across to where the forum is. Of course, in those days there was an entire legion stationed here. Long before my time – or yours, I would expect.'

'I have lived near Glevum for almost thirty years,' I agreed, 'and I don't remember it.'

'Nor do I. Our unit's only been here for a year or two. Of course, now that the countryside has settled down in peace – or something like it – they only keep a few hundred of us here to keep it going.' He looked around and added, with that same element of pride, 'But it's still impressive – what is left of it.' He seemed to remember suddenly that he was guarding me and he pointed with his blade to the commander's house. 'But I'm supposed to be taking you inside. I don't want to get mixed up with all of that!'

'That' was Scowler's detail struggling through the gates carrying the segments of the body from the cart. They had contrived a makeshift litter from a plank of wood and, though their burden was still shrouded in the soldier's cloak, one disembodied leg had become partially unwrapped, revealing all too clearly what was underneath. One of the bearers was keeping up a reluctant, tuneless drone that could – with imagination – be taken for lament.

'What are they going to do with him?' I said, fearing for a moment that they would let it lie in state, on view to the soldiers in some public place.

Emelius made a face. 'Put him in the infirmary, perhaps? That would be suitable, since he was – apparently – an officer.'

'From that unit that was stationed here from Gaul, I understand?' I was recalling what the commandant had said about that military belt. 'Or was that before your time as well?'

'The Fourth Gauls Half-Mounted Auxiliaries, you mean?' The centurion looked at me, surprised that a civilian had such a grasp on things. 'I remember them. That was part of the outfit that we took over from. They moved out in stages just as we moved in. Obviously there has to be a bit of overlap, to ensure that the takeover is smooth.'

'But your commander wasn't here then?'

'Oh, he came just after we were settled in. The previous one died.'

I nodded: in fact, it had been murder, which I'd helped to solve.

But Emelius was still talking. 'The commander's post is a praetorian appointment from above, of course. Men like him can be appointed anywhere, at any time – usually part of their bid to be senators in Rome. This present one is quite an oddity: he really has seen service in the field and when his statutory period of command was up, he opted to stay with military life and come and join us here.'

'So he chose to come to Glevum?'

He grinned. 'Not like the rest of us. This is the fourth posting I've had since I joined up. Another few years and they'll shunt us on again. We could end up like the Fourth Gauls ourselves – up on the northern frontier freezing half to death – or it might be Africa, or anywhere at all. Though, with any luck by that time I'll be able to retire.'

Someone came out of the guard-room as he spoke and directed the stretcher-party to a nearby barracks block. 'It is going to the infirmary, by the looks of it,' Emelius approved. He saw Scowler's party looking and he raised his blade again. 'And that's where you'll be going yourself, if you don't hurry up. This knife is not for decoration purposes. I am under strict orders to deliver you inside.' He motioned me towards the praetorium again.

I took the hint and turned into the court and for the first time got a full view of the house. It was pleasantly appointed, with a stable and what was obviously a bath-suite taking up one wing and – from the odours which emanated from the corner opposite – a personal kitchen and a small latrine. The court itself was paved and bare of ornament apart from half a dozen boundary trees providing shade and two large statues set on matching plinths: one a large and unremarkable image of the Emperor, and a smaller piece depicting someone on a horse – a sculpture of astounding vitality and form. I am no expert, but I recognized the skill.

There was no time, however, to admire that now. A young male orderly – he seemed to be the commander's personal slave – in a green tunic and with civilian sandals on his feet, came hurrying out to meet us from the doorway opposite. 'Citizen Libertus? I've been expecting you. Let me relieve you of that damp cape of yours. Then, if you would care to follow me?' With these words he left Emelius standing in the court and ushered me inside.

I had scarcely time to wonder how the young man knew my name and how – since his master had been out all afternoon – he came to be expecting me, before I was led into a sort of atrium, roofed-in, as is common in chill Britannia. I looked around. The room was sparsely furnished, but what

was there was of fine quality: a black polished table, made of
ebony and decorated with a single inlaid band of ivory; a pair
of matching vases on a pair of matching stands, framing a
niche devoted to the Lars; a series of fine mural paintings
depicting Jupiter, in a range of guises from soldier-god to
swan; and, taking the place of what would in Rome have been
a central pool, a tessellated pavement of Neptune and the
waves, of a quality which I recognized as excellent.

Most strikingly of all there were a pair of painted stools,
and on one of them there was a seated man. He was turned
away from me, busy with a dish of figs and cheese, which
had been placed on a folding table next to him, together with
a goblet and a jug of watered wine. Only the back of his mop
of fairish curls was visible. But there was no mistaking the
enormous seal-ring on his hand and the patrician toga with its
ostentatious stripe.

'Marcus!' I would have known that figure anywhere: even
without the heavy torc around his neck, given to him by a
grateful Celtic chief. What was he doing here?

My heart sank to my sandal straps again. Of course! Florens
had threatened to have him arrested, too, and brought here to
the garrison for questioning. I fought down a wave of panic
that made my skin turn cold. If my patron was a prisoner too,
he couldn't help my trial, and would almost certainly blame
me for having said too much and managing to get him involved
in this. I was not looking forward to this interview.

He raised his head and saw me, stretching out the hand that
did not hold the fruit. 'Libertus! There you are at last!'

I saw with relief that he was not annoyed. Indeed, he was
almost smiling as I knelt to kiss the ring. 'Patron!' The smile
emboldened me. I got slowly to my feet and dared to ask, 'What
brings you to the garrison?'

His first words were not encouraging. 'I had a visitation
to the villa earlier today. Some idiotic soldiers on the hunt
for Voluus's gold and other valuables, they said. Apparently
there's been a vicious robbery. For some reason they
supposed that I was part of it.' I braced myself for a torrent
of abuse and blame, but he was simply nibbling at his fig
with unconcern.

Oddly, that unnerved me more than curses would have done. 'Patron, it has all been an unfortunate mistake,' I burbled anxiously, 'the result of something that a page-boy overheard, when I was with you yesterday.' (It *was* only yesterday, I realized with a start – so much had happened since, it seemed a moon ago.) 'Then when the lictor's cart was set upon . . .' I began again, but he held up a restraining hand.

'I understand all that. I got the full story from Gaius earlier – he was so disturbed that you'd been dragged away that he came and told me everything. It seems that fool Florens had made up his mind, for reasons of his own, that I had the stolen gold – though how he expected to distinguish it from mine, Mithras only knows. Fortunately I had my house-guest with me at the time.'

'The senior Decurion from Corinium and his wife?' I said, remembering.

He dabbed at his lips with a napkin from the tray. 'Exactly so. In fact, it turned out that it was no simple social call – they wanted to persuade me to sell them our town-house there. It irritated me, but in the end I was grateful he was there.'

'But you didn't sell the house?' I had visited that residence and knew it to be fine – no wonder the chief councillor had wanted it. It had come to Marcus when he married Julia: part of her personal estate as the widow of a past Decurion.

'Of course I didn't. He made a reasonable offer and I was tempted for a while, but then he said that since I hardly use the house myself, it would make an appropriate residence for someone like himself. That changed my mind, of course. And he doesn't really need it. He already has a substantial dwelling in the town! Quite big enough to cover the property require-ments for a mere councillor.' Marcus turned away to select another fig – a delicacy of which he was particularly fond. 'But apparently his new wife does not like the one that he's got – there's always been a problem with the outlet to the drain and she declares it stinks. She insisted that he came to bid for mine. Travelling with him all that way – and on the Ides of March as well. Ridiculous. Though fortunate for me, as it turned out.'

'Because the Decurion spoke in your defence?' I said.

Marcus smiled. 'More than that! He put the soldiers firmly in their place, saying that, since he had been there as a witness all the time, almost ever since you left the house yourself, none of Voluus's treasure could have found its way to me. If they searched my house, they'd have him to answer to. Just as well, since there was plenty of my own gold in the place. And he had brought some of his as well, to make down-payment with, though fortunately Florens's people never learned of that. No doubt they would have thought it highly suspicious if they had.'

'So the Ides of March was not so nefas, after all,' I said.

That made him smile again. 'Except for the Decurion's wife, perhaps. All the travelling had made her most unwell. And it was a wasted journey anyway.' He tilted back his head and popped the fig into his mouth. 'By the way, I think the soldiers went to search your roundhouse afterwards.' He wiped his fingers in a napkin from the tray and then carefully lifted the goblet to his lips. 'Though I don't suppose there was anything to find.'

Except my poor Gwellia, I thought, imagining her distress as the soldiers rifled through whatever they could find! No doubt they had been bullying my slaves as well and harassing Junio's family in the roundhouse next to mine. But at least Marcus had not been compromised.

But in that case, I wondered, what was he doing here?

'Ah! Excellence!' a voice behind me said, before I managed to get the question out. 'They told me you were here. And Libertus, too. I regret I've been so long, but there has been disturbing news and I was obliged to take account of it.' The commander gestured to the tray. 'But I am neglecting my duties as a host. I hope that my servants have looked after you.'

Now that my worst fears were laid to rest, I had been rather hoping for a taste of fig myself, but it was not to be. Marcus made a broad, expansive gesture with his hand. 'Indeed, they have. Your slave was most attentive, but I told him he might go – my own page is waiting in your servant's ante-room and I could call him if I needed anything. I imagine that your man has other duties to perform.' He put down the goblet. 'As I am sure you do yourself. I will not detain you. You know why I am here?'

The commander assented with a little bow. 'The duty orderly informed me. I understand you are offering to act as surety for this citizen, and to take him into personal custody until he comes to court?'

This was such astounding news it took my breath away. I turned to my patron to offer him my thanks, but Marcus was already saying briskly, 'I meet all the legal requirements, of course. As magistrate I naturally have an apartment in the town and I will undertake to see that he is kept there overnight and presented tomorrow before . . . whoever it might be.' The words implied the junior status of whoever took the case. 'Of course, as his patron I can't in fairness conduct the trial myself.'

Even Marcus must have heard my sharp intake of breath. 'So there is to be a trial?'

He turned to me. 'There's no escape from that, Libertus my old friend. I don't believe that you had any part in this, but there has been a charge, and until you can prove differently, there's little we can do. I will provide a lawyer for you, if you wish – someone who knows the rules of rhetoric and can plead more effectively than you could do yourself. You can repay me at your leisure – if you're found innocent. If not, I will forgive you any debt, of course.'

Not a word about speaking in my defence himself, which would probably have guaranteed my acquittal on the spot. However, it was an enormous compliment that he should exert himself at all. Not many patrons would do as much for a simple tradesman protégé like myself. I bowed and murmured that he was very gracious.

He nodded his agreement with his compliment. 'Well then, commander,' he said complacently. 'I'll leave it up to you to have him conveyed to my apartment under guard. I shan't be there myself – I have a banquet at my country villa to attend – but my servants have instructions to keep a watch on him and my doorkeeper, in particular, was chosen for his strength. Libertus can't escape, but my slaves will provide him with anything he might require tonight. I shall return tomorrow morning and deliver him to you. I imagine that arrangement will be satisfactory?'

The commander made a little bow as well. 'You relieve me

of a slight embarrassment, Excellence. I was prepared to do something of the kind myself, but it would have stretched my rations rather thin. I would have dismissed the case entirely, if it were up to me. But Florens insists on bringing it before a curial court, composed of town councillors and civic magistrates – and these are people over whom he has some hope of influence. I'm sure he'll do his best to get the verdict he desires.'

Marcus nodded grimly. 'I agree. I fear, commander, that this is also personal. Florens knows that – even if I'm not arraigned myself – charging my favoured client with a crime would be an acute embarrassment to me.'

None of this promised very well for me! I asked, at once, 'What makes you say that, Excellence? Does Florens bear you some special grudge?'

He waved a lofty hand. 'Nothing of special consequence. He wanted to marry an Imperial ward, that's all – a young woman of some intelligence and rank.'

'And you opposed it?'

'She was unfortunate enough to have a massive dowry, under the terms of her late father's will, provided that she did not marry a particular young man. I was administrating her estate and I refused consent to Florens – who was three times her age and whom she could not stand. She chose the other path, which suited everyone. Everyone but Florens, anyway. The young man had sufficient for their needs so they were happy, and the Emperor was pleased to have her dowry confiscated to the Imperial purse – with a small deduction for my services, of course.'

'So Florens is now looking for revenge,' I said bitterly – realizing that I was going to be the means of it.

My patron looked affronted. 'I knew he was vindictive, but I am surprised, I own. Florens was not exactly inconsolable. It was purely a financial contract, on his part anyway. There was another woman that he'd hoped to marry first – some foreign heiress with a fortune that he'd met overseas – but she accepted someone else, and this ward was merely a convenient substitute. And now I understand that he has found another bride! I hear a formal promise was contracted recently.'

'To take a bride whose dowry was dependent on that cart!'
I said. I told him, briefly, what I knew of the affair, with the
commander nodding his assent to my account.

'Porteus's daughter? That ugly sow-faced lump!' Marcus was
insensitive enough to laugh aloud. 'And now she's lost her dowry
and he is stuck with her! Doubly ironic really, because he and
Porteus were at daggers drawn over nomination to the Servir's
post, but I suppose the promised dowry made Florens shelve
his pride. But if Voluus can't pay her father for the land, then
the money's disappeared. No wonder Florens has it in for me.'

'For me, in fact!' I pointed out.

That sobered him a little. 'Ah, indeed. Though I think he
genuinely believes that you're involved, you know. And
circumstances do look suspicious for you. However, I have
faith in your abilities. I believe you went out to the site this
afternoon. Did you discover anything of value?' He stretched
out a ringed hand. 'I sincerely hope you did. Florens will be
demanding the highest penalty. Especially since a Roman
citizen has been murdered, too.' He turned to the commander.
'Or that is what your servant led me to believe. That'll mean
crucifixion for the steward, I should think.'

He said it so calmly that I shuddered at the thought, though
of course that is the statutory penalty for robbery on the road,
and this was a particularly heinous version of the crime.

Marcus did not seem to notice. He glanced at me. 'Where
would you think to flee to, if things do not go well?'

SIXTEEN

I was too appalled by this casual acceptance of my likely fate to make any proper answer to this enquiry. But my patron was right: it was a decision I would have to make before the trial. Whatever my decision, exile would be bleak. It is much better than the alternative, of course – that is why it is a privilege reserved for citizens – but being excluded from the Empire is no easy life.

Perhaps I could arrange to flee to the faraway south-west where I was born. I had been a man of rank there, with lands and animals, before I was snatched away by pirates to become a slave, and there might be people there who still remembered my name and family. But even if any of the local elders were still left alive, would they accept me, after all these years? My house and property had been destroyed by fire, so what was there to live on if I went? And how would I get there, officially deprived of 'food and fire' – so that anyone who sheltered me became a criminal himself? It was probably the best destination I could choose, but it was an enormous distance, especially on foot – and I would be forced to travel penniless.

And if I went, what would happen to my wife? She could not be allowed to suffer with me on the way. Perhaps, if I survived, I could one day send for her?

I was so busy with these wretched thoughts that I hardly realized that the commander had begun to speak again.

'The murdered man was more than merely a citizen, Excellence. A retired auxiliary from this very garrison, we have reason to believe. That's why I took the trouble to inspect the scene myself.' He shook his head as if the memory caused him grief. 'But there was nothing to be learned.'

Marcus arched an eyebrow. 'Libertus was no help?' I should have been flattered that he sounded so surprised, but flattery was not going to help me now.

'Libertus has been his usual observant self, and pointed out things that I might not have noticed on my own,' the commander replied. 'But as to finding out who was responsible, I fear we are no closer than we were before.' He turned to me. 'Less so, if anything. I'm afraid that was the message which was awaiting me – the one that delayed me, when we first arrived.'

'Go on,' Marcus prompted, clearly wishing to assert his own authority.

The commander went on addressing his remarks to me. 'One of the riders that we sent on ahead to make enquiries found himself delayed on the way back again by wagons on the road, just as we were ourselves. He remembered that you had spoken about an ancient track – the one that you told us that you used yourself – so he asked directions to it and came that way instead. He made such good time that he got back here before we did ourselves.'

I was about to ask where the other rider was, but he prevented me.

'But there, Libertus, I'm afraid the good news ends. He reports that he and his companion visited all the inns along the road, within the distance which we specified, but the lictor's cart had not spent the night at any one of them, or even stopped for refreshments for their horses or themselves.'

'That is most peculiar!' I frowned. 'And no one even noticed it as it went by? I would have thought that, with that size of escort, it was remarkable enough.' It was very impolite for me to press like this, but Marcus was not asking and I could not restrain myself. Anyway, at this stage, what had I to lose?

Marcus gave me a warning glare, but the commander seemed unmoved by any breach of protocol. He answered, civilly enough, 'You're right. There is one person who remembers seeing it – a smallholder who was working by the road – and he is being brought in to me for questioning. But he only has a donkey, not a horse, so that will obviously take a little time, especially at this busy time of day. The other rider is escorting him to make sure he arrives.'

'So it will not be possible for me to talk to this donkey-owner?' I could hear the desperation in my voice. I turned to Marcus. 'Or Calvinus either, I suppose?' I had been hoping to persuade my patron to arrange an interview.

Marcus shook his head. 'Out of the question, my old friend. I have already stayed in Glevum longer than I meant, and I shall have to find a lighted litter now to take me home – I have a private banquet to attend. It is quite a small affair, but it is in honour of the visiting Decurion and so it is important that, as host, I am not late. My wife will already be looking at the water-clock and wondering where I am.'

The commander glanced at me, but it was to Marcus that he spoke. 'Perhaps, with your permission, Excellence, we could grant Libertus one of his requests. After all, his liberty is probably at stake. If I am providing the escort for the citizen when he goes to your apartment, then there is no need for you to wait. Visiting the jail will not be possible, but we could delay his departure long enough for him to interview this man who saw the cart. There is someone waiting in the guard-house to see Libertus, anyway.'

'Someone else to see my protégé?' Marcus looked affronted and amazed. 'I was not aware of that!'

I, too, was wondering who the visitor might be. Florens – or more likely Servilis – with additional 'evidence', perhaps? Porteus come to mock? Or even one of the other councillors? I looked at the commander nervously.

He was soothing the ruffled feelings of an important man. 'The other person arrived before you did, Excellence, but naturally you were brought in here and given precedence.' He smiled. 'I believe you know the young man in question, anyway. I understand he gives his name as Junio.'

I felt an overpowering wave of sheer relief. If Junio was present there was still hope for me. 'My adopted son! I sent him on an errand when I was first brought in here,' I explained. 'I was hoping he could question the lictor's other slaves. I did not expect to be away from here for so long, of course.'

Marcus was entirely appeased. 'Ah, Junio, of course! That's understandable.' He spoke as if I had no right to visitors, unless by his consent. 'In that case, I will leave you alone to talk to him. My town slaves have instructions; they are expecting you.' He turned to the commander. 'Commandant, I am obliged to you. I will see you in the morning when I bring Libertus back. Now, if I might have my attendant brought to me . . .'

The commander clapped his hands and his slave appeared at once, as if he had been waiting at the doorway for a sign. He was given orders, first to fetch my patron's page and then to bring Junio over to the house. The boy nodded eagerly and scuttled off again.

'You can let me know tomorrow if you learn anything of note,' Marcus was saying. 'Ah, here comes my servant now! And he has brought my cape. Splendid – I fear the night will soon be damp again.' He allowed his slave to drape it round his shoulders as he spoke. 'Now, page, go and hire a carrying litter that will take me home. And be quick about it. I will see you at the gate.'

The boy – who was dark and good-looking as Marcus's pages always are – bobbed an obeisance and hurried to obey.

Marcus fastened his cloak clasp languidly. When he was ready he inclined his head towards the commandant and then held out his ringed hand for me to kiss. 'Until tomorrow, then.' And attended by the commander's military slave – who was, of course, going to the guard-house anyway – he strolled away to host his private feast.

The commander watched him go and then said thoughtfully, 'You have a kindly patron, citizen. Offering his own apartment as a haven overnight! It indicates how highly he holds you in esteem. No doubt you deserve it – ah, here comes your visitor. If you will excuse me, I have duties to perform. Of course I will have to leave you under guard, and the centurion will continue to be stationed at the gate, but you might prefer this conversation to be a private one. Talk to Junio in here and when the man who saw the treasure-cart arrives, I will send for you. After we've finished with our questioning of him, Emelius can escort you to your patron's residence.'

He had spoken of Marcus's kindness but his own seemed even more remarkable. I could do no more than stammer out my thanks, for a moment afterwards the orderly appeared and Junio was ushered in to speak to me. It was clear from his expression that he was overawed and the bow he sketched to the commander was unusually deep.

The commander sketched a hand towards the vacant stools. 'Make yourselves comfortable, citizens. I'll have fresh refreshments sent and my slave will be on hand if there is something you require. Junio, of course, is free to leave at any time. I will let the sentry know to let him pass. Libertus, I will see you later on.' And he was gone, with Junio staring after him.

My son turned back to me, his eyes still bulging like shield-bosses, 'Did you hear that, Father! Who would have believed it? Guests of the garrison commander, in his house! And you are to go to Marcus's apartment afterwards?!'

I sighed. 'I shall be lucky to have a roof at all tomorrow night,' I said. 'Florens is determined to have me brought to court and things are looking very bleak indeed. Everything I did this morning can apparently be quoted as pointing to my guilt – even the hour at which I chose to set off for the town. And you may be fortunate to escape yourself. Did you manage to speak to Brianus?' I sat down on the stool His Excellency had used.

Junio sank down on the other one. He was looking stricken now. 'Father, I am sorry. I did not mean to jest. When I heard that you had left the town in the commander's carriage – and even more when I learned that you were visiting his house – I naturally supposed that everything was solved. I didn't think that Brianus mattered any more.'

'If only that were true!' I muttered bitterly. 'But you did speak to him?'

A nod. 'I managed to find him, though he wasn't at the house. And he was not keen to talk. While he was bringing that message over to your shop, apparently Porteus sent his private mob around with several of the guard. They muscled their way into the lictor's flat, arrested Calvinus and threw him into jail where he has been kept under questioning all day. It seems they are now only waiting for the lictor to arrive before they bring in the torturers to do it properly.' He saw my face and added, in a disappointed tone, 'But I see you knew all this?'

'I'd heard that the steward was in custody,' I agreed. 'But nothing about Brianus. They didn't seize him, too? I knew my letter had fallen into Porteus's hands, so I thought they might have taken him prisoner.'

Junio shook his head. 'He was afraid that they were going to. When he got back with your letter he found some of Porteus's men still waiting at the flat, wanting to ask him questions about exactly where he had been. That is when he handed them the writing-block – he really had no choice – but they realized that he couldn't read it and in the end they let him go.' He frowned. 'How did you know that Porteus had your note?'

I grimaced. 'Because he sent a copy after us.' I explained how Servilis had arrived with it. 'It was intended to convince the commander of my guilt – and so it might have done, if he were not so favourably inclined. It will certainly look bad if they produce it at my trial.'

'Dear gods! When do you expect to be brought before the court?'

'Tomorrow morning, by the look of it.'

He frowned. 'But surely there was nothing incriminating in the note? I saw it myself. You only wrote it as an excuse for delaying Brianus.'

'I know that, Junio, but it happens that the words I chose – to impress the steward – were most unfortunate. They can easily be interpreted to imply my guilt. Porteus had even had the message copied out – on vellum and in a fair hand by a professional *amenuensis* – so it didn't look remotely like a scribbled note. It was clear that he'd got hold of the original, probably in order to produce it to the magistrate in court.'

'Brianus will not forgive himself for handing them the writing-block – especially if the verdict does not go well for you – but it was bullied out of him.'

'I'm only glad he wasn't taken prisoner himself,' I said bleakly. 'I feel badly enough about the steward's fate. I don't want Brianus on my conscience, too. If only I could have talked to him myself.'

Junio looked a little bit abashed. 'I did my best for you.'

'I'm sorry, Junio, I'm sure you have done everything I asked you to and more. But you can't imagine what it's like for me – cooped up here, unable to get out, and having to rely on someone else to question witnesses on my behalf. I'm sure we could have learned a great deal more if both of us were there.'

He was slightly mollified. 'You would be lucky to find him by this time, anyway. I am certain that he was going to make a run for it.'

'But that would put him on the wrong side of the law.' That was an understatement. For a slave to run away was a capital offence. 'Isn't he in enough trouble as it is?'

Junio made a little face. 'He was terrified they were going to come back later on and drag him, screaming, to the torturers. He was hiding in the temple when I tracked him down, trying to propitiate the gods. It was difficult to get any sense from him at all, except that he blamed himself . . .' He broke off as the commander's servant came into the room, bearing another dish of figs and two more goblets of watered wine for us. There was a pause while the slave set down his laden tray and tiptoed off again.

'Didn't Brianus tell you anything of use?' I prompted, when the boy had gone. I was conscious of impatience in my voice. I felt sure that Junio was holding something back – some juicy tidbit which he was proud of having learned, and which he was saving till the last. 'Not even about the lictor's character and past?'

'Not much,' Junio answered. 'He refused to say anything directly about Voluus at all – simply kept repeating that the steward was being held in jail and if he didn't keep his own mouth shut they'd come for him as well.'

'I expect that's exactly what they threatened they would do,' I answered heavily. 'Well, never mind, Junio – I am sure you tried.'

'I put a few questions but he didn't really answer them – either because he didn't know the facts, or was simply too frightened to confide in anyone.' He picked up a goblet and took a sip from it. 'But there was one thing about Calvinus that might interest you. Brianus told me a story about a pageboy back in Gaul that Voluus accused of stealing from a purse.'

'The lad who was probably entirely innocent, but was flogged into confessing and then condemned to death?'

'You have heard that as well?'

'Calvinus told me about the incident himself. He was talking about how cruel his master's punishments could be. Is it relevant?' I could not see what this had to do with me – though I could see how Brianus would apply it to himself. I reached for the drinking vessel and took a doubtful sip, hoping that wine might soothe my jangled nerves. There was no effect. The wine was watered, and every bit as sour as I had feared.

'Did Calvinus tell you that the boy in question was his son? Or possibly his younger brother – Brianus did not know the exact relationship.'

'Part of his family?' I was incredulous. 'Calvinus certainly didn't tell me that! But how do you know? Surely he didn't mention that to Brianus?' The pompous steward confiding in the frightened slave?

Junio shook his head. 'It came from the slave-girl that Calvinus wants to buy. Pronta, is she called? The steward was trying to impress her with his rank, apparently – saying that he was not born into servitude himself, but was really a warrior of the Marcomanni tribe who was captured and sold to slavery after a defeat.'

'Really?' I was evaluating this. 'I can't imagine plump Calvinus as a fighting man.' But in some ways the tale was plausible. The Marcomanni are famous throughout the Empire. They have been defying the army in Germanica for years.

'Mounting raids on Roman property, rather than a fight,' Junio explained. 'He was caught setting fire to an army granary, so as a punishment they rounded his entire family up as well, and put them up for sale. At any rate, that's what Calvinus told the girl.'

Even in my current state of stress I was amused. 'And was she impressed? The fact that he was a barbarian by birth and an arsonist by choice?'

Junio laughed. 'I don't suppose she was. She doesn't much like Calvinus in any case, it seems, though she has a much better time of it than poor old Brianus. But you see where this is leading? The whole household were shipped off by a slave-trader to Gaul, where Voluus got a bargain by purchasing the lot and immediately selling on the ones he did not want. But he did keep one or two of them, apart from Calvinus.'

'Including this ill-fated page?' I whistled with surprise. 'I see! And since Calvinus was obliged to watch him die, he had a special reason for hating Voluus. I suppose it might be true. Have you checked with Pronta?'

'I would have liked to speak to her, but she's run away as well – and Brianus refuses to say where she has gone. I even tried to visit Calvinus in jail, but they wouldn't let me in, though I offered the jailer a considerable bribe to let me talk to him. But, if this story's true – and there's no reason to suppose it's not – might it not make a difference to your case? It would give Calvinus a motive for revenge. Do you suppose that Porteus was right, and the steward has been plotting against his master all along?'

'It has to be a possibility.' My brain was racing like a chariot. 'It would fit with what we know about the lictor's character. He has a nasty temper, but he's calculating, too. We heard that he plays cruel games with Calvinus all the time – dangling the dream of freedom and snatching it away.'

Junio nodded. 'And if the steward wasn't born in servitude, he must feel it doubly, I should think. So if that page-boy really was his son . . .' He left the words unfinished. 'Though it wouldn't be the case, officially, I suppose, after they were taken into slavery.'

That was true. A slave is legally a un-person, 'a vocal tool', owned like any other piece of household furniture and can no more have a family than a table can. I knew that to my cost. I had been married to Gwellia when I myself was seized – and I knew what it was to have one's feelings swept aside and all existing relationships anulled.

'Perhaps that's why the lictor accused the lad at all,' I said. 'Because he knew that Calvinus would have to watch him flogged. He may have even known the slave was innocent. He seems the sort of person who delights in causing pain.'

'That's exactly what Brianus said to me – and he's naturally wondering what that means for Pronta and himself, when Voluus gets here and finds out what's occurred. The poor lad is half-insane with fear. But it does give you some insight into Calvinus, doesn't it?' Junio drained his wine and set the goblet down. 'It would give him a motive for this crime.'

'Establishing a motive would hardly be enough,' I said, knowing that I sounded ungrateful as I spoke.

'Motive and splendid opportunity. As everybody says, he was right here on the spot, and knew all about the treasure-load. He probably knew exactly where it was going to be and when. If he wanted his revenge, it would have been easy to arrange an ambush on the cart in return for what was in it. Any rebel would have jumped at such a chance, and paid him for the information, too.' He looked at me in triumph. 'Will you be able to use that plea in your defence?'

'I doubt that it would help. They think I'm in collusion with the steward anyway. I wish you'd had the chance to speak to Calvinus direct,' I said, meaning that I wished *I'd* had the chance myself. 'But they wouldn't let you, even for a bribe?'

'He's in no condition to speak to anyone, that's what the warder said, though not until he'd taken the money anyway. I did get a sort of promise that Calvinus would get a better cell, with fresh air and daylight, and proper food and drink – though whether it will happen is another thing.'

'You had sufficient money?'

'I took some from the shop. I didn't think you'd mind. I didn't take it all, and anyway, I didn't spend the whole of it.' He scrabbled in his arm-purse and fished out some coins – a couple of *sesterces* and an *as* or two. 'I'll give the rest to you – tomorrow you may need it, although I hope you won't.' He put the money on the tabletop and slid it towards me.

I was grateful but I didn't pick it up. 'But surely you will need it for a hiring-coach yourself. You can't walk back to the roundhouse at this time of night. It will be dark in half an hour.'

He shook his head. 'I have already decided to bed down at the shop. It's dry and warm and I can curl up by the fire and there's still sufficient money left to buy myself a meal. And don't worry – my wife knows where I am. I gave Minimus that message to take back with yours.'

'But Minimus went home hours ago!'

He grinned. 'I could see that this business would take a little while and I didn't want her worrying that I'd been set upon by wolves – as she always does when I am in the forest after dark. You take the money, Father.' He rose and dropped a friendly hand upon my shoulder as he spoke, and with the other gestured through the open window-space. 'I see a soldier hurrying over here – no doubt that is the summons that you've been waiting for. I'll be in the workshop if you have need of me. Anything, Father. You don't have to ask. Otherwise, I'll be there in the court to speak for you.'

'But . . .' I was trying to protest that doing that was dangerous for him, but he'd already given my shoulder a quick squeeze and hurried from the room.

I just had time to scoop the coins into the draw-purse at my belt before Emelius came panting in, accompanied by the commander's military slave who was carrying my cape.

The centurion wasted no time on formalities. 'They've brought in the farmer who says he saw the cart. The commander wants you in his office instantly.'

SEVENTEEN

D usk was approaching now, and the courtyard was full of shadows as we passed. Next time night fell across this normal scene, I was likely to be a fugitive. I gazed about, trying to take in every detail, as men who are sentenced to the beasts are said to do.

Soldiers were busy with their evening tasks, squatting in doorways to buff their armour up or rubbing goose-grease on their leather tunic skirts. Smells of cooking wafted in the air as each contingent made its evening meal – of beef and cabbage, porridge or whatever it might be – while torches and oil-lamps flared in every barrack block and the air was musty with the scent of tallow-smoke. How long would it be before I would have a home again, and enjoy the right to light and food and heat?

I went into the guard-room, which had seemed so threatening before. It felt almost like a cosy haven now, so full of body warmth that it was hard to feel the fire. It was crammed to bursting, with clerical officers preparing their reports and rota-lists, and night sentries getting ready to relieve the duty watch. Tomorrow night – if things went against me in the court – all these men would be my enemies, sworn to cut me down if I was found within the boundaries of the Empire, and ready to execute anyone who gave me food or fire.

My only hope was that the man awaiting me upstairs had some information which might prove my innocence. It was not probable. I toiled up the bleak stone steps to talk to him.

The farmer was standing on the far side of the room. He was not prepossessing, on first appearances: short and swarthy and not very clean. He gave off a strong smell of mud and pig manure, and he wore a pair of 'country shoes' – uncured hide which is bound around the feet until it takes on the rough shape of a boot. The resultant stink is always terrible, and in the fastidious commander's office it was overpowering. The man looked up with sullen, fearful eyes as I came in, and rubbed a mud-stained arm across his grimy face – with no effect beyond creating further streaks on both.

The commander was sitting on the stool behind his desk, as far away from the pig smell as he could put himself. I was invited neither to take my cloak off nor sit down. He signalled the centurion to take up station at the door and waved a hand at me.

'This is the citizen Libertus,' he announced impatiently. 'The pavement-maker that I told you of. He is here to help me with the questioning, though Jove knows we're not getting very far. Libertus, this man is Biccus. He has a little farm and he thinks he saw the treasure-cart last night.' He turned to the pig-man. 'Tell the citizen what you have just told me.'

Biccus looked at me distrustfully. 'What is there to say? I saw a cart all right. You could hardly miss it, with an escort of that size. Went past my farm a little before dusk. Otherwise, I don't know what else I can say. Didn't take much notice. It wasn't my affair – I was busy digging up the ground for cabbages. I've said all this before. There's nothing more to add. And now that I have told you, am I free to go?'

The commander raised his eyebrows helplessly at me, as if to say, *What now?*

Biccus was chewing on his lower lip. I recognized the signs. He was reluctant to cooperate, but at the same time scared, so was answering all questions as briefly as he could; not refusing information – which would be an offence – but not volunteering anything of his own accord. He would tell us nothing that he was not specifically asked.

However, I had one weapon which the commander lacked. I said in Celtic, 'You're freeborn, I think?' The local tribal dialect was not quite the same as mine, but I knew from experience I would be understood. 'You own the land you live on?'

He looked at me, surprised. 'Yes, I do, though there's not much left of it,' he answered using Celtic, too. 'My ancestors had acres and acres of good land. Until these accursed Romans came and annexed most of it.' He jerked his head at the commander, with a scowl. 'They didn't call it that of course

– just paid a pittance and called it "purchasing" – as if my great-grandparents had any choice at all.'

'Good farming soil, you say?'

He made a snorting nose. 'Not the miserable corner that has been handed down to me! The Romans naturally seized the best land for themselves. And even what was left has been divided up, of course, as it was handed down. I'm only left with three remaining fields and one of those is pretty well a swamp for half the year.'

'Not very much,' I sympathized. It was a common story – farmland subdivided among surviving sons each time, so that in the end the meagre parcels scarcely paid their way.

'Hardly enough to feed my family on – and even then I have to use the forest for the pigs. Miles I have to walk. And then these accursed Roman soldiers come, when I'm busy planting out – won't even give me time to wash and change my clothes, but drag me in here like a stinking fool . . .' He checked himself and frowned. 'But I shouldn't talk like this. You must be one of them, because they brought you here and I understand that you're a citizen. How do you speak our tongue?'

'I am a Celt myself. I too had lands once, but I lost everything. I earn a living making pavements now.' I saw a new expression dawning in his eyes and I went on earnestly, 'I think that you can help me. There has been a dreadful crime . . .'

He broke me off with a derisive laugh. 'I thought as much. And now they've brought me here to pin the blame on me.'

I shook my head. 'Quite the opposite. They're trying to blame me! The army brought you here because, if you've seen this cart, you may have information which will prove my innocence.'

I saw him hesitate.

'Two rich and powerful Roman councillors are taking me to court, and I have no witness in my own defence,' I went on urgently. 'Won't you help a fellow Celt by telling what you know? I am just a humble tradesman, very much like you. They are members of the Glevum curia.'

Perhaps the commandant had recognized the last two words. 'Glevum curia' is similar in either tongue. In any case, he interrupted me. 'Libertus, I cannot allow you to go on with an interrogation which I do not understand. If you cannot use Latin, I must ask you to desist.'

So my most useful strategy was denied to me! I turned to him. 'Just one more question, commandant – then I promise that I'll stop. Of course, I'll tell you what's been said so far.' I gave a brief account of the nature of the farm – omitting the sentiments about the army's part in this. 'It's just that I think Biccus finds the Celtic easier.'

That was not strictly true, but the commander bowed his head. 'Very well. I can see that you have managed to gain his confidence. At least you are getting something out of him. But just the one more question, then you will use Latin, please. Otherwise, you could be coaching him to lie on your behalf.'

I turned to Biccus urgently. 'You heard what he said! This is our only chance. I know this commander. He is an honest man. This matter was urgent – not for him, for me. My trial will be tomorrow, probably, that's why they insisted that you come at once. I assure you, no one thinks that you're a fool. So it is up to you. Will you help me fight injustice by telling what you know?' I switched to Latin. 'You saw a cart accompanied by an escort, is that right? When exactly, would you say that was?'

A doubtful shrug. 'Yesterday, about an hour before dusk, I suppose. Perhaps a bit before.'

I saw the commander scribble a calculation on a slate. 'Around the eleventh hour, shall we say?' he interposed.

The pig-man shrugged again. Obviously the Roman system did not mean much to him. (It can be difficult to calculate – even with marked candles or a proper water-clock. Total light and dark, respectively, are each divided into twelve to make an hour. Thus as daylight gets shorter at this time of year, so does a Roman hour – and night hours grow correspondingly longer, of course, to compensate.) Obviously Biccus did not bother with all that; he simply used the general estimation which our ancestors had used. 'I can't tell you that. The clouds were gathering. No shadows to judge by, even, since it was going to rain.'

This was getting nowhere. 'Can you describe the cart?' I asked.

'It was a fairly big one. Heavy, too – you could tell from how low it was sitting on its wheels. Good thing it was on the military road or it would have been down to its axles in the mud. Left to me I would have pulled it with an ox or two, but they were using horses – for greater speed, I suppose. Splendid ones as well. Good ones on the cart – and four beauties for the escort, too.'

I shot a glance at the commander. He was nodding, looking grave. 'That sounds like the cart that we're enquiring about,' he said approvingly. 'Did you glimpse the cargo, or any part of it?'

Biccus shook his head. 'Something weighty, that's all I know. No telling what it was. It was all done up in bags and boxes and even then it was mostly covered with a cloth. Not surprisingly. Like I said, it was coming on to rain.'

I tried again. 'So the cart wasn't travelling towards Glevum very fast? Fast enough to get there before nightfall, would you say?'

I saw a hesitation cross the pig-man's face. 'Very likely not, supposing it was coming to the colonia at all. Though that was the direction it was going in when it passed me, certainly!'

I looked at him keenly. 'Why do you say that? You think that it was headed somewhere else?'

He shook his head. 'I aren't saying that.' His Latin wasn't good and his grammar left a lot to be desired. 'I wondered, that is all. I can't be positive. It's just that when I had finished with the cabbages and I stood up again, I couldn't see it further down the road.'

'And you expected to?' It was obvious that he'd stood up especially to gape.

He was not at all abashed. 'The area's slightly hilly, but the road is pretty straight and my top field is right up on the rise, so – except where odd stands of trees get in the way – generally you can see anything, either way, for miles.'

I nodded. Roman roads are always built as straight as possible, unless there is actually a river or mountain in the way. 'So you are telling us the cart had somehow disappeared?' My mind was racing – had the ambush already taken place and the empty wagon been hidden in the trees?

'I don't believe in Roman magic. But it was puzzling.'
Biccus was still attempting to justify himself without admitting
that he'd meant to spy. 'They might have speeded up a little,
I suppose – as you say, in an attempt to get to Glevum before
dark. Though they'd have had to move a lot more quickly than
they were. Or perhaps they just found somewhere to stop
before it rained. That's probably what happened.' He nodded,
satisfied.

'Is there an inn nearby they might have used?' I asked. The
scouts had reported denials from them all, but frightened people
have been known to lie.

Biccus shook his head. 'There is only one place I can
think of that they could possibly have gone. There's another
farmstead at the bottom of the hill, with a lane that leads to
it – runs along the wooded valley by the stream. Part of what
was once our tribal home. I suppose it's possible the travellers might have turned in there – for shelter anyway – though
I would not have thought they'd choose to force themselves
on to a private farm.'

'Private farm? I thought you said those lands were part of
our *terratorium*?' the commander challenged him, and then
explained – since Biccus was obviously mystified, 'Didn't you
say the land was annexed by the garrison, in order to grow
provisions for the soldiery? The travellers might have gone
there looking for some troops.' He glanced at me. 'Protection,
possibly?'

Biccus shook his head. 'The army stopped farming out there
years ago, when the full legion left. Most of the fields are
back in private hands.' He glanced at me and added in muttered
Celtic, 'Didn't come back to our family of course – the
confounded Romans bought it for a fraction of its worth, but
when they sold it they asked the market rate – and naturally
we couldn't raise the price.'

'Do you know the present owners?'

He gave a bitter laugh. 'Never met them, and would not
wish to if I could. Roman sympathizers, all the lot of them.
Anyway, the owner's moving on. He's already sold his stock
and produce – not that there was very much of it to sell. Some
ex-soldier who used to have the place but never made it pay.'

'A legionary veteran?' That would be logical. Legionaries were often given land (in addition to a handsome sum) when they had served their term. 'Part of his retirement settlement, I suppose?'

Biccus shook his head. 'Not this one. I hear he bought it for himself. Of course, I never personally asked him, so I can't swear to it – but you know how people talk.'

I knew by this time how Biccus talked, when he felt encouraged to! I could imagine the pig-man's family exchanging views and news about the incomers who'd usurped their lands. I nodded silently.

His next words confirmed my thoughts. 'My cousin met him once and found him disagreeable. Not the first idea of how to run a farm. No, though no doubt he got it at a bargain price – if he really was a soldier once, he would have known the appropriate officers to bribe.'

The commander gave a warning cough. Of course, we'd slipped into our native tongue again. I glanced at him, suspecting that he'd taken offence, but the insult to the army had been lost on him. I gave him a more tactful version of what had just been said and he turned back to Biccus. 'Very well. Go on with your story. And this time stick to Latin, if you please.'

Biccus ran his grubby arm across his face and again attempted to comply, although he sometimes struggled to find the proper words. However, it was intelligible enough. 'Why the fellow wanted it is anybody's guess – he's done almost nothing with it and the lands have gone to ruin – but now he's found a wealthy buyer to take it off his hands. Offering a small fortune for it, as I understand, and doesn't even want the equipment or the stock, because he wants to build a brand-new villa on the site.'

I turned to the commander. 'There you are!' I cried triumphantly. 'That's the solution! It must be Voluus! In which case that's obviously where the wagon-party spent the night! I must get out there! Commandant, I beg you to arrange some transport for me at first light: I must go and see the place before the trial.'

In my enthusiasm I had said too much. He looked at me

coldly. 'There is no "must" about it, citizen. You know quite well that I can sanction nothing of the kind. I might be swayed sufficiently to send a scout, perhaps – if your patron will defray the cost, and if you can persuade me that the trip will be of use.'

EIGHTEEN

I should not have been surprised. It was sufficient concession
for him to have allowed me to stay here and speak to Biccus
at all.

'I apologize, commander, if I sound presumptuous,' I said,
forcing myself to sound properly contrite. 'But you can see
that this might solve the mystery of where the cart was overnight. If Voluus has just bought property of his own nearby,
it would be an obvious place to stop: he could arrange to have
the horses and the men provided for. And being on his own
land, he'd assume that it was safe. Much safer than stopping
at any public inn . . .' I trailed off. I was not convincing him.

He shook a disbelieving head at me. 'But did Biccus not
just tell us that the purchaser intended to build a villa on the
site? Doesn't that suggest that it *wasn't* Voluus? Why would
he require a second country house when he's already bought
a site from Porteus? And I'm assured he has. Forest-lands on
the other side of town. I believe I mentioned it to you.'

I could only say feebly, 'Perhaps he's changed his mind.'

'Then he has changed it since I spoke to Florens earlier
today. He says the lictor has sent on detailed instructions for
the plans, and asked Porteus to set his slaves to work to finish
clearing off the land. He's even listed the materials he wants
– marble and all sorts of expensive building stone – and
requested Porteus to buy them in for him, so that construction
can begin as soon as he arrives. Obviously he's anxious to
oversee the actual building work himself. I simply can't believe
that he's bought a different site instead. When would he have
had a chance to do it, anyway?' He shook his head again. 'It
must be someone else. Even another moneyed veteran perhaps.
Plenty of people are anxious to settle hereabouts, and Biccus
tells us that the land is good.'

I had to concede that the commandant was right. No one
builds two brand-new villas outside of the same town, and

certainly not both within an hour's easy ride. That would be
a pointless exercise, quite apart from the phenomenal expense
it would entail. But I was reluctant to give up my idea that
there was some connection between the farm and Voluus. I
could not believe in pure coincidence.

'Perhaps the story about wanting to build a country house
there isn't true. Or . . .' I was struck by an interesting new
idea, '. . . perhaps the new owner isn't actually Voluus
himself, but someone that he knows.' I turned to the pig-
man. 'Biccus, do you know any more about this purchaser?'

The pig-man shrugged. 'Only that he is a foreigner. That's
all I know for sure. Somebody said they'd heard he might
have come from Gaul.'

'Gaul!' I pounced upon the word excitedly. 'Then it could
easily be a friend of Voluus.'

The commander raised an eyebrow and said wearily, 'A
friend who robbed him and murdered all his slaves? Or
betrayed them to the rebels – which comes to the same thing?'

I stared at him. 'Great Mercury! Then perhaps it's not a
friend at all, but an old enemy? You don't suppose those threats
that Voluus received . . . ?' I turned to Biccus.

The pig-man seemed to positively blanch under the furrows
of dirt upon his face. 'Did you say threats?' He looked beseech-
ingly at me. 'You can't blame me for that. Look, citizen, I
admit that I once stormed down to the farm and shouted to
the owner that I would burn his ricks if he didn't stop his dogs
from harrying my pigs. But I'm just a humble freeman and
I've already told you everything I know. I've never heard of
this man Voluus – whoever he may be – and I've certainly
never sent him any messages.'

'No one is accusing you,' I said. 'Voluus is the owner of
the treasure-cart and he is on his way from Gaul. I simply
wondered if the man who's newly bought the farm could be
the person who wrote the threatening note, especially if he
comes from over there.'

'A note!' Relief spread over Biccus like a water-stain, and
seemed to give him sudden confidence. 'Well, in that case,
citizen, I can prove it wasn't me. I don't know how to read
or write. Besides, if you'll excuse me saying so, I think you're

flogging the wrong ox. Would this Voluus – whoever he may be – deliberately arrange to have his treasure go to the home of a man who sent him threats?'

He was right, of course. It would be like walking deliberately on to someone's sword. I murmured something to that general effect.

'I don't think the new man's there yet, in any case,' the pig-man eagerly went on. 'And I'll tell you something else. This Voluus person couldn't have made arrangements in advance for his cart to call there. The old owner was due to leave there just before the Ides. And, as I say, the new one hasn't come. So when would a message have the chance to reach the person it was intended for?'

'But Voluus is a lictor who has just retired from Gaul. Isn't it . . .' I began, still unwilling to extinguish the only glimmer of a theory which I had.

The commander gave that cough again and shook his head at me. It was a warning not to say too much. Too late! I could already see Biccus pricking up his ears. The pig-man would have another story to tell his relatives and another grudge against the conquerors. Even though there were no lictors in this colonia, they were known by reputation everywhere and ranked even above taxmen as the most hated officials in the Empire. It was likely that the story of the lictor and the threats would be all round the countryside as soon as Biccus got back home.

The commander pushed back his stool and got slowly to his feet. 'I think we've learned everything we're likely to from this. It's been a stressful day for all of us. However, I concede that this farmstead should be searched. The lictor's cart may still have gone there to shelter from the rain, as Biccus originally said, and – even if this was purely by chance – there may yet be something to be learned.'

'A thousand thanks, Mightiness!' I cried. I was ready to fling myself at his feet in gratitude. 'I promise you'll not regret your confidence in me. I think it is possible that's where they were attacked, and I swear that if there's any clue at all I will find it . . .' I had spoken eagerly, but the commander waved a hand to silence me.

'Libertus, I said nothing about permitting you to go. What I will do, for your benefit, is send a man out there at first light tomorrow to have a look around, in case there are any of these signs that you are hoping for. There is no question of your going out there yourself. Now, let me hear no more about it. Is that understood?'

I nodded ruefully.

'Can I go home now, in that case?' Biccus enquired, in a plaintive tone, adding without conviction, 'I was promised a reward.'

The commander shook his head. 'It is far too late for you to journey home tonight. I'll make arrangements to have you put up at the hiring-inn, where they can accommodate your donkey, too. That is your reward for coming here and what you've said so far. If your information proves to be of use, we'll consider if there should be something more. Tomorrow you can accompany my scout and show him exactly where the lane and farmstead is.' He turned to me. 'As for you, it's getting late. Time I delivered you to Marcus's, before his servants start to wonder where you are. Besides, my slave will have started to make my evening meal and I still have other duties to perform.' He sat down at the desk again and unrolled a document, calling as he did so, 'Centurion, are you there?'

Emelius, who had been standing outside all this while, bustled in and snapped smartly to attention. 'Present and awaiting orders, sir.' He smacked his centurion's baton on his leg, as if for emphasis.

'Accompany Libertus to his patron's flat and when you have delivered him, report back here to me. Take Biccus downstairs with you and find a man to take him to the mansio and have him fed, then send to the hiring-inn and request a bed for him. Say I sent you and the garrison will pay.' He glanced at me. 'I hope your patron is as generous as he claims to be and will meet all these expenses made on your account.'

It was obviously the best that I could hope for now and I bowed my thanks before allowing Emelius to escort me down the stairs, with Biccus trailing reluctantly behind.

The pig-man was given into the hands of an octio downstairs, who looked him up and down with ill-concealed disgust. 'We'd

better get you cleaned up first of all, I think. I can't deliver
you to the mansio to eat smelling like a pig-enclosure. And
I'll have to burn those clothes before I take you to the public
hostelry – even there you're likely to disturb the other guests.
Doubtless there's a cleaner tunic somewhere you could use,
though there's not much we can do about the shoes.' A deep,
reproachful sigh. 'You'd better come with me!' And Biccus
was seized roughly by the arm and hustled off in the direction
of the military baths. The last I saw of him, he was protesting
all the way.

There was scarcely time to take in this little scene before I
was hustled off myself, out of the fortress and back into the
town.

I turned to the centurion. 'Would it be possible for us to
stop briefly at the jail? I would like very much to have a word
with Calvinus.' It was worth a final try.

Emelius did not even condescend to answer this. He simply
drew his dagger from its sheath again and held it closely to
my ribs, jerking his head towards the route he wished to take.
'This way, citizen. I'm walking at your heels.'

I thought for a mad moment of attempting an escape and
making my own way to the jail, but an instant's reflection
showed me what a stupid thought it was. Emelius was plump
and sometimes lumbering but he was not only much younger
than I was, he was a serving soldier – and anyone who can
do a route-march in full kit was going to be a good deal fitter
than an ageing shopkeeper. Besides, there were too many
people in the streets, any of whom could be legally required
to chase after me, if I did anything so foolish as to try to run
away.

The town is always very busy around dusk, and it was so
tonight: creaking wagons making those delayed deliveries;
bakers cleaning ovens and resetting fires; people who could
afford no other flour queuing up to purchase the grit-filled
sweepings from the miller's stones. Traders darted to and fro,
bringing in their stock for safe-keeping overnight, some of
them shouting curses to their slaves, who brushed down the
pavements outside the premises with little whisking bundles
of tied broom, but they all made way for the man in uniform.

The very dray-horses seemed to sidestep as we passed, snuffling gently in their clanking chains.

We turned down a dusky side-street to avoid the crush, though it was not much better here. The taverna on the corner was packed with customers who were already beginning to spill out on to the street, and the soup-kitchen next door was also doing a boisterous trade: its open door and window-space aglow with smoky light, while a noisy crowd gathered round the entrance, trying to push their way into the steam and smell. But even they reduced their clamouring and stood aside to let the soldier and his prisoner through.

At length we came out on to the major street which skirted the forum and led towards the baths. Marcus's town apartment was at the other end – one of the most prestigious such properties in town, though (as with the lictor's residence nearby) there were poorer folk crammed into the attic floors above – one of the reasons why my patron rarely used the place.

This area was a good deal quieter, but we were still delayed. We ran into a funeral heading for the gates: no doubt some worthy freeman paid for by his guild, since there were professional mourners and musicians accompanying the bier and a long procession trailing after it. (In Glevum such things still happen after dark – just as all funerals used to, years ago, in Rome. The practice has survived here, I have often thought, not only because of a natural preference for old-fashioned ways, but because it means the other members of the guild can continue to work throughout the day.)

Mourners have a natural precedence – no one is anxious to offend a corpse and have the angry spirit haunting them – but it was amazing how the sight of the centurion was enough to make them pause. Most simply stared in silence as I was marched along, though I was conscious of some sympathetic whispering. The undertaker's women carried baskets of sweet herbs – no doubt intended to be added to the pyre – and I caught the sweet smell of lovage as I passed.

Emelius had obviously smelt the herbs as well, for though he did not for a moment drop the dagger at my back, I realized that he'd paused to spit on his free hand then pull his ear with it. Hipposelinum – lovage – once it has been picked, is said to bring ill-fortune if you cross it on the street, but I did not bother to do the self-protective ritual myself. I felt that my own luck could not get much worse, as we found ourselves outside the block where Marcus had his flat.

The wine-shop was still open and a gang of youths was clustered at the door, blocking the pavement and getting in our way. They were dressed in togas and had obviously been sampling the wares – but being quite clearly the sons of wealthy men, they were not afraid of mere centurions. They ignored us totally. One of them was swinging from the painted wooden sign – which showed the nature of the establishment for those that could not read – while his comrades urged him on and the wine-shop owner protested feebly from within.

Emelius muttered something to the nearest youth, who paid no more attention than if he had been a dog. I felt the centurion stiffening with rage, but he obviously did not want to cause an incident, and – putting up his dagger – he gripped my elbow and steered me off the pavement, intending to walk on the roadway round the group of youths.

However, as we did so the fellow dangling from the sign abruptly lost his grip and tumbled to the paving right in front of us. He was too drunk to care and lay there giggling. The sight of the centurion had no effect on him, though his friends seemed suddenly sobered by the accident. They stole sideways looks at Emelius's stony face and one by one slipped silently away, leaving their comrade lying in the road. He was tittering inanely, but seemed mercifully unhurt.

Emelius stood over him and ordered him to rise, but the boy just looked up at us with a foolish grin. 'Will do in a minute, need to sleep, tha's all.'

The shopkeeper came out. 'Thank Mercury you've come! You see what state he's in. He could have killed himself. I want him arrested and taken home at once. I'll tell you where to take him – his father is a customer of mine. I'll write out a bill for you to take as well. Someone's got to pay. Emptied two *amphorae* before I got to them, and didn't have a quadrans between the lot of them.'

The lad on the pavement gave a little grunt, rolled into the gutter and promptly fell asleep.

The centurion turned him over with his foot, though he never slacked his grip upon my arm. 'I'll deal with him later. He won't stir from there. In the meantime, I've got work to do. I'm delivering this . . . citizen . . . to His Excellence's flat.'

'Up those stairs and first door at the end,' the shopkeeper supplied, obviously wishing to be helpful to the authorities. 'But I don't think Marcus Septimus is there. I saw him leaving an hour or more ago.'

'All the same . . .' My escort pressed me on, making no further effort to explain.

The wine-shopkeeper looked doubtfully at me. 'Well, please yourself, of course. Don't say I didn't warn you. Either way, I will be waiting when you come down again. In the meantime, I'll keep watch on him.' He gestured to the snoring figure lying in the road, whose mud-stained toga had half-unwrapped itself and whose hair was now full of fragments from the mire.

Emelius nodded and marched me to the entrance to the upper floors. The stairwell was poorly lit and I almost stumbled as we hurried up the steps. Unusually, there were no other inhabitants about to stare, a fact which I put down to the late hour of day. Secretly I was rather grateful, though, as it spared me the embarrassment of further scrutiny.

But as we reached the landing the explanation for this lack of bystanders became clear. Marcus's town doorkeeper was awaiting us. This was a man that I hadn't seen before, and he was enormous – huge, hairy and malevolent, with pointed yellow teeth, like one of the performing bears that you sometimes see paraded through the streets. His hands were enormous and so covered with matt fur that they might almost have been designed as paws. He held one up to challenge us as we approached. It was holding what appeared to be a twig – though it would have been a baton to any other man.

'This is the citizen my master told me of?' His eyes were small and close together, giving him a squint. I thought that I had never seen an uglier man, but his credentials as doorkeeper were in no kind of doubt. The gold-edged scarlet uniform in which my patron dressed his slaves only served to emphasize the giant's strength and power: the flimsy tunic strained across the muscles in his chest and failed to hide the bulges in his arms and legs.

'This is Libertus,' Emelius agreed, ever the proper Roman officer. 'I was instructed to escort him here.'

'Then you can leave him with me. I'll take good care of him.' The bearish doorman directed a leering smile at me. 'Welcome, citizen. If you'd just like to step inside?'

NINETEEN

Emelius said nothing further – even a centurion does not argue with a bear – but he transferred me silently, and a moment later I heard his hobnails clip-clopping down the stairs as he hurried off to deal with the drunken youth outside. I felt like a rabbit that's been let out of a noose only to find itself on the butcher's block, as I looked up at the doorkeeper who had now become my guard.

He was still giving me that yellow-fanged smile as he raised the heavy latch on Marcus's front door with one of his massive paws, and with the other steered me sharply in.

I had visited the town apartment several times before but not since my patron had come back from his recent trip to Rome: I knew that the place had been refurbished since, so it was no surprise to find it somewhat changed. It had always been luxurious – even more opulent than the lictor's rooms and in huge contrast to the commandant's ascetic residence – but now it was exotically crammed with ornaments and furniture. Here in the entrance-hall alone there was a table and a chest, two marble statues, an altar in a niche and a set of painted murals on the wall, depicting Jove in various guises capturing pretty girls. Bowls of dried rose petals gave off their musty sweetness to the air and lighted tapers flickered from a dozen sconces on the wall, throwing mottled shadows on the mosaic floor. That floor was almost the only feature that I recognized. It was a modest creation of my own.

I was not permitted to stand and look at it. The doorkeeper was still impelling me inside: through the lighted atrium, where there was a team of silent slaves lined up to welcome me, then – with the troupe of servants following – I was whisked on to the dining area beyond. Here again, the oil-lamps were already lit. Before I had the chance to say a single word, I found myself being simultaneously lowered to a folding chair, expertly relieved of my sandals and damp cloak and having a bowl of perfumed water placed before my feet while a hot stone from the brazier was dropped, sizzling, into it.

I was a little anxious about that heated stone: I had not seen it done before and was alarmed that some kind of painful questioning lay in wait for me, but I need not have been concerned. It was simply intended to warm the water up – surprisingly effective, as I soon found out. A pretty little page was already on his knees, solemnly washing my gnarled old toes and legs, while an older one performed ablutions on my hands and face.

I tried to wave them off, a little embarrassed by all the attention being showered on me. 'There's no need to cosset me,' I spluttered, as the servant rinsed my face. 'Give me that towel. I can manage for myself.'

The handsome attendant gave me a little bow. I recognized him as the page who had escorted Marcus from the garrison. 'If you are quite certain citizen,' he murmured, though he looked aggrieved, as though it were an insult not to be allowed to rub me dry. 'Our instructions are to treat you as a guest.' He handed me the cloth.

I buried my forehead in the linen towel and rubbed my cheeks and eyes, feeling the tension seeping out of me as if it had been sloughed off with the dust and perspiration of the day. The moment that I raised my head again, the cloth was whisked away – even before I had the chance to wonder what I was supposed to do with it. Meanwhile, thanks to the efforts of the kneeling page, my clean and newly-perfumed feet were dried and my deftly cleaned sandals were laced on again, quicker than I could have refastened them myself.

'Then, if you are ready, there is a meal prepared,' the page went on. 'Nothing very fancy, just pork stew with leeks and some bread and cheese and figs for afterwards. I hope that will suffice? His Excellence assured us that your tastes were simple ones, but if there is anything extra that you might require, we are empowered to fetch it for you, if it can be had.'

'His Excellence is very good,' I said, with warmth. Someone was already tucking a fine napkin round my neck, while another servant hovered with a pitcher and some wine. If this was the lifestyle of a wealthy man, I thought, it would be easy to become accustomed to these little luxuries.

I wondered if I was expected to recline, as Romans do, to eat the promised meal – one of the three couches had been pushed up into place and cushioned pillows had been laid on it. I decided that – as His Excellence's guest – I should conform to Roman ways and I began to rise, with the idea of doing so.

The pressure of a heavy hand prevented me. 'Stay right there, citizen.' I looked up and saw the doorkeeper still looking down at me. He flashed his yellow teeth. 'There's no need for you to move. Your meal will come to you. The serving slaves will see to it at once.'

It was clearly a command. A folding table was instantly produced and a tray appeared, as if from nowhere, with a covered dish on it. One of the servants removed the metal lid, and I was presented with more steaming stew than I could reasonably eat. I felt my stomach growl. I'd had almost nothing for the day and this smelt ambrosial. There was a helpful spoon provided and I picked it up, though I noticed there was no sign of any knife – as there would have been for any other dinner guest. Marcus was taking no chances that I might put up a fight.

'Very nice.' I dipped my spoon into the stew.

'There is some garum if you wish it, but we were told that you would not.' The page was anxious and solicitous, as if he could not quite believe that he had heard aright.

'That's true,' I assured him, 'I've never cared for it.' That was an understatement. I detest the salty stuff. The Romans' enthusiasm for covering everything with a sauce of semi-decomposing anchovies is something I have never understood.

The boy was looking politely scandalized by my refusal of the sauce. 'Whatever your preference, citizen, of course. But there's some in the kitchen if you change your mind.'

I was too busy eating pork stew to answer him. I was so hungry that I would have eaten almost anything, but the meal was as delicious as it smelt – with just a touch of spice to liven it. Sometimes Roman dishes are cooked with garum in the mix, but this tasted only of coriander seeds. Marcus's cook-slave had obviously been briefed.

After I had eaten much more than I should I pushed back my plate, only to find it immediately replaced by a platter of fresh bread and cheese and figs. I did not need it – I had eaten far too well – but I took some anyway, excusing my behaviour inwardly by telling myself that it was not a case of simple greed. If I were condemned to exile by tomorrow's court, at least I would have eaten substantially tonight and I would not be seriously hungry for a day or two.

At length I washed down the last crumbs of my extensive meal with yet another cup of watered wine, leaned back – as far as I was able – on my folding chair, and indicated to the servants that I'd dined sufficiently.

The page-boy was at my side at once, to whip my napkin off and offer me a bowl to rinse my fingers in. 'Then, citizen, unless there is anything else that you desire, I will show you to your bed.'

I hesitated. There *was* another thing which I desired, of course – apart from the luxury of talking to my wife. I wanted a chance to make a visit to the jail in the faint hope that somehow I could prove my innocence. Would it be possible to persuade the slaves of that? I did not expect to be allowed to go alone, of course, but the presence of an escort might prove to be a help. Arriving at the prison with a snarling bear in tow might persuade the warder to let me talk to Calvinus. However, looking round at the faces of the slaves, I was not certain that I dared to ask for this. It was obviously not the sort of thing that Marcus had in mind, and I did not want to antagonize the page by suggesting something that he very likely could not grant. Most of all I did not want to infuriate the bear. I glanced towards the little altar in its niche, wondering if the household gods would favour my request.

The page-boy saw my glance and misinterpreted. 'You need not concern yourself about libations, citizen. The master has already dealt with that.'

Nothing had been further from my thoughts, but I managed to stammer something half-appropriate.

'So, citizen,' the boy went on, 'if you would care to follow me? The master has decided that you should have the mistress's room, and it has already been prepared for you.'

A guest in the second-best chamber in the house? Soft pillows and a proper Roman bed – a wooden frame with a goatskin stretched across so that the mattress did not touch the floor! I was really being favoured like an honoured guest. Marcus had never treated me so well before. In fact, my general reception here had been so warm that I decided, after all, that I could take a chance. I put on my most ingratiating smile.

'You asked if there was anything more I might desire?'

The page-boy sketched a bow. 'Name it, citizen. My owner's orders were explicit on the point. You are not to want for anything we can provide.'

'Then,' I watched him nervously, 'I had wondered if it might be possible for me to leave the house – not without an escort, naturally. I want to ask some questions of someone in the town. It might improve my chances before the magistrate.'

There was a dreadful silence. The shock I'd caused was almost palpable – enough to make me wish I'd never said a word. I saw the page-boy glance towards the doorkeeper, who was still hovering somewhere at my back. 'What should we do with him?' he said. 'Lock him in the bedroom or send out for chains? The master said to treat him as well as possible.'

The bear's voice growled, 'You leave this to me.' I was so paralysed with sudden fear that I did not dare to turn, but I heard the doorman's footsteps – like a roll of drums – coming towards me across the pavement floor.

One, two, three – and then a hairy hand had seized my shoulder and swivelled me around – chair and all – as though I were no heavier than a fly.

'Did you really think that we would let you out of here?' The grip was painful and I flinched away, but the pointed teeth were grinning down at me, and the close-set red-rimmed eyes were leering into mine. 'And have you get away? After the master's promised to deliver you to court? And don't tell me that you weren't planning to escape. Do you think that I was washed in on the high tide yesterday?' It was not a question; it was a sort of threat. Any moment, I expected, he would pick me up and shake me, as a dog will shake a bone.

My voice – which had led me into this predicament – entirely deserted me now that I needed it, and all I could manage was

a strangulated squeak. I essayed a foolish smile. 'I didn't mean
. . .' I stammered.

The grip on my shoulder tightened even more – so painful
that tears came springing to my eyes and I gave a whimper.
I tried to stifle it, which only made it worse and it came out
sounding like a mocking laugh.

The result was unexpected. The bear let go of my arm and
gave it a playful punch – so hard that he almost knocked me
off my chair. 'The citizen is jesting!' He let out a braying
laugh. He bent down and stared into my face, breathing sour
wine and bad fish over me.

I did the smile again as the page put an unexpected word
in my defence.

'Master warned us that he had a mocking wit. It's my fault
for using such a form of words. He was offered "anything"
and he made a jest of it – as he might have asked us for the
sun or moon.'

I knew when I had been given a reprieve. I sent up silent
thanks to the good old household gods and nodded eagerly.
'Just my little joke.'

The doorman laughed again and slapped his thigh as if this
tickled him. I was not sure if he genuinely found my words
ridiculous, or if he was delighted by his own cleverness in
manoeuvering me into withdrawing my request. Either way,
there was clearly no hope of leaving here. The bear was more
intelligent than I had first supposed and every bit as dangerous.
He was still chuckling and I feigned a laugh myself.

There was an uneasy titter among the other slaves, then the
boy who had served me stepped forward from the rest. 'Of
course, citizen, I should have realized. You would not abuse
your patron's hospitality by asking for something we could
not provide.' He came across to help me to my feet. 'I will
show you to your bed. I have lit a lamp for you.'

He picked up a little oil-lamp made of bronze, shaped like
a woman's shoe and, holding it aloft, led the way back through
the atrium and into the passage where the bedrooms lay.

He paused outside the second door and pushed it wide.
'This will be your chamber for the night. I trust you find it a
comfortable one. The bed is aired for you and I shall be

sleeping right outside your door, in case there is anything that you require.' He gave a sideways grin. 'Anything within the realms of possibility, that is. Would you care to have assistance to undress?'

I took the lamp from him and looked around the room. If this was to be my last night as a free man, it promised to be a very comfortable one.

The bedchamber – like that of many other Roman wives – was well appointed, with an adjoining door, which I knew led into the master's sleeping space. (Roman couples very rarely share a room at night, though they may often share a bed for a part of it.) Here in town there was no hypercaust to heat the floor – as there was in my patron's country house – but there was a brazier, and a woven mat beside the bed, which itself was heaped with cosy rugs and furs. There were painted shutters at the window-space – stout ones which not only stopped the draught, but also reduced the noises from the street.

'My patron is most gracious,' I acknowledged to the page. 'I am sure that I have everything I need. As to undressing, there's no need for it. I shall sleep in my tunic, as I always do. However, if you have a fuller's pot . . .'

He nodded. 'In the master's vestibule. Or I could bring you something in here, if you prefer . . . ?'

I shook my head. I used to keep a fuller's pot myself when I lived in town – the fuller will collect it to use for cleaning clothes, when it is full of urine – though now we're at the roundhouse we've constructed a latrine. 'I'll use it where it is.'

I was happy to do that for more reasons than he thought. I had never been in the sleeping area before, and was not sure where the vestibule might be, but a mad notion was forming in my mind. As the boy led me to it, I made a mental note of where it was in relation to that intervening door, and how far it was to the main entrance way from there.

I was already planning that, when the slaves were all asleep, I might elude the doorkeeper and slip out into the night.

TWENTY

It was not nearly as easy as I had hoped that it would be.

In the first place it was ages before I was left alone. The slave insisted on assisting me to bed, wrapping me in blankets and blowing out the lamp – which I had hoped to keep burning to light me on my way. I pleaded that I might require the fuller's pot again, but it did not change his mind. He would be right outside the door, he said, and if I called him he would come at once, with a lighted taper, to accompany me.

'The braziers in the passageway are left to glow all night and there is always one oil-lamp burning in the atrium so there is no problem about lighting a candle any time you wish,' he said, standing in the doorway holding a fresh-lit taper of his own. 'Shall I clean your sandals properly while you are asleep?'

I had to think quickly as to why I should refuse. I did not want to be barefoot if I got out into the town. I hit on a solution, of a kind, though it was rather thin and unconvincing, even to myself.

'Tomorrow I am due to appear before the court,' I said. 'And I want to look pathetic, as tradition demands, so that the judge is as lenient as possible. I do not have a *toga sordita* – a special old soiled toga – to wear.' In fact, the toga that I had at home would almost qualify, according to my wife; she was always complaining that I did not keep it clean – but I didn't say that to the page-boy. Instead I pointed to the patches on my work tunic. 'The garment that I'm wearing will have to do instead, and a pair of dirty sandals will obviously help.'

The young man nodded sympathetically. 'Perhaps the master will allow me to rub some ashes from the lamps on to your hair and forehead, too. It is generally taken as a sign of penitence.'

'Penitence does not come into it,' I said, more sharply than

I meant. 'I want to look humble and downtrodden, that's all. I am innocent of all the charges – as Marcus is aware.'

He gave me an exasperating, knowing smile. 'Of course you are, citizen,' he said, in a tone which suggested quite the opposite. 'But worrying about the trial will be a strain for you. The master has left a draught of poppy-juice for you to take to help you sleep. I will fetch it for you, and when you've drunk it, I will let you rest.'

This was an unexpected complication to my plan. I knew my patron's sleeping-draughts of old. If I was forced to drink a single sip of it I would fall into a sleep and then I'd never manage to elude my guards. Perhaps that was Marcus's intention!

There was only one strategy that I could see. While the page was hurrying away to fetch the promised cup of poppy-juice I turned myself towards the wall and closed my eyes. When he came back, I did not stir.

'Citizen?' he murmured.

I did not reply, merely continued breathing with deep, even sighs. (I forbore to make an actual snoring noise, although I was almost tempted as the moments dripped away.)

After a long silence, he said, 'Citizen?' again, then came over to the bed. It was hard not to stiffen as he peered into my face. I feared I would suffer the irony of being 'woken up' to take a sleeping-draught, but after a little he tiptoed off again and I heard him very softly close the door.

Even then I lay unmoving for what seemed an age. The bed-frame was a fine one but it was apt to creak. I knew that the servants would be busy for a while with their evening chores and I could not make my move until the house was still. What is more, it was likely that the page-boy would return and look in on me again, before he settled down to sleep himself.

I was right on both counts. For what must have been the best part of half an hour, I could hear the clatter of dishes in the front part of the house, then laughter in the rear room where the cookery took place. (There was no proper kitchen in a place like this, because of the possibility of fire, but – as I knew from previous visits to the house – a room with a cooking brazier set on stone flags against the wall, where simple things, like the stew I'd had tonight, could be prepared.) From the merriment I guessed the slaves had done their tasks and were enjoying the remains of the altar sacrifice: by tradition the household staff can generally eat whatever food offerings the gods have not consumed themselves.

I began to wonder if the household ever went to bed, but one by one the voices died away and all the movements ceased. I sat up cautiously and – in the dark, since the page had taken my oil-lamp away – began to feel with my feet for my sandals which were underneath the bed. I had just located one of them and was about to lace it on, when I heard a muffled creaking from the door. I snatched my feet up – sandal and all – and lay quickly down again, pulling the bed-rug up about my ears.

Just in time – the page appeared again, holding the lighted taper high to peer at me. I could just discern his silhouette against the candle-glow outside, though I took care to keep my eyelids almost closed.

I closed them tighter as he came over to the bed. 'Still fast asleep,' he murmured to someone waiting in the hall.

'Then I suppose it's safe for us to go to bed ourselves.' I recognized the doorman's growling voice. 'If there's any hint of trouble, you know where I am.'

This was not an encouraging exchange to overhear, since I was still hoping to get out of here. I was no match for the slaves, if it came to struggling – Marcus likes his boys athletic as well as beautiful – and as for tangling with the bear! My blood ran slower at the very thought.

Still, I would deal with that problem when I came to it. In the meantime I was struggling to keep completely still. At last, after what felt a lifetime, the light retreated and the door was closed again. I heard the scuffle as the page rolled out his sleeping-mat. I dared not make a move till I was sure he was asleep, though I was increasingly impatient at the wait.

Every moment made it harder to get around the town: people shut up shops and houses after dark and the streets were shadowy and dangerous. Few people did much work by candle-light, so unless they were feasting or attending funerals, respectable families went to bed betimes and stayed there until dawn. The night was the province of the underworld, in every sense: thieves, beggars, paupers, prostitutes – and ghosts. I did not want to leave here any later than I must.

Finally I judged that it was safe to move. I still had one sandal halfway on my foot and with a little effort I found the other one. I was about to lace them up, when I had another thought. My hobnails would inevitably make a noise – I remembered the centurion clattering down the stairs – much safer to wait until I was outside. I picked my sandals up and resolved to carry them.

I did not attempt to leave the bedroom by the passage door. My expedition to the fuller's pot had taught me that, by going the other way, I could get out through the master's room – provided that I did not walk into anything – and emerge further down the hall, nearer to the atrium and the outer door. My eyes had got accustomed to the darkness now and I could make out the corner of the bed, the outline of the cupboard and the chest, by the faint glow of the brazier by the wall.

Gingerly, carrying my sandals by their straps, I edged towards the intermediate door. It opened at my touch and I was pleased to see that here in Marcus's bedroom the shutters were not closed and a faint light was filtering from the street. I tiptoed over to the window-space and looked out of it. There was still a group of would-be purchasers around the wine-shop door, though most of them were honest slaves by now, clutching the amphorae that they'd filled – to carry home to whatever master might have sent them there. Slaves in cloaks and tunics! That was good for me. I could attempt to merge with them when I got out. Supposing that I ever managed that!

Very cautiously I crossed the room and opened the outer door into the hall. In the shadows I could see the humped shape of the slave, wrapped in a blanket outside my former room. He had his back to me, which was doubly fortunate, so I closed the master's door behind me and stole silently out into the deserted atrium.

There was a single oil-lamp as the page said, and in the darkness its rays spread very wide, though it was placed before the altar and did not light the route which I would have to follow to gain the outer door. There were compensations – it was safer to confine my path to the darker areas – but several times I almost barged into a table or a chest, and once I over-turned a little statue from its plinth and only just managed to catch it as it fell. I held my breath lest I'd disturbed the page, but he only sighed softly and rolled over in his sleep.

The servants had taken my cloak when I arrived and I did not know what they had done with it, though I was hopeful of finding it in the outer vestibule. So when I reached that area, I was busy peering round to see if I could see it anywhere – and almost walked into what was right in front of me.

The doorman was lying stretched out on the floor. He looked even bigger than he'd looked when standing up – his massive body seemed to take up all the space there was and he was blocking the entire entrance-way. He lay diagonally, as though the area was not long enough for him: his head (which was towards me) was resting on my rolled-up cloak and the bulk of him was wrapped up in an outsized blanket-cape. He was lying on what might have been a rug and he looked so comfort-able that I wondered if he slept here every night.

Certainly he was sleeping now. He was snoring – not an imitation snore but a whistling snuffle which would be hard to feign – so I crept forwardly hopefully. But (and it was a considerable 'but') his feet were actually pressed against the outer door, so that – even if I could have somehow stepped across his sleeping form without disturbing him – any attempt to open it would wake him up at once. What's more, I real-ized, peering at the hinge, it was designed to swing inwards, and there was no room for that. There was not the shadow of a chance of getting out this way.

As I stood there considering what to do, the bear began to stir. Perhaps he was somehow conscious of my presence, as I had been of his, but I did not tarry to find out. I slipped back to the shadows of the atrium and hid there in the darkest corner, trying not to shiver audibly.

There was a shuffling and a grunting and the bear appeared, but to my great relief he did not come into the room, simply stood in the doorway looking up and down – mostly at the passage opposite, where the page-boy was still asleep. I did my best to look like a piece of furniture but he hardly glanced in my direction anyway, simply wrapped his cape around him, grumbling, and went back to his post. I heard him lowering himself on to his mat, and shortly afterwards the snores began again.

After a moment I risked letting out a sigh. I'd been standing so motionless I hadn't even breathed. Then, slowly – and even more cautiously than I'd come – I stole back the same way. The door of Marcus's bedroom squeaked alarmingly as I pushed it open and I slipped into the little vestibule inside, ready to protest that I had come to use the pot. But nothing happened. The page-boy did not appear and after a few moments I felt safe to move again.

It was the open shutters that gave me the idea. I knew that the window-space looked out on to the street, Perhaps, with a little enterprise . . . ? I went to have a look.

The wine-shopkeeper was in the shadows locking up his shop. The last of his customers had evidently gone and he'd snuffed his candles out, though there was still a lot of noise and light from the direction of the hot-soup stall and more shouts and laughter from the taverna down the street. If I was really going to scramble out, I'd have to do it quickly, before everyone went home. I did not want to draw attention to myself: any late straggler on the street was liable to be suspected of nefarious intent and questioned by the watch. I leaned a little further through the window-space, trying to judge how far I'd have to jump.

Too far, I decided. We were on the first floor up, and there was a solid granite pavement underneath. If I got through the window-space and hung on by my hands, it would still leave me six feet or more to drop – with every likelihood that I would break a leg. And once I'd left here, I could expect no help from anyone. I would be in breach of every law there was and the whole machinery of state would be my enemy. I would also be abusing the commandant's faith in me, to say nothing of my patron's hospitality. Marcus, in fact, was legally responsible for me, and would be liable to a substantial fine and public humiliation if he could not produce me to the court. It was clearly nonsensical to even think of it.

I went back slowly into the other room and sat down on

the bed. In the gloaming my eye fell on the rug. It was not a very big one, but it would have to do.

I picked it up and rolled it into a sort of tube, so that it was approximately the same length as me, then put it carefully into the bed and covered it with rugs. It did not look much like a sleeping person when you were close to it, but at a distance it was good enough, especially in the dark. Then, remembering to take my sandals in my hand, I crept back into the master's room and eased myself – with some difficulty – through the window-space so that I was sitting on the sill, my bare feet dangling above the street below.

TWENTY-ONE

I f I had been a hero in a story of some sort, no doubt I would have leapt lightly from the ledge and scampered off, but I am an old man and no longer as fit as I once was. For a moment I did not move at all. The drop seemed even greater now than it had looked before and I was tightly wedged into the narrow window-space. I could not see how I could turn around and dangle from my hands as I had so hopefully supposed.

I was beginning to think that I would have to spend all night sitting on this uncomfortable ledge until I died of chill, when I heard something moving in the wind and I suddenly remembered the existence of the sign. It must be here somewhere, because it was hanging near the wine-shop door, and I was sitting almost over that. It had been strong enough to support the young drunkard earlier. If I could locate it, would it take my weight? If I could manage to balance with my feet on that, perhaps I could manoeuvre myself round the other way and do my dangling after all.

I leaned forward – very gingerly – and caught a glimpse of it: a foot or so below the level of my feet and slightly to one side. I eased one buttock forward and found that I could touch the bracket with my still-bare toes. Another inch and I could get my instep on to it – having no sandals on would make it easier – so that I could swivel round and grab the window-ledge.

The result was not as I'd intended it. My instep reached it, fairly easily, but in leaning forward I dislodged myself. The iron stanchion was slippery with wet, and as I lurched forward my bare foot slipped on it, so that – far from standing on the bracket with my weight upon my hands, as I'd hopefully supposed – I found myself astride it, like a rider on a horse, with my tunic riding up disgracefully around my thighs. My descent to this position had been so abrupt, and the iron post had caught me in such a painful place, that I gave a shriek, let go of my shoes and clung with both hands to the sign instead.

My own shriek alarmed me. I was afraid that I'd disturbed the house, but my eyes were watering and I could not move. No light flared in the window-space above and no angry voices shouted down at me. The only sound was that of loud laughter further down the street, and I realized that a group of people were approaching fast. I held my breath, praying that they would not look up at the sign, or stumble on my sandals, which had fallen to the street, though it was far too dark to see where they had gone.

But the gods had something else in store for me. There was a creaking, cracking sound from somewhere near my ear and – very slowly – the bar began to bend, tipping me forward as the bracket parted from the wall. I slid down it like a snowball running down a hill and landed with it, on the pavement, in a heap. I was so winded that I could neither speak nor move, so when the revellers reached me I was lying there, together with the shop sign and little bits of pebble from the wall.

One of the passers-by had stopped to look at me, holding his torch high to get a better view. 'Swinging from the shop sign by the look of it. You'd think that he'd know better at his age, wouldn't you?' He reached out and turned me over with his foot, just as I had seen the centurion do to the drunk youth earlier.

I could do no more than lie there, looking up at him. This was the end of my little escapade! I thought. Any minute now I would be dragged off to the watch for causing damage to the wine-shop property. I would be questioned, the story would come out, and this time I would be locked up in the jail. At least, I told myself, I still had Junio's money in my purse. It might buy me the opportunity to talk to Calvinus.

The man with the torch was bending over me and I could detect the smell of cheap wine on his breath. He wore a tunic not a toga, I was glad to see, and so did his companions, by the look of it, so these were not people of great authority. A group of freemen, possibly, united by a trade, coming from some bibulous meeting of their guild? In that case, they were probably not natives of the town – freemen born within these walls are citizens by birth and entitled to wear togas when they go out to dine.

'Leave him, Hilarius.' One of the others was impatient to be off. 'You don't know who he is or where he's been.'

Hilarius giggled – it was not difficult to see how he had earned the name – but he had the stubbornness which comes with too much wine. 'You can't be sure he isn't one of us.' He leaned right down and stared into my face. 'Not a carpenter, are you, by any chance? Though I didn't see you at the banquet, come to think of it.'

I relaxed a little. 'Different trade,' I muttered, with what breath was left to me. 'Though I work with buildings, too.'

Hilarius looked triumphant. 'There you are, you see!' he cried exultantly. 'He may not be a carpenter but he's the next best thing! Come on, old fellow – you can't stay here all night.' He grasped me by the arm and hauled me to my feet, though he was by no means steady on his own. 'Can't have a fellow drinker picked up by the watch. No doubt you've got a family who'll reward us for returning you – say a cup or two of Rhenish, or something of the kind, or better still the means to buy it with? Or are they pleased to see the back of an old reprobate like you?'

I shook my head. 'My son will pay you, but I live outside the walls.' My mind was racing now. Clearly I could not let them take me to the shop, any more than I'd identified my trade – that would make it easy to work out who I was – but with their protection I could walk the streets of town and not draw further attention to myself. Even if the bear and page-boy woke and noticed that I'd gone and sent the household out to hunt for me, no one would be looking for a man in company. 'Perhaps if you could just escort me to the gates . . . ? I'll see you get the money for your Rhenish wine. Just tell me where you live.' I had enough wit left not to mention that I had money in my purse, which might have been an invitation to be robbed.

My rescuer was rocking – with laughter or with wine, it was difficult to tell. 'Outside the walls, eh? You should have thought of that a little earlier, my friend. All the gates are guarded at this time of night, and only official business gets you through – though of course easier getting out than in. But as it happens, it's your lucky day. We're on our way to see a funeral – one of our members died and the guild's providing him a pyre. We've just been to the pre-cremation feast.'

'Then you will be going out through the northern gate,' I said. Bodies of adults cannot by law be laid to rest within the city walls and the northern road was the site of most crema-tions and even burials. It was lined with the graves and memo-rials of the great, and there was also a funeral *columbarium,* a so-called 'dove-cote' wall, comprising little niches in which the ashes of the dead could be immured. 'That would be most convenient for me. Though I mustn't keep you from the pyre.'

Hilarius was not so easily deterred. 'Oh, that's all right. We didn't know the man. He happened to be a member of the guild. We've only recently arrived in town – we used to have a busi-ness near Corinium,' he said, confirming my guess in all particulars. 'But we heard that opportunities were better around here. More now, since this fellow fell off the scaffolding. They put him on the pyre at least an hour ago – we're merely going to see them put the fire out and collect the ashes up into the urn. Only polite since we were invited to the feast.'

One of his companions interrupted him, giving a hiccough that was supposed to be a laugh. 'Trouble is, we're not exactly sure which way to go.'

Hilarius shrieked with mirth. 'We lost track of the proces-sion, I'm afraid. Stayed behind to help the servers finish up the wine. But if you say the north gate, that's good enough for me, though we can always ask. Someone must have seen the funeral – the guild provided musicians and all sorts.'

It occurred to me that I might have seen it pass myself – in which case it was going the other way, towards the south. But I didn't say so. For one thing, I did not want them talking to the watch, and for another I wanted their company till we left the town. 'Then the north gate it is?'

There was a murmur of agreement from his friends. 'Well, we'd better hurry,' one of them remarked. 'Or it will be all over before we reach the pyre. Hilarius, if you insist you're going to bring your pal, you'd better see he's quick. Here, I'll support him on the other side.' He thrust his shoulder under mine and went as if to lift me off my feet.

'But I've lost my sandals,' I managed to protest. It sounded like a bleat.

'Fell off when you were swinging on that sign? Silly person!' Hilarius chided me, but he took his torch and hunted for my shoes. It didn't take him long. He picked them from the gutter and handed them to me. 'Full of mud and muck and the gods-know-what. Still, it serves you right.' He gestured to the shop sign which was lying at his feet. 'Don't know what the wine-shopkeeper's going to say, when he comes back tomorrow and sees what you've done. Just as well he didn't catch you in the act.'

He didn't know how very true that was! And I wasn't out of danger yet. I had just sat down to put my filthy sandals on, when there was a noise above our heads and a flustered page was shouting down at us.

'Hey, you!'

My heart stopped in my chest.

'What's all this noise? You're waking half the street – there are people here who need to get some rest! Go on, be off with you, before I call the watch.'

He was holding his lighted taper in one hand but since Hilarius had a torch and I was sitting very close to him without it actually illuminating me, I realized that I'd not been recognized. What is more it was clear that I had not yet been missed.

Hilarius almost gave the game away. 'Sorry!' he hollered cheerfully, waving an explanatory hand at me. 'Our friend here had a little fall, that's all.'

'Then take him home before he falls again, and let respectable people get a little sleep!' The taper disappeared and there was the sound of shutters being sharply closed.

There was a lot of wine-fuelled giggling from the carpenters, one of whom suggested going upstairs to 'sort it out' but eventually our little party lurched away. I was supported by an arm on either side but in fact I was the least fuddled person in the group, despite the several cups of wine I'd swallowed earlier. The fright the page had given me would have sobered me, if I'd drunk twice as much – and the night wind blowing through me kept me wide awake, since I did not have the benefit of a cloak, of course.

That was a double inconvenience, in fact, not only because my skin was coming up in pimples with the cold, but because a man out on the street without a cloak at night is noteworthy, especially if he is supposed to be attending at a pyre – and the last thing that I wanted was to be conspicuous. Perhaps the best defence was – after all – appearing to be drunk. People look away from inebriated groups, I told myself, so I permitted my companions to half-carry me along.

They themselves were nothing if not jovial. I was treated to a song with a dozen choruses – none of which the carpenters could totally recall, though they continually urged me to join in. I dared not offend them, so I made a droning noise and in this fashion we made it to the walls.

There was, of course, a soldier on duty at the gates and I was worried lest he'd seen me at the guard-house earlier, but he scarcely glanced in my direction. His attention was entirely on Hilarius, who asked directions to the cremation pyre.

'Guild of carpenters? There has been a funeral come this way tonight, but I'm not sure it was that one, from what you're telling me. All the same you're welcome if you want to go and look.' He pointed to a faint glow in the distant dark, far beyond the suburb where my workshop was: a pyre had been set up among the monuments.

I had an inspiration. I hauled myself upright, and turned so that the soldier couldn't see my face. 'I'll go and ask some questions if you like. Save the rest of you traipsing all that way, if it turns out that it is not your guild at all. I did see a funeral, come to think of it, going out of the southern gate a little earlier. Might be the one that you were looking for. Shall I go and see?'

And without waiting for an answer, I slipped out of their arms and was through the open gate before Hilarius could object.

It was not enough, however, to have got outside the walls. I had to give an answer before I disappeared back to the workshop, or the carpenters might have all come out after me. I was ready to invent one, on the strength of what I knew, but there was a beggar lurking in the shadows by the wall and he sidled over to beg an as from me.

'A quadrans if you tell me who that funeral was for,' I told him, whispering.

He shook his head. 'I don't know. It's no concern of mine. I keep away from funerals: the mourners never give you anything and they're likely to report you to the authorities – not that I'm actually breaking any laws, I'm not within the walls.'

'A quadrans,' I reminded him, jangling my purse.

'Wife of some merchant, that is all I know. Probably died in childbirth from the wailing that's going on.'

'That is worth a quadrans,' I told him, fishing out some coins. 'And here's another for forgetting that you ever saw me here.'

'A bargain, sir!' He snatched the money from my hand and vanished into the dark.

I went back to the gatehouse, taking care to stand in the shadows so that the sentry could not see my face. 'It's not the one you want, Hilarius,' I called. 'Try the southern gate.' Then, I added, to the soldier who had opened up to let me in again, 'I don't think I'll bother now, thank you very much. It's too far to go. My home's in this direction.' And I trotted quickly off, before anyone decided to prevent me doing so.

TWENTY-TWO

I t isn't easy, walking through the unlit northern suburb in the dark. The lesser roads are horribly uneven here – not the paved surfaces that you find inside the walls – and even when there hasn't been a lot of rain, the gutters run with mire. The area is full of shops like mine and little factories – many of them hot and smelly businesses, candle-makers, brewers, tanners and the like – all of whom get up at dawn and lie down with the sun, since (having no armies of servants to command, nor banquets to attend) they are careful to save money on unnecessary heat and light. These streets are unlit and treacherous at night: there was scarcely even the glimmer of a taper to be seen.

It took me a long time to pick my way along and several times I stumbled in the mud. My sandals, which had been dirty before all this began, were caked by now in things unspeakable, and my tunic was also much the worse for wear. I was freezing cold by this time, and my teeth were chattering. But I knew the streets by daylight and I persevered and finally I found myself outside the workshop door.

It was likely that Junio would be abed himself, on some makeshift mattress on the floor beside the fire, and I was ready to have to hammer for a long time at the door. But the shutter to the workroom was still a bit ajar and I was able to edge down the adjoining lane and look inside.

The room was so familiar that a lump rose to my throat. Suppose that this mad enterprise of mine had no result? Suppose that I discovered nothing, and was dragged up before the court to be found guilty, not only of the crimes involving Voluus, but of breaking bail as well? This might be the last time that I ever saw the shop.

Junio was sitting on a stool beside the embers of the fire, clutching a beaker of something in his hand and staring gloomily into the coals. The remains of a street-vendor's pie was lying on the hearth. Of course, he did not have a servant here with him tonight and he would have had to make his own arrangements for a meal.

I tapped the shutter softly and it made him jump. He picked up a length of wood and came across with it, clearly ready to protect the premises. 'Who is it?'

I had forgotten that I would be invisible. 'It is I, your father. Let me in.' I was shivering so much that speech was difficult.

The transformation in his face was wonderful to see. He dropped the plank and bounded to the door and I heard him throw the bolt and open up the latch. 'Father!' He threw his arms around my neck. Then he looked down and saw the state of me. 'What has happened? What are you doing here?' But he stood back as he spoke to let me in.

I sank down on the stool that he'd been sitting on, letting the warm embers thaw my ageing bones. Without my asking Junio was already refilling his cup and handing it to me, and I recognized that he had warmed and spiced some wine beside the fire – he had not been raised as a child-slave in a Roman house for nothing. Warmth flooded through me with the unfamiliar brew and already I was feeling much more like myself, but Junio hadn't finished. He had taken a candle and was ferreting upstairs, and when he came back I saw that he'd been searching through the rags and had found a patched and ancient tunic of my own which I had put aside to give to some deserving pauper by and by. Tonight, however, I had need of it myself, and with that and the spare birrus – the hooded woollen cloak – which I always kept hanging up behind the door, my teeth stopped chattering and I could talk again.

Junio, who had lit a taper by this time, and poked the embers into life again, would also have urged his piece of pie on me, but I explained that I had dined extensively. 'At Marcus's expense,' I told him, with a smile, and gave him an account of my adventures of the night.

'So you climbed out of the window and ran away from there.' Junio shook his head. 'You realize if they catch you, there'll be Dis to pay?'

I nodded. 'But I can't believe this farm is just coincidence. If Voluus sent his cart there, it must have been arranged.'

He poured me another beaker of warm, watered, spicy wine. '*If* he sent his cart there. But you're not sure that he did. Even this Biccus isn't sure it stopped there, after all.'

I shook my head. The beverage – far from interfering with my brain – seemed to be helping me to think. 'Then where else did it go? He says himself that there isn't anywhere. But there seems to be no way that the owner of the land could possibly have been expecting it. However, there may be some connection, all the same. If, for instance, the new owner was someone Voluus knew, who'd already told him he was going to buy the farm.'

'More likely an acquaintance of someone that he knew, since Voluus hardly knew anyone round here?' Junio thought for a moment. 'A friend of the retiring governor of Gaul, perhaps?'

I seized on this at once. 'That would make a kind of sense. A governor would have sufficient influence to request a favour on Voluus's behalf. He might not even trouble to arrange it in advance, simply sent a message with the cart. "Citizen so-and-so, I commend these travellers to your care. I request that you give them hospitality" – that sort of thing. Sent under seal, of course, but certain to arrive. Much more secure than any messenger.' I was warming to this theme. 'Besides, if the traveller's on the doorstep with your letter in his hand citizen so-and-so cannot very well refuse.'

Junio frowned. 'So what do you suppose? That this host saw the treasure on the cart and the temptation was too much for him?'

'Or someone else had followed them and killed them while they slept?' I countered, though I didn't really believe it as I spoke.

'Then chopped up the bodies, dragged them out and tried to make it look like rebel handiwork? And slaughtered the horses for good measure afterwards? It does not seem a very likely tale to me.'

I shook my head. 'All the same, I am convinced there is a link. There is only one way to find out. You and I have to get out to that farm tonight. And perhaps we could look in at the jail as well, and have another try at seeing Calvinus.'

'Tonight!' Junio couldn't have looked more startled if I'd stabbed him through the hand. 'But you must surely see that that's impossible! They won't let us near the jail. It's much too far to walk out to the farm, and anyway it's dark and you aren't even certain where you're going.' He picked up the jug and drank the dregs from it, as though he needed alcohol to steady him. 'Besides, you're tired. You've had a busy day. And surely now Alcanta's here it alters everything?'

'Alcanta?' I murmured. Surely I had heard that name somewhere recently. Then I remembered. 'Great Mars! You don't mean Voluus's wife? She is here already? Has the lictor come as well?'

His expression was one of disbelief. 'So you didn't get my message? I thought that's why you'd come.'

'Message?' It was my turn to frown.

'I sent Brianus with it, to your patron's flat. Didn't you receive it?'

I shook my head. 'How long ago was that?' I was having mental visions of Marcus's servants coming to my room and finding I was missing, long before I'd hoped. If they had already called the watch and set a search for me, this evening's enterprise was going to be even more difficult than I had supposed.

Junio's answer allayed that fear, at least. 'Not long after I left you at the fort. When I got back here he was waiting at the shop, almost paralytic with anxiety. He'd gone back to his apartment and found it full of slaves – the ones that Alcanta had brought with her from Gaul.'

I was puzzled. 'I thought he'd run away?'

'He had, but the temple priests persuaded him that it was safer for him to go back home, saying that – since Calvinus was in prison and Voluus wasn't here – it was unlikely that he and Pronta had even yet been missed. However angry Voluus might be when he discovers that his treasure's gone, it couldn't be as dreadful as the penalty for a captured fugitive.'

'That was sensible,' I echoed. 'Did the boy take Pronta back with him as well?'

Junio shook his head. 'He could not find her, so he went alone, thinking that she might have done the same. But when he got there he found these other slaves. They had no idea who he was, which was fortunate. When he said that he belonged to Voluus, they thought he was some sort of messenger, so they gave him directions to where his mistress was. He might have gone there, too, except that he enquired for Pronta, and was told that she was listed as an official runaway, the watch had already been told to hunt for her, the guards had been given her description at the gates and she would be shown no mercy if she was ever found.'

'That must have upset Brianus,' I observed. It meant that the lictor would have her put to death. 'The boy was fond of her.'

'What upset him even more was realizing that the same applied to him,' Junio said with vigour. 'He had half-intended to go to his mistress and confess: say that he'd been absent from his post and take the punishment – he expected a beating or no rations for a day – but once he understood what was in store for him, he changed his mind again. He was lucky there. They still thought he was a messenger from Voluus – he hadn't told them otherwise – so they just let him go.'

'Go to his mistress? So she wasn't at the flat?'

Junio shook his head. 'Apparently she arrived in Glevum late this afternoon. The ship that brought her here had favourable winds and made much better speed than anybody thought. She sent a message to the apartment, naturally, to say that she was on her way – but there was no one there, of course, and nothing was prepared. She hadn't even heard about the treasure-cart. There's been a dreadful fuss. Somebody at the building was keeping watch on Voluus's behalf and sent the news of all the day's events back to her with the messenger – including the information that Calvinus was in jail.'

'That watcher was one of Porteus's spies, no doubt,' I said. I was beginning to see what this was leading to. 'And I suppose he also managed to report that the lictor's other two slaves were on the run?'

'Exactly. Poor Alcanta! What a welcome to receive. You can imagine what a dreadful shock it was for her – and with

an infant, too. If one of the councillors had not stepped in and
offered her his hospitality for a day or two, she might have
had a dreadful time of it.'

That councillor was presumably Porteus again, and he would
doubtless want paying for his solicitude, but I did not linger
over that. I had a pressing question. 'How do you know all
this?'

'Brianus told me. When he discovered that he was a wanted
runaway, he ran away again, more terrified than ever, as you
might suppose. He came to beg for help – he had nowhere
else to turn, he said, and you had been kind to him.'

That would teach me to give oatcake crumbs to slaves! 'So
where is he now?'

Junio looked stricken. 'Father, don't you see? That's just
what I don't know. I sent him to tell you all this news, but
you say he didn't come.'

I thought a moment. 'If there was a search for him, I expect
the watch have picked him up and put him with the steward
in the jail. In that case you'll be lucky to escape the courts
yourself. You know the penalty for helping or harbouring a
runaway.'

'As I pointed out to Brianus himself, it is no crime to assist
a fugitive if you can prove to the satisfaction of a magistrate
that his master was unnaturally cruel and that he has only
come to you for sanctuary – Brianus's weals and bruises might
convince a court. Anyway, if not, what difference can it make?
We are likely to be in exile tomorrow anyway.'

I frowned at him. 'You? I am, certainly, but you are not.
Though you could always blame me for his coming here, I
suppose.'

Junio made a face. 'Do you suppose that I would let you
face the hardship of exile all alone? Of course I shall come
with you.'

This was so unexpected that a lump came to my throat, but
I managed to say gruffly, 'Of course you will do nothing of
the kind. What about the women? And your infant son?'

'We would have to leave our wives and send for them later,
if things go well enough. If not, they could scrape a living
where they are. They have sufficient crops and animals to live,

and I don't imagine Marcus will permit them to starve if times are hard – even if he has to take them back to servitude.'

Both our wives had been slave-girls in their time, and it was not something that I would ever wish on them again, but Junio was right. A life in Marcus's household, even as a slave, would not be half as harsh as a life in exile, or struggling alone against the winter elements to eke a meagre living from the small-holding. As the old adage has it, 'better serve than starve'.

All the same I shook my head. 'I could not permit it. Anyway, it might not come to that. Help me find out what I need to know, and maybe I'll be able to prove my innocence.'

'Help you by encouraging this mad enterprise of visiting the farmstead in the middle of the night? It would take you hours to walk all the way out there – even longer, since you'll have to walk for miles around the outside of the town-walls before you start. The gates are shut and guarded at this time of night.'

'Then we'll have to get the sentries to open them,' I said. 'And some form of transport to get us to the farm. So listen carefully, I've got a sort of plan . . .'

TWENTY-THREE

A few moments later we were damping down the fire, blowing out the tapers and locking up the shop. Junio had managed to contrive a torch by dipping a bunch of dried rushes in some oil, and – having lit it in the embers – he was now holding it aloft as we made our way back to the gates. It was a great deal easier with a light.

But instead of turning in towards the town, I led the way out to the monuments, where the funeral was just coming to a close. The funeral offerings and perfumes had been added to the pyre (as it was easy to discover from the smell) and it was burning down. The presiding priest – a doddering old man – was in the act of pouring wine on to the fire to douse the flames, and the funeral women stood by with their urn, ready to put symbolic ashes into it – the rest would be dealt with when the pyre was cold. Two or three people turned to look at us, but evidently decided that we'd merely moved to get a better view: there was already a considerable crowd, many with torches very like our own, and a couple of extra hooded mourners created no remark.

There was an awkward moment when the aged priest scattered a handful of earth upon the pyre and invited the funeral guests to come up one by one and make their farewells to the departing soul. Something was obviously expected of us all and I did not even know the corpse's name. When it was my turn I walked up to the fire and murmured something pious-sounding underneath my breath. In fact, my address to the departed was composed of a short list of the different kinds of stones we used in the workshop, which was all my scrambled brains could think of at the time. But I got away with it. Nobody was listening, apart from Junio, who came behind me and did something similar.

Then it was time for the funeral visitors to depart, leaving the relatives and priest to finish at the pyre and select a bone for symbolic burial. (In old-fashioned Roman families, even nowadays, one tiny fragment of a cremated corpse is ritually interred, in ground specially purified by the offering of a pig.)

None of this required the rest of us, so a torch-lit procession soon formed behind the flute and we wound our way back to the gates again. The sentry did not even blink as he stood back to let us through.

As the portals closed behind us, Junio turned to me. 'Well, we've got into Glevum – what do we do now?' he murmured under cover of the crowd.

'Follow the flautist to the centre of the town, then we'll lose the other mourners and decide what we do next.'

Losing the other mourners was not difficult: they were all returning to their homes, as fast as possible, anxious to perform ablutions to wash bad luck away, so by ducking down an alley we soon found ourselves alone, though several of them actually called a warm 'goodnight' to us.

The warmth of that farewell was the only warmth there was: the alleyway was damp and dark and smelt of midden-heaps, but the manure-collector I had noticed coming into town had clearly done his work this evening and the worst was gone, so it was possible to walk along the passageway with care – especially since we had the luxury of light. Junio was fretting about his sandal-soles but I was anxious to keep out of the major throughfares, because by now we were close to the forum and the wine-shop block again.

It was still necessary for us to cross that very street, of course, but when we came to it there was not a soul in sight. The windows in my patron's flat had all the shutters closed and even the staircase entry was shadowy and dark: there was no sign of the disturbance I had feared, and even less of any kind of search. I began to breathe more easily.

'Well?' Junio demanded. 'Shall I lead you to the jail, so you can try to talk to Calvinus, or do you want to go directly to this farm?'

I made a calculation, looking at the sky. All the light had faded from the west and the first stars were twinkling in the gaps between the cloud. 'It is getting very late. If we propose to go out through the southern gate, we had better do it straight away.'

He glanced at me, the torchlight dancing in his eyes. 'You don't expect to play the funeral trick again? I know the carpenters have got a pyre, but no one will believe you're attending it so late.'

I shook my head. 'I've got another plan – it all depends who is on duty at the gate.' I grinned at him. 'And since it seems that no one's on the hunt for me, we can use the pavements and the wider streets from here. No more horrid alleyways like this.' I gestured to the one from which we'd just emerged.

As I did so I felt my mouth go dry. Someone had seized the corner of my cloak and was tugging me back into the narrow space again. 'Citizen Libertus?' a whispering voice accused.

I whirled around, shouting to Junio to flee. He, of course, was carrying the torch and I squinted in the dark trying to make out who my captor was. It was not a large person – I could see as much that – but the grip was determined and my best efforts could not pull my clothing free. 'Is that the pageboy?' I muttered, angry with myself. I'd been a fool to think that I could get away so easily, and I'd been careless, too, ceasing to take enough precautions to defend myself.

'Come into the alley; I want to talk to you. It's very important.'

I recognized the voice. 'Brianus!' I was whispering, too – not so much for fear I might be overheard as because I was breathless with relief. I gestured to Junio, who had crossed the road and was standing watching me – defying my instruction that he should run away – and he came back to us.

Brianus was crouching in the corner of a doorway and even when we stepped into the alley where he was, he was most unwilling to let go of me. He was also clearly terrified of the illumination from the torch and he was not happy until Junio took it further off. By that time, though, I had caught a glimpse of him – thin, strained and dishevelled, his pale face streaked with tears. He wore the cape and tunic that I'd seen him in before, but this time his garments positively stank.

'You had a message for me?' I began. 'Quite an urgent one. But it didn't reach me. What prevented you?'

'Forgive me, sir,' the boy said tearfully. He did not release my cloak. 'I did try to bring it. I got right to the corner of the baths – but I didn't realize that the place that I was looking for was so near to where my master has his flat.'

Of course! I hadn't really worked that out myself. I had known that the two were fairly close, but the implication for Brianus had not occurred to me. 'So you were afraid that somebody from there would notice you? And hand you to the authorities, I suppose?'

He gave me a grateful smile. 'I knew you'd understand. And it wasn't only that. I went another way and tried to get there down this alleyway, but just when I was about to cross the road, I saw a soldier at the wine-house door. An important one – you know, the kind that has the sideways crest.'

'That would be the centurion who escorted me,' I said.

'He was not escorting you when I caught sight of him.' Brianus was gaining in confidence again. 'He was arresting someone who'd been lying on the floor. I knew that my mistress had proscribed me as a runaway, and all the soldiers would be looking out for me. So I stayed where I was – intending to bring the message when he'd gone away – but then the watch appeared and I actually heard them ask him if he'd seen a pair of missing slaves.'

'And you thought . . . ?'

He shook his head. He sounded desperate. 'It wasn't specu-lation, citizen. They gave a description and there could be no doubt – they were talking about Pronta and myself. A reward had been offered, by the order of some city councillor, to anyone who captured us and brought us back. Dead or alive, that's what the watchman said.'

'And what did the centurion have to say to that?'

'He said he hadn't but he'd keep a watch. So they went away and started asking everybody else – even a snooty private slave who was sauntering past the lane. They asked the people gathered round at the wine-shop door and all the people standing on the stairs. Well, of course I couldn't go there after that. I did not know what to do – I had to find some kind of hiding place. In the end I found an empty meat-stall just along from here, and I went in there and hid among the straw.'

That explained the smell, I thought. 'And then you heard me talking to my son and recognized the voice?'

He shook his head. 'It wasn't as simple as all that. A little later on, I heard the watch again. They were searching the row of stalls that I was in, rattling the doors and poking with their swords. I thought my end had come. And then I heard the leader of the watch let out a shout. 'There's one of them, at least! And there's a piece of luck. Someone's saved us the trouble of dispatching her. Run and get a stretcher and we'll take her home and claim for the reward.'

I was staring at him. 'Pronta!'

He nodded bitterly.

'Are you telling me she's dead?'

Another nod. 'She had been strangled, by the look of it.'

'You actually saw her?'

'Well, of course I did. I couldn't just go away and leave her there. When they went off to get their wretched stretcher, they only left one watchman keeping guard on her and he was patrolling the street where people walk, not keeping watch in the alleyway itself. I chose a moment when he'd marched the other way and stole in to take a look at her. They'd left a pitch-torch burning in a wall-bracket nearby, so it was possible to see. It was Pronta, though I hardly recognized her at first. You should have seen her face.' His voice failed him as he blinked back his tears.

There was nothing I could say to comfort him. I've seen the effects of strangling, and I knew what he meant. 'So there was nothing you could do for her?'

'I put three handfuls of dust on to the corpse – I remember that's supposed to symbolize a burial if nothing better is available – so at least her spirit will have rest. But I could not linger. I was in danger as it was. The watch could return with their stretcher any time – so I went back to my stall. I reasoned they'd be busy with the stretcher, first of all, so while they were in there with it, I slipped out myself and I've been hiding in doorways ever since, wondering what on earth I was to do. I thought in the morning I might manage to get word to you somehow – and then to my amazement you went walking by.'

'So you seized my cloak – and almost frightened me to death by sneaking up behind me in the dark?'

The boy reluctantly relaxed his grip. 'Not at first I didn't. My plan was to wait until you were alone. I began to follow you – I still had that message to get to you – but then you stepped into the street and I saw who you were with. Then I knew that it was safe to talk to you, though you would have already heard the news I was supposed to bring. But I could not imagine what you were doing here. I thought you were supposed to be sleeping at that apartment opposite.'

'I was, but I had business in the town,' I said. I did not want to further panic Brianus by telling him that I was wanted, too! 'And I must deal with it. I'm glad to find you safe – I feared that you'd been recaptured and locked up by now – but I have serious troubles of my own and I must go and try to sort them out.'

The hand shot out and gripped my cloak again. 'Let me come with you, citizen. No one will take me for a runaway if I am with two citizen tradesmen like yourselves.' He must have sensed that I was weakening. 'Your son told me that it was not a crime to appeal to another master for sanctuary, if your own was unnaturally harsh. So I appeal to you.' Without relinquishing his grasp upon my clothes, he threw himself before me and kissed both my muddy feet. 'Afford me your protection. You will save my life. I am willing to have you take me to a magistrate and I'll show him my weals.'

The last thing that I wanted to do at that moment was to see a magistrate or have a frightened childish slave to think about! But the boy was right. I was his only chance – and, on reflection, there might even be advantages for me. Having an attendant gave a person dignity, and made one's presence on the streets more unremarkable. 'Very well,' I said ungraciously. 'I'll let you come tonight. Though I warn you that tomorrow you will have to go. I'll pass you to my patron – it's the best that I can do. I'm likely to be exiled before the day is through. Especially if I don't get on with what I need to do. So let go of my clothing and stand up, for Juno's sake!' I said it more

sharply than I meant, for Brianus was covering my feet with
kisses now. I raised my voice a little. 'Junio, bring the light
here. It is time to go. Give the torch to Brianus. Let him carry
it. It seems I have acquired a temporary slave.'

The boy let go of me and scrambled to his feet. 'At your
service, master!' The bunch of reeds was burning down by
now, but as he took them I could see his face. It was alight
with joy. 'And I'll follow you into exile, if you'll let me stay.'

Poor misguided fellow, I thought. He did not know how
much trouble I was in. 'You can start by leading us towards
the southern gate,' I said. 'And when we get there, don't say
anything until you're spoken to. We'll go down the main
thoroughfare – it's the quickest way and very probably the
safest, too. And never mind the watch – you're quite right,
they won't be looking for a group. Do you know the way?'

He nodded and without a word set off along the street,
proudly holding the torch to light the way.

TWENTY-FOUR

We did have an encounter with the watch. We passed them as they came out of a lane across the street, their pitch-torches ablaze. I saw Brianus stiffen and look nervously at me.

'Don't stop, don't look, just walk on as you are,' I hissed at him, and rather uncertainly he did as he was told. I raised my voice and called across the road: 'Good evening, gentlemen. All quiet on the streets?' It was more than mere bravado: I felt safe enough in company but I was keen to know whether there was yet a search for me.

It appeared there wasn't. 'All quiet in Glevum, except that we are looking for a slave. Rather like your own, from the description that we have.'

Brianus froze, despite what I had said, and I urged him gently forward with my hand. 'Well, this one's ours,' I called out cheerfully. 'But if we find any stray ones we'll be sure to let you know. Is there a reward?'

I saw the members of the watch exchange a glance. 'You bring him to us and we'll make sure you're recompensed.'

'We'll keep our eyes open,' I promised, and was about to move away when the leader of the watch called after me.

'If you do come across him, see you come to us. Don't take him to the garrison – they've got their hands full there. There's been a body found. Something to do with that wealthy lictor who was coming here. He hasn't had much luck. You heard his treasure-cart was set upon by thieves?'

I knew more about it than they did themselves, including the death of Pronta – presumably the body that they were talking about – but I did not tell them that. I said, 'I heard his wife has got here, anyway.'

'It's their slave that's gone missing,' one of younger men put in, and earned himself a warning kick from all the rest. Obviously the team had claimed the full reward for bringing

Pronta in, and were hoping to do the same again with Brianus
– even if they had to pay a little to whoever found him first.

And there was their quarry, carrying my torch! It would
have been quite funny if his life were not at stake. 'We'll look
out for him,' I told them, 'but we can't stop and help you
search. We've been to a funeral and it's a long way home.'

The watchman nodded. 'Well, see that you take care, if
you're going outside the walls. It's obvious that rebels are
active in the woods again.' He paused. 'Here, wait a minute!
Let me look at that.' To my alarm he strode across the road
and went straight to Brianus, who was standing with his eyes
shut, paralysed with fear.

I closed my own eyes, preparing for the worst. This was all
my fault for talking to the watch. I thought of protesting that
the slave was claiming sanctuary with me, but I held my
tongue: better to argue when we were in custody – as I surely
would be for harbouring a runaway, although it hardly mattered
any more. I was already as good as exiled. There was no hope
of achieving anything tonight.

'There!' the leader of the watch was sounding satisfied.
'You'll be better off with that.' I forced my eyelids open and
saw with amazement that he was taking the guttering reed-torch
from Brianus and substituting a tar one of his own. 'Can't be
too careful, with all these rebel thieves and murderers about.'

Brianus was a silent statue, mystified with shock – and so
was I. Only Junio had sense enough to burble out some thanks.

'Oh, that's all right. We've plenty at the store and we're
going back anyway. It doesn't cost us anything: the curia
provides them for the watch. If you really want to thank me,
find that slave for us.' And he went back to his fellows and
led them down the street.

I had to lean against a wall a moment to recover from my
fright. My knees had turned to butter and my hands to ice. It
was Junio who brought me to myself.

'If you've got your wits back, you two, it is time we went.
We'll only draw attention to ourselves by standing here. And
now, at least, we've got a decent light.'

He was right, of course, so we set off again and pretty soon
were at the southern gate.

As we approached it, Junio turned to me. 'I think you said you had a strategy?'

I nodded. 'I hope that it will work. I think there's every chance – I recognize the man on duty at the gate.' It was the soldier who had waited on me in the guard-house earlier and poured me the cup of wine I never drank. 'You stay here with Brianus and let me talk to him. If there's any trouble, slip away again.'

Junio nodded, rather doubtfully, and Brianus looked as if I'd volunteered to die. I squared my shoulders and strode up to the gate with as much false confidence as I could summon. 'Good evening, octio.' I had deliberately promoted him.

The soldier looked at me. 'Don't I know you, citizen?'

'Of course you do,' I told him breezily. 'I was falsely imprisoned earlier today, but the commander saw to it. I was invited to my patron's residence tonight – His Excellence Marcus Septimus Aurelius. Perhaps you've heard of him?' I could see by the man's expression that he had. 'I have just come from there. I have an urgent message for a certain Biccus, a freeman who was brought in to the garrison for questioning. I understand that he has been released and might have been eating at the mansio. It is imperative I speak to him at once.'

The soldier looked nonplussed and then his features cleared. 'You mean the pig-man?' he enquired, suggesting that the forced visit to the bath-house had produced a limited effect. 'He was at the mansio earlier, but only for a meal. We've billeted him and his donkey at the hiring-stables just outside the gates. If you want to catch him before he goes to bed, you'd better hurry. He's been there a little while.' Even as he spoke he was opening the gates, so I beckoned to Junio and Brianus to come and we passed together through the arch and out on to the road.

It had been simpler so far than I'd dared to hope. Brianus was speechless with admiration for my guile, but Junio simply grinned. 'I told you that my father would work something clever out. Though he could have just told them that we wanted to go home – it is no secret that the roundhouse is this way.'

I shook my head. 'We are the only pedestrians around, and this torch is visible for a long way from the gate. The sentry would soon spot where we were making for – this way at least it will be no surprise, and he won't send someone running to drag us back again. But he's right: we'd better hurry or we'll find that Biccus has retired to his bed. Bring the light here, Brianus, and let's see where we're going.'

The value of a tar-torch was a considerable one. Not only would it last a good deal longer than our own, but the pitch burned with a brighter, more consistent light. It lit the darkness better than the moon and we were able to walk the distance to the inn with confidence.

There was an oil-light still burning when we approached the door, so someone in the household was clearly still awake. I knocked and heard a scuffling from within and then a window was thrown open on my right. 'What's all the racket?' A man in a long-sleeved tunic was peering out at me, the oil-lamp in his hand. 'Can't you see we're closed? We haven't got a room. If you are looking for a bed, you'd better try the mansio.'

'You have a man called Biccus here, I think. The army . . .'

He cut me off. 'I should think I have, and most inconvenient it has turned out to be! Stinks of pigs – although he swears he's had a Roman bath – and no one else will share a bed with him. Yet the army says I've got to have him here. It's all very well them saying that they'll pay. Cost me a fortune with the trade I've turned away.'

'Well, I've come to requisition something else, as well,' I said. 'I think you have a cart which carries torches, haven't you? I believe I've ridden on it once.'

He held his lamp a little higher so he could look at me. 'And what if I have?' he said suspiciously.

'I want it fitted up for use at once. I'll need a driver, too. We are to be taken to where Biccus lives. On official business. As soon as possible.' I tried to make it sound like a command. I took a mighty gamble. 'The garrison will pay.' Behind me, I heard Junio catch a startled breath. I only hoped the innkeeper had not heard it, too.

The shrewd eyes glittered in the lamp-light. 'On whose authority?' He looked me up and down. 'You don't look much like an army officer to me.'

'Talk to Biccus, then,' I countered. 'He knows who I am. I

helped to question him. I was called in by the commander of
the garrison – with whom, incidentally, I rode out this afternoon, in one of your vehicles. The driver who took us will
vouch for that, I'm sure. Ask him, if you doubt me, but don't
keep me standing here. And be quick about it; I have important
work to do.'

The man was still grumbling but he pulled back the bolt
and very reluctantly allowed us to come in. It was clear what
he'd been doing when we knocked on the door: the table,
which on one end was littered with half-empty bowls and
mugs of wine, was covered on the other by small piles of
coins. Open beside them was a large box with a key. He had
been counting the takings for the day.

He saw me looking and swept the cash away, locking it
firmly back into the chest. 'I'd better get Biccus to take a look
at you, I suppose. Though the wretch is probably in bed –
sleeping away my profits, since he's in there all alone.'

'I'll take him with me, if I helps,' I volunteered, as though
this were a favour I'd decided to bestow – though in fact I'd
planned to do so all along. Only Biccus knew where we were
going! 'And we'll leave his donkey with you as a pledge
against the cost. It's worth at least as much as the hiring-fee
would be – that way you can't lose.'

The innkeeper weakened, though he went on tetchily, 'Now
he takes the pig-man – when it's far too late! We won't get
other travellers at this time of night. And we'll have the donkey
feed to find as well. Well, you'd better put that torch out –
you'll need it later on.' He lit a taper from his lamp and went
off, muttering. Soon we heard his padding footsteps on the
floor above our heads and the sound of rapping on a distant
door.

Brianus smothered the tar-torch expertly in a jug of wine.
He was bursting to say something, I could tell, but I held my
finger to my lips – and only just in time. The innkeeper was
already clattering down the stairs, followed by Biccus, who
was now moderately clean and wearing a coarse tunic that
was far too big for him, though he was still carrying his horrid
footwear in his hand. It was clear that he'd been wakened
from his sleep and he was far from pleased.

The innkeeper pointed an accusing hand at me. 'You know this person?'

Biccus cast a jaundiced eye at me. 'I do – at least, I met him at the fort. I can't recall his name. He's some sort of Roman citizen. I don't know the other two.' He was in his uncommunicative frame of mind again.

'Members of my household – my son and slave,' I said impatiently. It was no good trying Celtic here – the innkeeper was clearly from the local tribe himself, so the only people not to understand would be Junio and Brianus, who had both been raised as Latin-speaking slaves. I tried a different approach. 'You agree we met. In the commander's office, isn't that the case? When you were brought to him for questioning? And who was it that persuaded him to let you go?'

Biccus looked resentful. 'I suppose that it was you.'

'You see?' I murmured to the innkeeper, though what Biccus said was not really proof of anything. 'So, now will you provide the lighted cart to take us to the farm?'

Biccus glanced up sharply. 'So you did persuade them to let you go out there, after all? And you must have talked them into letting you go home as well; otherwise you wouldn't have your son and slave with you. I don't know how you do it – I thought you'd been refused. You must have influence.'

I did not know how to reply to this, except to murmur, 'It took a little time,' but the effect on the innkeeper was immediate. He snatched up his taper and hurried off again, this time out towards the courtyard where the stable was. We could hear him shouting and hammering on the wall, and the sleepy answers of the waking slaves.

I caught the pig-man's eye. 'Count yourself lucky,' I said cheerfully. 'You wanted to go home and now you are going to get a cart ride all the way.'

'And what about the donkey?'

'Don't worry about him. They're going to keep him here – and we'll bring you back to pick him up another time.' I spoke as though that were a certainty, although of course it was nothing of the kind. If things went badly for me, I would have to ask Marcus to sort that out as well.

Biccus sat down on the bench and began to tie his dreadful shoes around his feet. The smell improved at once.

Brianus edged over and whispered close to me, 'What are we going to do, master, when we arrive out at this farm? We won't be able to get in – everybody will be fast asleep by now.'

It was a question I hadn't really asked myself – my sole concern had been to get there and see what I could find. Clearly even that was not easy in the dark, and the owners were likely to set the dogs on us. But I couldn't help it: my freedom was at stake and things had gone too far for me to change my mind. I could already hear the clatter of the horses in the yard, and the slaves complaining as they pushed out the cart. More and more tapers were flaring into light, and men were fetching a harness and strapping it in place.

'You'll see when we get there,' I said to Brianus.

Junio caught my eye. 'And you'd better relight that tar-torch in the fire, if you want to see anything at all. I think our transport is awaiting us – and here is the innkeeper, no doubt to tell us so!'

It was not quite as simple as he made it sound. The innkeeper insisted that I scratch him a receipt, agreeing that I'd taken the cart and that Biccus had occupied the bed; otherwise he would not get the payment, he declared. 'It's most irregular, in any case.'

I scratched the words he wanted on a piece of slate and he, still grudgingly, showed us to the cart. Biccus was helped up to the front – beside the scowling driver, so that he could point the way – though it was quite a squash, since two blazing torches were set on iron spikes each side to illuminate the road as much as possible, and there were unlit replacements stacked up behind the seat. Our own torch was thrust into another holder at the back, where its flickering light would cast its glow on us.

Then, with a final clattering of hooves, we were out of the courtyard of the inn and on our way.

TWENTY-FIVE

It was a long, cold, bumpy journey and long before it stopped my teeth were chattering again and my bones were stiffer still. There had been little conversation while we were on the cart – I think that I was not the only one to listen to the distant howling of the wolves or wonder if there were bears or bandits in wait round every bend.

If there were, they did not trouble us and at last we found ourselves deep in the countryside. We came to a little valley with a stream and a lane that led along it off the road. There the cart rumbled to a halt. Biccus scrambled down and came round to talk to us.

'That's the farmstead I was telling you about. What do you want the driver to do now?'

'He can drive us down there and then take you home.'

Biccus shook his head. 'No point in doing that. My wife will have given up expecting me tonight. She'll have bolted all the doors and put the shutters up, and is no doubt sleeping with an axe beside the bed. She'll have let the dogs out, too – though that would be all right – but she's likely to attack me with it if I turn up in the dark. I think it's safer if I stay with company and go back in daylight, if it's all the same to you.'

'Then we'll all go to the farm together.' I was glad of that, in fact. Biccus was the one who knew the area, and if we did run into anyone there was at least a chance he would be recognized.

Biccus nodded and we heard him scrambling back into his seat.

The lane was a narrow one and extremely dark, the more so as the torches were beginning to burn dim, and it took a little time to reach the house. When we did so, it came as a surprise. The driver came round to help us from the cart, but even as I got down and looked around I could scarcely take it in. The building was a mere dark smudge against the night,

and the barns and stables ghostly silhouettes. There was no
sound at all: no noise of animals, no warning honk of geese
and not a glint of light – nothing but the hoot of owls and the
burble of the stream.

'The place is deserted,' I murmured in dismay. If the place
was empty there was nothing to be learned.

Biccus was standing beside me in the gloom. 'I told you
that the owner had just moved away. Obviously the new man
has not yet arrived. Well, that solves one problem. If there's
no one here, at least we can find a place to bed down in the
barn. It will be warm and dry there, if nothing else.'

Brianus was lighting us another torch from the dying flickers
of the old. He brought it to me, joyous. 'And we've even got
a light so we can see where we are going.'

I took it from him and led the way into the nearest barn. It
was entirely bare – it had been swept and limewashed recently
– but it was dry, as Biccus had observed. I had been in less
comfortable lodgings on this very day. 'This will do,' I said
resignedly. 'Brianus, there is another barn next door. It looks
as if it might have been a store for straw or hay. Go and see
if there is any in there now. It's possible that some was left
to feed the horse before it went. If so – and if it is reasonably
clean – bring a few armfuls here. We'll make a mattress out
of it and then we'll sleep like kings. At first light we'll have
a quick look round before we travel back.'

The cart-driver, who had followed us inside, looked bale-
fully at me. 'Are you including me in that proposition, citizen?
If so, you'll have to think again. I've got a comfortable bed
awaiting me at home, and horses to think of. I was instructed
to bring you over here. No one said anything about waiting
overnight. So, if you'll excuse me, I'll be getting back, while
I still have enough torches for the trip. I don't want to run
into those rebels on the way – I heard what they did to that
poor lictor earlier, and I don't want it happening to me.'

'What happened to the lictor?' Junio and I exclaimed in
unison.

The driver raised an eyebrow. 'Don't say you didn't hear?
The body was found not far away from here by a customer
of ours, hacked to little pieces and without a head. They would

not have known him, if it wasn't for the toga-clasp and the ring.'

'The ring?'

'A seal-ring. They found it on the finger of a severed hand. It was brought in to the curia and one of the councillors identified the seal – the lictor had written several times to him.'

'Porteus?' I murmured.

'I couldn't tell you that. All I know is they had to use one of our hiring-vehicles to go and pick the pieces up – they couldn't leave a lictor out lying on the road, but no one else had a vehicle to spare and the army death-cart was busy somewhere else.' He frowned at me. 'I'm surprised you didn't know. There was an awful fuss. Surely you were in the garrison tonight? Didn't they send you over to requisition me?'

This was an unexpected awkwardness! 'I went home to get some items from my household first,' I answered hastily. 'This must have happened after the city gates were closed.'

To my surprise he seemed satisfied by this. 'Pretty close, I think. I know they had to open up to let us bring the body in. Apparently the man's wife had only just arrived by sea, and they had to go and let her know the news. Poor woman. She identified the toga-clasp and is going to organize a proper funeral – though she hasn't even moved into her home. In the meantime the body's lying in the fort.' He shook his head again. 'I'm still surprised they didn't tell you when you went back tonight.'

'I did hear something,' I replied, remembering suddenly what the watch had said. Of course, it was the lictor's body they had meant, not Pronta's, as I'd thought! 'Only I thought they were talking about someone else – a person who'd been murdered earlier.'

'Ah, the driver of the treasure-cart!' he said. 'That's another citizen the rebels killed today. To say nothing of the escort, and those men were armed. You can see why I am anxious to get home.'

'In spite of the rebels being on the road?' Junio put in.

'There's nothing on my cart to steal and I'm clearly not a Roman, so I hope to Juno that they'll let me pass. If not, I won't give up without a fight. I've got a knife about me and

I'll use it, too. Take one of them with me, if I do no more.'
He spat on his hand and rubbed his ear for luck, then made
an unexpected dash into the court. We heard him jumping up
on to the cart.

'Wait!' I shouted after him, but he was gone and we could
only stand and trace the disappearing flicker of the lights as
the cart rattled down the lane again. We three were left in
darkness – Brianus had our torch – and with one accord we
groped toward the other barn.

The door was open and we could see inside. This barn
wasn't empty like the other one. Brianus had found a sconce
to hold the torch and was using his hands to rake together a
few remaining strands of hay that were scattered around the
bottoms of the wall – ignoring the pile of heavy sacks and
boxes which took up the whole of the centre of the floor, and
which were roughly covered by a huge coarse sacking cloth.

I glanced at Junio and saw that he had read my thoughts.
'The treasure!' he murmured. 'Will you look, or shall I?'

I stepped forward and pulled the cloth away. One of the
sacks rolled clanking to the floor. Together we seized it, tore
the rope away and tipped the contents out. Bowls, pans, spoons
and metal jugs spilled around our feet: good but not expensive,
normal household wares.

I stared at Junio and he stared at me. He picked up a ladle,
went over to a box and used the heavy handle to prise the lid
away. The wood snapped, creaking, and we looked inside.
This time it was clothing – tunics, rugs, a pair of ancient boots.
We turned to find Biccus, who was peering at our find with
a look of satisfaction on his ugly face.

'Well done, citizens, I would not have thought of that. We
can use the rugs as coverings to keep us warm. And you've
found beakers, too – there is sure to be a well, so we will
have water in the morning if we're thirsty then. Pity there's
no food here, by the look of it – I expect the departing owner
took the crops with him and I know he sold or slaughtered all
the animals – but there's enough at my house, and it isn't far
. . .' He broke off, seeing the expression on my face and
Junio's. 'You are disappointed? I thought you would be
pleased?'

I shook my head. 'This isn't what I'd really hoped to find.' I said it bitterly, chilled by the cold reality of my present plight. I had run away and broken bail, and now I was stranded miles away from town with little prospect of returning there before the court convened – so Marcus would be subject to a heavy fine and my sentence doubled, if that were possible. And all for nothing! I had been so keen to come and see the farm, certain that the place would hold a clue, or at least a person who had seen the cart – instead of which the whole estate was cold and dark and the hoped-for treasure proved to be a pile of packed-up household goods.

Biccus was shrugging. 'Well, it's hardly a surprise. I told you that the owner was packing up to leave. In fact, we're lucky that he hasn't come back for this load of luggage yet – at least we have the chance to make use of it tonight.'

I nodded grimly. There was nothing to be said. Junio was already foraging for rugs and blankets in the box. He found a bunch of home-made tapers, too, and I picked up the piece of sacking cloth – it was big enough to make a base for all of us. Brianus, meanwhile, had finished raking straw and came over with an armful – and a triumphant smile.

'This is all that I can find that's clean,' he said. 'There's just enough to make a bed for you – the rest of us will have to make a mattress of our cloaks. Now you've found those blankets we shall not be cold.' He glanced nervously at me. 'I wondered about looking in those sacks, myself, but you had told me to collect the straw.'

He said it simply, as though my word was law: if the barn had been on fire, I thought, he would have continued with his task until it was completed or I ordered otherwise.

Biccus, though, did not seem satisfied. 'There's more straw over there beside the ladder to the loft. Quite a lot of it.'

Brianus shook his head. 'That isn't any good. I had a look at it. Someone has been killing animals, by the look of it, and the straw was put down to mop up the blood.'

I turned to Junio. 'Animals? I wonder! If this is the place where the escort stopped the cart – whether it was all arranged before or not – that is much more likely to be human blood.'

Junio looked doubtfully at me. 'That's a lot of "maybe's",

Father. There isn't any proof that the cart even came in here to the farm. And as Biccus has just told us, the farmer butchered his remaining stock. Where else would he do it?'

'Outside in the yard?' I countered. 'Isn't that more likely, even in the rain?'

'When he was going to scrub and limewash the shed, in any case?' Junio replied. 'And wouldn't he have made a final sacrifice to ensure the blessing of the gods?'

'So where's the meat?' I argued.

Junio shrugged. 'If there was any extra he would have taken it – either to the market or to salt in his new home. Even if he's moving to another farm, he can't expect fresh produce for at least another year.'

What he was saying was wholly logical, but I could not let the matter go. 'But bloodstains, in the only place the convoy could have stopped – on a farm that's been bought by a customer from Gaul? It's too much like coincidence. Let me see that straw.'

Brianus dutifully took the torch and led me to the place. He was right, the top straw was just speckled, but lower down the stalks were steeped in blood – dark red and sticky right down to the floor. There'd obviously been some previous attempt to clean the area – there was no trodden mess or droppings, just the bloodied straw – and the floor around it was swept reasonably clear: no sign of the struggle that murder would have caused. I hated to admit it, even to myself, but it was exactly what you might expect if someone had been butchering a couple of old cows to sacrifice.

I stooped down and ran a finger across the bloodstained floor. One small patch was particularly wet – as if the blood was fresher there than all the rest, though maybe it was simply that more had settled there. From an oil-anointed creature with severed neck, providing its owner with a last blood sacrifice? Or a dying escort-slave? If only it were possible to tell the difference!

I looked up to find Junio standing over me. 'You still think this was where the treasure-party died? In that case it must have been a very swift attack.'

I got up and slowly shook my head. 'Perhaps it was the

rebels, after all. Perhaps the travellers were betrayed. Perhaps they were surprised. Perhaps they were murdered while they were asleep – because they'd stumbled on a rebel hideout by mistake . . .'

'More maybes, Father?' Junio squeezed my arm. 'I can only hope you're wrong. If rebels have been here, we're in danger, too. And I suppose that it is remotely possible – a deserted farm would be a splendid place to have a hideaway. But would you not expect an escort to stand guard, if they were sleeping in an empty place – especially with a cart-load of treasure to defend?'

I shook my head stubbornly but decisively. 'We are going to keep somebody on watch, at any rate,' I said. 'We can take turns to sleep. Two people at a time. Me and Biccus, then you and Brianus. We'll take these things and bed down in the barn next door. Bring those tapers – we'll need to keep a light.'

And for a long, restless and uncomfortable night, that is exactly what we did.

TWENTY-SIX

I was awoken from a fitful dream by Brianus's urgent whisper
in my ear. 'Master! The bandits! I think that they are here!'
I struggled to sit upright and looked stupidly at him. He
was holding a taper, but faint light was filtering though the
spaces in the eaves and I realized that it must be almost dawn.
'There are people in the courtyard!' He hissed the words at
me. 'Your son has slipped into the other barn. He's searching
through the sacks to see what weapons he can find. He told
me to wake you, so we are prepared.'

I was already shaking Biccus into wakefulness. The pig-man
had faithfully kept watch with me for hours and he was inclined
to be resentful that I'd disturbed him now. 'What in Pluto's
name . . . ?' he hollered, then saw the finger I was holding to
my lips. 'What's the matter?' he murmured, suddenly subdued.

I did not need to answer. The sound of voices just outside
the door was an explanation in itself. I simply jerked my head
towards the sound, and busied myself with doing up my sandals
and my belt. It might be necessary to make a quick retreat.

Biccus's pig-eyes were wide open with alarm. 'Dear gods
– I do believe the owner has come back. Or perhaps the new
one's come. I can hear a woman – that must be his wife.' He
had already risen to his feet and was beginning to put his
frightful footwear on.

I paused in the act of putting on my cloak and realized he
was right. I could hear a female laughing, rather mirthlessly
and her ringing voice exclaiming, in a martyred tone, 'Well,
councillor Florens, thank Juno we've arrived. What a frightful
journey. Thank Mars we had your gig. I did not realize this
place was so far from town.'

'Florens!' I was so startled that I said the word aloud. 'These
are no rebels. That's the man who wants me brought to court.
He's found out that I'm here and he's come to drag me back.
Well, I'd better go and face him. You two stay here. It's better

if you do – there's no need for you to be involved in this.'
And before Brianus could voice the protest that was clearly
on his lips, I pushed the barn door open and stepped into the
courtyard and the first cold light of day.

I was expecting to find the place awash with slaves and
guards and carriages, but there was only a solitary gig with a
rather sullen Servilis in the driving-seat. He was engaged in
driving it away – evidently intending to unhitch the horse –
and he did not look my way. Standing in the gloom were his
erstwhile passengers, a man and woman both in mourning
clothes, dark against the semi-dark of dawn: the man in full
toga pulla, with a black cloak to match, and the woman in
a cape and stola of Ligurian grey.

If I'd not known that it was Florens, I might have been
deceived – the light was dim and he looked quite different in
his funereal dress – and the woman was not anyone I'd ever
seen before. She was young and lively, despite the sombre
cloth, and her hair – which should have been hidden by a veil
– was escaping from its jet-encrusted pins and plaits and
cascading in delightful light-coloured ringlets round her face
(which should also have been covered, if the Roman rules of
strict decorum had been met).

Her jewelled hand was resting on her companion's arm and
she was looking boldly up at him. (He was small and portly
but she was smaller still.) 'It's very lonely here.' She shivered.
'Are you quite sure it's safe? There are no real rebel bandits
in the vicinity?'

He looked into her face and gave a pudgy smile. 'The fact
that it is lonely is exactly why I chose it as a hiding place.
And as for being safe, my private guards will be here in a
little while. Their wagon is already on the road – though of
course it does not travel as quickly as a gig. They'll stay here
when I go back to town, and see off any unwanted visitors.
But who is going to come out here, in any case? The man
who used to own the farm is unfortunately dead, as you're
aware, and all these buildings now belong to me.'

I felt a tingle running down my back. My assumptions
had been wrong. Florens was not here in search of me at
all. This was some secret assignation of his own. I tried to

melt back into the barn again, moving as slowly and noise-lessly as possible. I wished devoutly I had stayed there all along. At any moment one of them would look up and notice me.

It was Junio who attracted their attention first. He must have crept out of the other barn without me noticing and seen me standing there, in danger as he thought. He dropped the sack that he was carrying, which fell with a startling clatter to the ground. The woman shrieked in terror and fled towards the house, but Florens whirled around.

'Father, there's danger. Make a run for it!' Junio shouted, as all eyes turned to him – and I realized that he'd made the noise on purpose to let me get away.

I might have tried to calm him – an illicit assignation is embarrassing, no more – but the barn door behind me was opened suddenly and Biccus and Brianus were standing at my back – armed with the iron ladle and a burned-out torch, which they were fiercely brandishing. Brianus had a bucket in his other hand, and he tossed that to me, saying, 'It's empty but it's heavy. If it hits them, it will hurt. I'm sorry, master, this is all the weaponry we've got. Unless Junio's found something better in . . .' He broke with a gasp as Florens flung himself upon my son and threw him to the floor.

The councillor was plump and ageing and Junio was young, but the attacker had the advantage of surprise. As Junio lay there winded on his face, Florens grabbed his hands and knelt on him, then – to my horror – he seized the heavy sack and brought it crashing down on Junio's skull. The victim gave a little moan and then lay ominously still, a small red trickle oozing from his head.

We three lunged forward as one man to accost the councillor, who was standing up and coolly dusting off his hands, but before we reached him Florens gave a whistle through his teeth. Instantly Servilis came running from the field, like a sheepdog summoned by his master's signal-call – except that this sheepdog had a dagger in his hand.

'Arrest these people, Servilis.' Florens was the picture of authority again, dignified and solemn in his mourning black. It was hard to believe what we had just seen him do. 'Put them in the shed. And take this body somewhere and take care of it – by this time I imagine you know what to do.'

I stared at him, astounded. Pieces of pattern snapped suddenly in place. 'You!' I said. 'You are the owner of this place. You knew there were bloodstains in there, didn't you? So you set out to silence Junio. Well, you haven't silenced me. You killed those people with the treasure-cart – or you had them killed – and now you've murdered Junio as well. Don't think I'll let you . . .' I was prevented from saying any more. Servilis had seized me by one arm and was twisting it savagely up into my back, while his other hand held the dagger to my neck.

I thought of swiping at him with the pail, but a sudden pressure of the blade dissuaded me.

'Put that bucket down.'

I dropped it instantly.

He turned to the others. 'And drop those stupid weapons. Get into the barn. One false move from you two and your master's dead as well.'

Brianus and Biccus sheepishly obeyed, but I hadn't finished yet. After what had been done to Junio, I hardly cared what happened to myself. I shouted to Florens as we were marched inside, 'You lured the treasure-cart in here and murdered all of them. How did you do it? Laced their wine with poppy-juice and stabbed them while they slept? Or even poisoned it? That would account for the stab-wounds after death . . . Ahhh!' This as Servilis increased the pressure on my arm.

'You want me to despatch him, master?' my tormentor asked. Florens had followed us into the barn.

'Leave him, Servilis, the man is just a fool. The courts will deal with him when we take him back. We've caught him outright now. Look at all the extra charges we can bring to bear: escaping from the fortress – as I assume he did – breaking into buildings, trying to attack a Roman citizen and impugning the honour of a councillor. The wretch I caught stealing isn't even dead. I can see him breathing. So there's another thing. Accusing me of murder, in front of witnesses! I wonder what my friend the magistrate will make of that.'

'You attacked a Roman citizen yourself,' I said, braving the threat of further damage to my arm. Now it was relief that made me bold. 'The man you set on was my adopted son. If you didn't kill him, it was merely chance. And don't think that you'll avoid the charge by just arraigning me. If I'm consigned to exile, my patron will bring the matter of the assault to court.'

Florens was entirely unmoved. 'You mean that wretch I brought down in the court? But, my dear Libertus, he was just a thief. I caught him escaping from my private barn with a bag of my possessions in his hand. The lictor's widow is a witness to the fact. The law permits me to defend my property. No court is going to punish me for that.'

His air of outraged reason made me furious, but with the dagger at my throat there was little I could do. Junio was obviously seriously hurt – I thanked the gods that it was nothing more than that – and I was certain to be exiled for life. Everything I'd worked for was slipping from my grasp.

I was not the only one. Behind me I could hear the smothered sobbing of my slave. Brianus. Of course, he was under threat as well. If he was discovered now, he was in danger of his life – my testimony as a criminal would be no help to him. But there was a chance for him. Brianus was purchased in Britannia, so Voluus's widow did not know his face, and neither Florens nor Servilis had seen the boy before – it was Porteus's bodyguard who caught and questioned him.

I looked Florens in his pink-rimmed eyes. 'Well. You have caught me. Take me to the court. And you have a case against my son, if he survives. But let the others go. They have done nothing.'

Florens looked scorning. 'Nothing except break into my property.'

'They broke into nothing. The doors were all unlocked. They simply sought shelter in a deserted farm. How could they possibly have known that it was yours?'

I could see that he was tempted. There was nothing to be gained by his detaining them – he could not pretend that they had helped me with the crimes, because they almost certainly had witnesses to prove that they had not, and in any case they could not be tried with me. As non-citizens they would need a separate court – at, of course, additional expense.

Florens frowned. 'Who are they anyway? What are they doing here?'

'This man is Biccus, from a farm nearby,' I was already beginning to explain.

But Brianus interrupted me. 'He doesn't know me, master, but I've seen him before. I saw him at the mansio, when Voluus was here.'

Florens pounced on the implication instantly. 'You are the lictor's slave! The one that ran away. So, Libertus, in addition to his other crimes, has been harbouring a fugitive as well. More indication – if we needed it – that he had friends within the household who could have helped him plot!' He smirked. 'And when Voluus is murdered you are both found nearby! I think the court will find that quite significant.' He turned to me and smiled. 'So, citizen, I don't think we can agree to your request. I think we'll have your two companions taken to the jail. Gagged and bound, I think, so they can't run away. And listen – there is the sound of wheels and hoof-beats in the court. Here are the very people to take care of it. I think you've met my private escort, citizen?'

My throat was too dry to make any reply, Behind me, Brianus was weeping quietly. 'I am sorry, master, I have let you down.' Biccus was saying nothing, as was often the case.

Florens was already striding to the door, raising his voice and shouting to his men. 'Come in here, lads, and take these three away. Don't be too gentle, they're thieves and murderers – we caught them in the act. Make sure you bind them most securely and keep them at knife-point all the way, though if your hand should slip I shouldn't fret too much. We'll claim that they were trying to avoid arrest.' He peered out into the strengthening light. 'Come on, then. Get on with it. We haven't got all day.'

TWENTY-SEVEN

There was a rattling of hobnails and half a dozen running men stormed in. I braced myself but it was not the shattering surge of Florens's brutal bodyguard. This group was in formation and were carrying drawn swords, and their leader was a breathless and plump centurion.

'Emelius!' I breathed. I had never been more relieved to encounter anyone. 'What are you doing here?' Then I remembered my conversation at the garrison the evening before. 'The commander has sent you to investigate?'

'Nothing of the kind,' he said without a smile. 'I was sent here to arrest you. You were supposed to be sleeping at your patron's flat, but you got out somehow. When they found you missing, they came back to us and the commander guessed where you had gone. And when we went to requisition a larger vehicle . . .'

My heart sank, but I nodded. 'I'm sorry about that. And, of course, your suspicions were confirmed.'

Biccus was gaping at me. 'You mean you didn't have permission to take that cart at all? Dear Jupiter! And to think that I agreed to come with you! I hope you're satisfied. Look what troubles you have made for all of us.'

Emelius looked stern. 'Well, he won't be making trouble for you any more. I'm under instructions to take him to the court. No doubt there'll be a few more charges to answer after this.' He turned to me. 'I hope for your sake that we get there before your accuser does; otherwise your patron will be liable to a fine. He won't be happy – he is threatening to disown you as it is.'

I was past desperation, so I simply said, 'My accuser will be there. He's standing right behind you.'

The centurion whirled round. 'Of course. I recognize the face. The councillor who brought you to the garrison. A thousand pardons, Worthiness, I did not know you in those mourning robes.' It was understandable. Without the resplendent purple stripe, Florens looked almost insignificant.

His personality was undiminished, though. He waved a lofty hand. 'I am expecting a cart-load of my slaves to arrive at any time. I was going to escort this villain to the courts myself, and his companions, too. I am going to charge all three of them with robbery and assault – but now you can deliver them instead.' He nodded to Servilis. 'You can let the prisoner go. Go and guard the lady until the others come – fortunately I'll be able to leave them here with her, as planned.'

'Lady? What lady?' Emelius looked around in puzzlement. In other circumstances, it would have made me smile. Even Servilis was smirking as he bowed and left.

'The lady Alcanta is under my protection now that her husband is unfortunately dead, centurion,' Florens told him rather haughtily. 'She has been enjoying the hospitality of my residence in town, but of course that cannot decently continue very long. Voluus did leave an apartment in the town, but after what has happened she's afraid of living there – especially with an infant child to think about. It happened that I recently acquired this farm . . .'

'You?' I interrupted. 'Biccus told me that it had been bought by somebody from Gaul, who was intending to build a new villa on the site.'

Florens looked pitying at me. 'I assure you that it's mine. Her husband did express an interest in obtaining it – his wife, he said, would like a country property – but at the time the owner was not prepared to sell. When I heard it was available I purchased it myself, hoping I could tempt him into it. But when Alcanta came, and it was obviously unsafe for her to move into the flat, I brought her out here to see if she would like it as a temporary home, until more permanent arrangements can be made for her. No one but ourselves would know that she was here. Even so, with all the threats to Voluus, I thought that she required a guard.'

It was so sweetly reasonable that I almost believed the words myself. Emelius, though, had practical concerns. 'But the lady will surely have a guardian under law, under the terms of

Voluus's will?' he said with courtesy. 'Should he not be consulted, before such plans are made?'

'Voluus has left everything to his wife and child, and I am nominated as their guardian in Britannia,' Florens said. 'I can produce a document, under Voluus's seal, confirming it. And here is the lady now; she will tell you the same thing.'

I turned. Alcanta was coming through the door into the barn, framed in the first golden rays of sun and I heard a stifled gasp as the soldiers took in how beautiful she was. Beautiful, but perhaps indecorous, it was not her fault that she was not at home, but a mourning widow should wear a veil and weep, not wander freely round the premises when there were men about. Calvinus had called her 'wilful', I recalled.

'Florens!' She went to him with little tripping steps. 'I came to warn you that the boy you hit is slightly stirring now. Servilis is with him to make sure he doesn't bolt. It's just as well we went to look at him. I got tired of waiting for you in the house. What has detained you?' She looked around and seemed to notice the armed soldiers with alarm. 'Who are all these guards? What are they doing here? They haven't . . . ?'

Florens held up a hand to silence her. 'Nothing to concern yourself about, Alcanta. I will handle this. They have simply come to take our unwelcome visitors to court.'

He had spoken very firmly and I saw her set her lips. The pretty chin was raised in a defiant jut. 'Well, make them go away. If we are to be married and go back to Gaul when I am out of mourning . . .'

I interrupted her. 'Married! But Florens is contracted to marry someone else.'

Florens had turned from pink to scarlet now. 'Not so, citizen. I don't know how you came to hear of that, but in any case the contract will be void. It depended on a dowry that will not now be paid.' He turned to Alcanta. 'Take no notice, lady. The citizen is wrong. All will be exactly as I promised you. You and your infant will be safe with me.'

The girl in widow's mourning stole a doubting look at him. 'If you say so, Florens.' She sounded unconvinced.

The councillor propelled her by the arm and led her briskly to the door, though she did not look as if she cared for that.

'Then, centurion, if you would care to bind and take your prisoners under guard, I will follow in the gig and see you at the court. Alcanta, I will have to leave you here a little while – I'll make arrangements for the funeral while I am in town and have your husband's body moved into the flat, where I suppose a servant should start on the lament – but my escort-slaves will very soon be here and then you'll have a guard. In the meantime, look around the place and see if it will suit you as a temporary home. I will return as soon as possible. The trial of this miscreant should not take very long.' He was already striding off with her across the court.

Emelius watched them go, then jerked a thumb at me. 'Very well, then. Let's have you on our cart. It won't be a very comfortable ride for you today! You two soldiers on the end can bring the other pair – and I suppose we'd better take the one that's over there, as well.' He gestured two more of his men towards where Junio was still lying in the court, with Servilis standing over him. Florens and the lady had also stopped to look.

'That is my adopted son,' I said. 'He is a citizen, and Florens attacked him. He almost broke his skull.'

The centurion made a little face. 'Tell that to the court. The councillor claims that you were robbing him. And the lad's not desperately hurt – you heard they'd seen him stir.'

'Then let's try and revive him, not drag him like a sack,' I pleaded. 'A splash of water might help bring him round.'

'Oh, very well,' he said reluctantly. 'It's easier to manage a man when he's awake. I noticed that there was a bucket at the door. I'll get my men to fill it with water from the well and fling it over him. That should do the trick. See to it, soldier.' He nodded to one of his two remaining men.

The fellow nodded and ran off to the well, carrying the bucket. I was wishing that I'd had the wit to use it as a weapon when I could, but it was too late now. Emelius had his centurion's baton in his hand, and was prodding me towards the open hiring-cart – probably the very one I'd ridden in last night, though the driver was a man I didn't recognize. Biccus and Brianus were shoved up after me, their hands bound behind them with a piece of rope. As a citizen, at least I was spared the indignity of that.

I craned to see if they had managed to wake up Junio, but the soldier with the bucket was standing helplessly, looking round the court as if searching for the well. Florens made no move at all to help.

Biccus saw the problem. 'The well is in the corner over there,' he shouted, gesturing in the right direction with his head. He turned to me and added, in the Celtic tongue, 'I ought to know. I almost fell into it when I came before – to tell the owner to control his dogs.'

The soldier nodded an acknowledgement and trotted over to fill up his pail, but Florens gave a roar and rushed across to him. 'Stop! What in Hades are you doing! Keep away from there.'

The man stopped, bewildered. 'But the centurion said . . .'

Florens's manner altered instantly to one of unctuous charm. 'I think the well is poisoned. It's not safe to use. If you want water, get it from the stream.' He smiled apologetically at Emelius. 'I'm sorry, officer. That well is dangerous. One of the first things that I propose to do is fill it in and dig another one.' He turned to Alcanta and smiled down at her. 'I can't have anything happen to the lady here.'

Biccus was scowling and grumbling audibly. 'Shouldn't be anything the matter with that well. My family had this farm for centuries. Perfectly good water from it all that time. Someone has been careless and let something rot down there. I told you that ex-soldier did not know the first thing about how to run a farm.'

Alcanta threw a look of purest hate at him and Florens looked furious, but Emelius simply shrugged. 'Well, it hardly matters what the water's like. He isn't going to drink it anyway. We only want to throw a little over him to bring him round. Jump to it, soldier!'

The man saluted smartly and started to obey, expertly tying the pail onto the waiting chain, ready to lower it gently down into the well, but Florens stepped forward and intervened again. 'I told you, it's poisonous – you'll get it in his mouth!'

The soldier hesitated in his task and looked to his superior to advise. As he did so, I had a wild idea.

'Tell him to do it, Emelius!' I cried. 'I think I know what is hidden down that well.'

Florens would have slain me, if a look could kill. But he
essayed a casual laugh. 'Nonsense! Of course there's nothing
hidden in the well – except the water which, as I say, is
dangerous.' He looked around, as if appealing to the gods, before
he said, 'I expect that's why the previous owner was so keen
to sell the farm but, as the law says, the buyer must beware.'

I realized what question had been niggling in my brain.
'But I thought that he was dead?' I challenged. 'You told
Alcanta so. I overheard you when you first arrived. So how
did he sell you the farm so recently?'

Florens's face was almost purple now – more purple than
his usual patrician stripe. For two quadrans, I could see, he
would have lunged at me, just as he had lunged at Junio earlier.
But the soldiers were watching and he controlled himself. 'The
two things are not contradictory. He sold it to me just before
he died. Probably poisoned by the water from the well!'

Alcanta clutched at him. 'Florens, is that true? I thought
. . .' She tailed off as she saw the fury in his face.

I turned to Emelius. 'Another useful coincidence, centurion,
don't you think? Murder seems to follow the councillor around.
The treasure-cart just happens to be passing his new farm the
night it is attacked: the lictor names him as guardian of his
wife, and then just happens to be murdered on his way. And
now we learn the previous owner of this house has also died,
just after selling it to him. All a little too convenient, wouldn't
you agree? I have no proof of anything, of course, but if we
should happen to find treasure in that well . . .'

I said no more. Emelius, who had been gazing speculatively
at me, gave a brisk command. 'We shall soon find out. Water,
soldier. Dip the pail at once.'

This time there was a rattle as the chain ran down and the
soldier shook it to make the bucket tip. 'Almost ready, sir,' he
muttered, shaking it again. 'But I can't get it up again. There's
something blocking it.'

I looked at Florens. 'What do you think we'll find? Statues,
chests of money, gold and silver bowls?'

'There's no treasure in there,' he muttered stubbornly.
'Probably just a bit of wall collapsed. It's obvious the well
has not been used for months.'

'Yet it managed to poison the owner of the farm!' I said, earning another, still more vicious scowl.

Emelius took a quick decision. 'The citizen is right. There is something very odd about this story of the well.' He signalled to the soldiers who were guarding us. 'Leave the prisoners and come and lend a hand. And you . . .' This time it was Servilis that he was talking to, '. . . find a bowl or something and get water from the stream.'

'You may find something useful in that sack,' I said, pointing to the one which had felled Junio. 'It comes from a pile of household goods we discovered in the shed.' Servilis looked as though he had been struck by sudden lightening. He glanced sideways at his master, who shook his head at him. Emelius strode over and picked up the sack himself, and as he did so Alcanta gave a moan and slumped on to the ground beside my newly stirring son. One of the soldiers – on his own initiative and seeing she was faint – found a pool of rainwater in a stone feeding-trough and used his helmet as a makeshift cup to splash it on her face. Then, sheepishly, he did the same for Junio.

Meanwhile, everything was happening at once. The soldiers at the well-head gave a triumphant cry and began to haul in quickly on the bucket-chain. Emelius put a hand into the sack and let out a cry as though he had been stung. Florens picked up the corners of his robe and dashed off in the direction of the gig – surprisingly sprightly for a portly man – calling out to Servilis to follow him, while two of the soldiers raced off after him.

Junio, revived by the water on his face, stirred and started to sit up. He looked up, blinking, at Emelius. 'Treasure!' he said weakly. 'Off the lictor's cart. Sacks and sacks of it. Buried under all the household boxes in the other barn.'

Emelius nodded, producing a fine gold statue from the sack. No wonder it had been heavy enough to stun.

I confess that I was startled. I had thought the treasure would be in the well. I got down off the cart – there was no one near me to prevent me now – and hurried over to see what was being winched up in the pail. I almost wished I hadn't. As it emerged it was very clear what had obstructed it. In the bucket was a severed head, bearded and bushy and surprisingly intact. I turned away from it.

The centurion was less squeamish about this sort of thing, the result of serving on the battlefield, I suppose. He came, lifted the horrid object by its hair and appraised it with some care. 'Not been dead for very long,' he said judiciously. 'A day or so at most. Bit swollen with the water, but you can see it hasn't started to decay at all.'

'Well, it didn't have the chance. It's Voluus the lictor, surely?' I replied. Then, seeing that Alcanta was rousing from her faint, I added sharply, 'Don't let his widow see the head.'

But it was too late. She had already seen it as I spoke. She clutched her throat and gave a strangled cry, 'My love! My husband! Florens cheated me!' and fell back again into a swoon. The soldier with the water helmet knelt down to her at once, took the pretty head on to his lap and began gently patting both the lovely cheeks – clearly very happy with his self-inflicted task.

Emelius looked at me and rolled his eyes. 'It seems that you are right. This must be the lictor, though I must say I'm surprised. Doesn't look quite old enough to me – though it's difficult to tell. Death seems to suit him, though. Looks almost handsome, in a swarthy sort of way, though I heard that in life he was an ugly brute. It reminds me of someone. I can't think who it is.'

'Master!' Brianus was calling from the cart. 'Can we get down and have a closer look?'

I looked at Emelius, who nodded to his men, and one of them went over and helped my companions down. Brianus, his hands still tied behind his back, came sidling up to me. 'Biccus thinks he might know who that is. It's not my master, though, I'm quite sure of that!'

TWENTY-EIGHT

'What?' I found myself shouting. 'Not the lictor? But Alcanta has just told us that it was!'

'Well, it isn't.' Biccus was gazing intently at the grisly face. 'But I can tell you who it is. I only glimpsed him for a moment once, when he set his dogs on me, but I'm fairly sure that is the man who used to own this farm. I never knew his name. Antonius, Antoninus, Antolinus – something of the kind.'

'Dear gods!' This time it was Emelius who spoke. 'Antolinus! Of course it is! Didn't have a beard and lots of curly hair when I last saw him, but that's who it is. I thought that he was dead. But there's no doubt about it. Antolinus Gallus. Octio in the Fourth Gauls Half-mounted Auxiliary Regiment.' He shook his head.

I was still struggling to make sense of this. 'So you think he was the driver of that treasure-cart? The owner of the belt that someone recognized? And this is what happened to the head?'

The centurion shook his head. 'Not a chance of it. You saw that body that the death squad found. That man was forty if he was a day. Antolinus was comparatively young – as you can still see by the look of him. But I thought he had been murdered by rebels long ago – they said they found his body . . .' He trailed off. 'But obviously it wasn't him at all.'

'Certainly it wasn't, if this really is his head. I agree with you – this fellow is relative young and has not been dead for long. If it is your Antolinus, he must have been living some- where in disguise. Oh, of course! Out here in the country, it's quite obvious – running a farm he didn't really understand and hoping the army would never think of looking there for him. A clever ruse, in fact. Often a runaway is better hidden very close to home. People always expect the opposite.'

'Especially when they think he's dead,' Emelius said. 'I expect there was an ambush but he managed to fight free. It must have been a rebel he hung up on the tree, dressed in his uniform and hacked to pieces to match the way they treated us. No doubt his companion was murdered in the raid and he just deserted, knowing that we wouldn't look for him.'

'No wonder he kept dogs to frighten neighbours off. It would have been certain death if they discovered him.' I looked again at the bearded handsome face. 'Though somebody obviously did kill him in the end. Probably Florens – though I don't know why.'

I gestured to the requisition cart, where Florens and Servilis were being bundled in at sword-point, just as I had been – the councillor still protesting that he was innocent. 'Is it my fault if rebels use my well?' he was demanding, of no one in particular. 'Libertus is talking nonsense when he accuses me. Like the rest of his assertions, it's quite preposterous. Of course I didn't kill the escort of the cart. How could I have done so? On the Ides the basilica was closed, but I was in the public baths all afternoon and in the evening Gaius had a special sacrifice to mark the day – half the curia was there! And you know yourself that I was in Glevum all day yesterday. And why should I kill the previous owner of this farm? I'd just bought it from him – there are records of the fact. What would I have to gain by killing him and chopping off his head?'

That was the problem with all of this, I thought. I could understand the murder of the lictor, possibly: Florens stood to profit, as Alcanta's guardian, and more so if he took her as his wife, as she seemed to have agreed. So why bother to steal from the treasure-carts at all, let alone kill the escort in that appalling way? And what had this deserter got to do with it? Yet I was convinced that Florens was at the heart of this.

Emelius was looking equally perplexed, for reasons of his own. 'But if this is Antolinus, where's the body gone and, if this is not the lictor, where is Voluus?' He gazed at me suddenly. 'You don't suppose we'll find he isn't dead at all?'

That would make nonsense of all my theories, I thought wearily. Florens would get nothing if the lictor was alive – indeed, he would be forced to marry Porteus's girl. I had a sudden inspiration. 'Wait a minute!' I said the words aloud. Without waiting for permission I ran over to the cart. 'You didn't meet the lictor, but you went to Gaul? Don't I remember that you told me that?'

Florens still had self-possession left. He looked disdainfully at me. 'I met his family, as I told you. I never met the man.'

'And yet he nominated you to be guardian for his wife?'

He raised an eyebrow. 'He knew my reputation as senior councillor, I suppose. Perhaps he learnt about me while he was over here. He sent a sealed message to me afterwards, inviting me to act in that capacity, should the need arise. Only while she is in Britannia of course; otherwise she goes back to her brother's potestas. Is that so surprising? I can produce the letter if you like.'

'So you only met his family while you were in Gaul? What family was that? I heard that Voluus had no other relatives. So was it his wife that you're referring to? A foreign heiress that you hoped to wed? Only by then it was too late, of course – a binding contract had already been made with Voluus.'

Florens couldn't answer; he was blustering. 'I don't know why you want to make an issue out of that. Of course I would have married Alcanta if I could. Who wouldn't want to do so? She is very beautiful. But she was already promised and, as I say, I never met the lictor in my life.'

Brianus by now was standing at my heels and he tugged my tunic sleeve. 'But he did know him, master. I told you so before. I saw them dining at the mansio.'

'And he's already told us that they discussed the farm!' I pointed out. Then I realized what Brianus had said. I whirled around to him. 'You mean it was this councillor who dined with Voluus at the mansio that night?' I'd gone on thinking that Porteus was the dinner guest.

Florens was flustered. 'Ah, of course. I had forgotten that occasion. There was such a fuss. We were in the mansio discussing the matter of the farm, but Voluus received some sort of threatening note and he lost his temper. It was embarrassing.'

Hardly an occasion to forget, I thought. Aloud, I said, 'I hear you saw the contents of the note?'

He waved a vaguely self-important hand. 'Vague threats – "you will be killed and all goods destroyed if you come to Glevum, I've not forgotten you" – that sort of thing. Not signed or sealed, of course. Voluus was simply furious. Swore that he would have the writer caught and brought to trial or even kill him with his own bare hands. I had to calm him down.'

Brianus was nodding. 'That's quite true, master. I saw it for myself. And master – my other master – must have been alarmed: he told me to get his luggage packed at once, because he'd changed his mind and was going straight back to Gaul. He wasn't even stopping to acquire a horse – he was going to borrow one so he could start at once, and I was to join Calvinus and Pronta at the flat and he would send instructions as to what to do.'

Emelius and the soldiers – except the helmet man – had gathered round us and were listening to all this. 'And did he send instructions?' the centurion asked.

'He sent them all the time,' Brianus replied. 'I couldn't read them, but Calvinus could. Proper letters, sealed and everything. All the details about him moving over here: how many carts we were expecting and when they would arrive and what we could expect in every one of them.'

'So it looks as if Calvinus really was involved?' Emelius remarked. 'I was beginning to wonder if we were mistaken about that.'

'I think we've all been making a mistake,' I said very slowly. 'I don't think the lictor wrote those messages at all.'

'But he must have . . .' Brianus began, just as Florens snorted and said, 'Who else would have written them? They were fastened with his seal.'

I looked into the pink-rimmed eyes again. 'Exactly, councillor. The seal that was found on the finger of that severed hand last night. Obviously it was meant to suggest to us that this was Voluus's corpse, when it was actually someone else – in this case Antolinus, I suspect. I should have realized that it was peculiar. Why rob a man and leave his toga-clasp and seal – both of which are likely to be valuable things?'

'Well, it was not the first time,' Florens pointed out. 'One of the bodies of the escort still had a ring on it.'

'Did it now?' I asked him. 'And how do you know that? I seem to recall that you were in the public baths all day and then attended a sacrificial banquet afterwards. How did you come to see the fingers of a corpse?'

Florens was fidgeting. 'Servilis must have told me. He took a letter out there, when you were there yourself.'

Servilis said nothing. He was sitting silently, looking at his owner as if he hated him.

'I don't think so,' Emelius observed. 'The bodies were already in the death-cart when he came, and he went nowhere near it. I was there, also, and I can swear to that.'

'You see,' I said. 'The councillor clearly did not see it for himself, but he knew that it had happened. And I think that I know why. It was all part of the plan. Leave one ring, and then another will not seem so strange, and chop the head and limbs off, so that people are much more difficult to identify? Who did it for you, Florens? Antolinus, I suppose? He had the knowledge to dissect a corpse, and a soldier would have a better stomach for the task.'

Emelius was shaking a bewildered head. 'Why leave a ring at all?'

'Because Florens had the lictor's ring, that's why, and he intended to leave it on a corpse for us to find – so we would believe that Voluus was newly dead. He took it from the body when he murdered him, of course – not recently but months ago, when he took Voluus to his villa on the promise of a horse. Brianus has just told us that his master borrowed one, and who more likely to have lent him one, than the councillor that he was dining with that night? But he never rode it. He was murdered then and there, and no doubt buried somewhere on the property. He wasn't missed, of course. Everybody in Britannia thought that he'd returned to Gaul and those in Gaul supposed he was still here – especially when a series of sealed messages arrived. Most of them written by the councillor, no doubt, though Alcanta must have written some herself, saying what was in the carts and when they would arrive.'

Brianus looked hurt and mystified. 'But why would my ex-mistress do a thing like that?'

'Because she hoped to be united with the man she called her "love", her so-called husband, by whom she'd had a child. She thought herself betrothed to him and would have married him – but her brother disapproved and had him conscripted before they could be wed. Perhaps they wrote in secret – I rather think they did – and she contrived to let him know that she was now with child.'

Emelius whistled. 'So that's why Antolinus faked his own death in that rebel raid? So he could run away to her? I recall the commander saying that the bodies that were found were still in uniform, but so badly hacked about, that if we had not known who was missing we could not have identified them for a burial.' He shook his head, remembering. 'He must have loved the lady very much.'

'The trouble was, I think she heard that he was dead, and there was the coming child to think about. Her brother might have thrown her from the house, so she was desperate to marry anyone as soon as possible. I think that's where Florens's role came into it. He discovered Antolinus – I'm not certain how, perhaps he really did want to acquire the farm from him – and worked out that he was a deserter in disguise. But instead of betraying him to the garrison, he listened to the story and, seeing an opportunity, cooked up a plan. He would go to Gaul, contract to wed the girl, bring her back and keep the huge dowry as his own reward, while she went off with Antolinus to his farm. I've no proof of that of course, but it seems the likely explanation of events. And Marcus told me that Florens tried to wed a foreign heiress once.'

'You are quite right, citizen.' Alcanta had regained her feet and had come – unnoticed – to listen in. Her face was drawn and stained with recent tears, but she held her head high and spoke with dignity. 'That's exactly what he did.' She gave a little sob – not of grief but fury, I was amazed to realize. 'Florens is very good at little plans like that. But when he got to me, it was far too late. My brother had contracted me to Voluus by then.'

Florens gave a roar and tried to lunge at her. Three soldiers pounced on him at once, and this time – councillor or not – they bound him hand and foot: none too gently, either, using the ties of his own tunic to secure his knees.

Alcanta blinked at him. 'Don't hurt him too much. I still owe him a little bit of gratitude.' She turned to me. 'Have you ever met the lictor, citizen? I wish I never had. He was a brute, a monster – he loved to cause you pain. When Florens told me that Antolinus was alive and that there might be a chance of seeing him, I pleaded with my husband to give me a divorce. He only laughed, of course, twisting my arm until he forced the truth from me – or most of it. I managed to hold out and not to tell him where Antolinus was – he would only have had him hunted down and put to death for desertion. Neither did I tell him that I was with child, because he would have realized that it was not his own. But Florens had a plan. He wrote to Voluus, inviting him to come here to Britannia – promising a future on the curia, a welcome banquet and all sorts of things. Voluus was flattered – he was always vain. He came to Glevum practically at once. It worked out splendidly. I had the child in peace.'

'While Florens met him here and arranged to murder him!' I said, casting a triumphant look towards the councillor. 'Having contrived to be nominated as your guardian?'

She shook her head. 'It should not have happened exactly as it did. The intention was to poison him after we'd all arrived in Britannia – these things can happen with unfamiliar food. But Voluus had spies. One of my servants wrote to him while he was here and told him of the child – I had meant to pass it off as belonging to a maid until after Voluus was dead.'

'I see! So that was the letter that Voluus received that day in the mansio?' It was making sense at last. That kind of fury comes from jealousy, not fear. 'Not a threat at all!'

She nodded. 'He was so furious that he threatened to return home that very day. He would have murdered me. Fortunately Florens intercepted him.'

Brianus was pawing at my arm again. 'But I'm sure I heard that the letter was a threat. It was discovered afterwards, at the mansio.'

'Not that letter, Brianus,' I told him solemnly. 'That message was destroyed. You told me Florens read it – and it gave him an idea. He had already planned to murder Voluus, but if he wrote another letter and left it to be found that would start the rumour of the threats. I imagine he wrote sealed letters to the house in Gaul, apparently from Voluus himself, explaining that the lictor wasn't coming back, and making arrangements for moving all the goods. No one but Alcanta would have known about the truth, and she was quite content. She hoped to be reunited with her love in exchange for everything she had. But there had to be a body, representing Voluus, or some awkward questions would be asked. That's where the threats came in. The authorities would look for ancient enemies.'

I looked at Alcanta. She didn't disagree. 'We never thought
of Calvinus as a likely suspect. He had an ancient grudge
against his master, it appears – but with a man like Voluus,
there were sure to be others that we didn't know about. His
death was not a loss to anyone. It was a clever thought.'
   Florens sighed. Suddenly the fight had all gone out of him.
'It might have worked, as well, if Antolinus had kept things as
simple as we'd planned. Arrange to have the treasure-cart come
in here overnight, give the escort poppy-wine and steal the
treasure while they slept to make the threats seem true. But there
was a sudden problem – Antolinus sent to me, saying that he
had been recognized. The driver of the treasure-cart was somebody he knew. There was only one answer. We had to kill the
man. Antolinus did it – poison in the wine – but we still wanted
people to know about the threats. He came up with the scheme
about the bogus rebel raid. I was at a banquet, and I couldn't
help. He did it the same way as he'd done before, except that
this time there were five corpses to arrange. He couldn't do it
on the road – it would have taken too much time – so he cut
the bodies into pieces in the barn and put them on the cart. Then
he had the problem of the horses, too. If he kept them here it
would excite remark, so he took them to the roadside and simply
slaughtered them as well – except for the one that he kept back
to ride. Spread the blood around to make it look as if the party
had been stabbed and hacked to death. It was a risk, of course,
but he got away with it. Rode off into the forest as soon as he
spotted the first witness on the road. He was an expert horseman.
Just as well – he could not have managed six horses otherwise,
even if four of them were towed behind the cart.' He shook his
head. 'It wasn't meant to happen. It was an accident of fate.'
   'How do you know all that? You must have talked to him.
And suddenly he's dead! Was that an accident?' Alcanta's eyes
were blazing and she clenched her pretty fists. 'So close, and
yet I missed him. And you used his body as my husband's
corpse, when you promised me that it would be some name-
less criminal! I can't forgive that, Florens. I don't care if they
feed me to the beasts. I'm going to tell the truth.' She turned
to the centurion. 'He wrote to me – under my husband's seal,
of course! – about a moon ago to tell me that Antolinus really

had been killed this time. Lies, of course, but he promised that, if I continued with the plan, I could come to Britannia and he would marry me himself and give the child a home, since of course I had no husband now. I, like a fool, believed him and went along with it. I even thanked him when he offered me the farmstead as a home, when all the time my lover's head was in the well. He must have put it there.'

'I didn't kill him,' Florens said. 'How could I have done? I was in Glevum all day yesterday – Libertus was with me a great deal of the time – and in the evening I was looking after you! When did I have time to kill him, tell me that? I couldn't ride out to this farmstead in the time I had.'

She thought for a moment and then hissed angrily, 'But you knew that he was dead. You had already told me that he was. And all that time he was actually alive. I don't know how you did it, but it must have been your plan.' She shook her head. 'And I can't imagine why. You already had the treasure – it was out here on the farm. You didn't even have to move it once the escort-men were dead.'

'But it's as clear as daylight, lady.' Biccus found his voice. 'He'd seen you by then. It was you he wanted, not just the contents of the treasure-cart. And who could blame him? I would marry you myself.' He sank back into silence.

'And I think I know who murdered Antolinus for him,' I observed. 'Someone who would not be wanted at the banquet feast. Someone who was doubtless promised a reward and, like Calvinus, is hoping someday to be free and rid himself of his uncomfortable name. Somebody who killed the maid-servant as well, so she could not swear that the body was not Voluus at all. Is that not true, Servilis?'

Servilis scowled. 'They both deserved the penalty, even under law. One was a deserter and one a runaway. There is an auto-matic death penalty for both, and I was acting on the orders of a magistrate. I don't think that you can punish me for that.'

I turned back to Emelius. 'Centurion, I think we have the answers now. You are under orders to present me at the court. I would like you to do so, and bring these people, too. I believe I shall be able to prove my innocence. Though I may be in trouble for requisitioning a cart.'

EPILOGUE

I was sitting in the garden of my patron's country house, where Marcus had been sitting when the whole affair began. Marcus was lolling on a folding chair nearby, watching his infant with indulgent eyes.

'Well,' he said, 'I suppose we can call that satisfactory. I am relieved that you managed to redeem yourself and did not cause me any more embarrassment. And they cleared you on all charges, even of the cart. Finding the lictor's body helped, of course. How did you manage to work out where it was?'

'Where would be more obvious than in the garden of Florens's country house, where I would duly cover it with a pavement floor? He must have put it there the night that Voluus died – after he'd removed the ring and toga-clasp, of course. But it would not be really safe till I'd put the pavement down. He even had his servants flatten out the place, so that I would not disturb the grave by accident.'

'Unfortunate that he actually murdered Voluus himself; otherwise he might have got away with just a fine. But a Roman citizen? And planning all the rest? No wonder he was sentenced to instant exile.' He threw a padded ball for little Marcellinus to retrieve. 'After being a wealthy councillor, he'll find it hard, I think, though he's taken that servant with him, I believe. Don't know why the fellow went – the court decided that he was justified in killing two runaways whom the law condemned.'

I made no answer, too full of sugared dates to speak. I had been given a whole plate of them entirely to myself, which I took as a kind of edible apology for his not volunteering to speak up on my account. It didn't matter: Alcanta's testimony had been more than enough to sway the magistrate, but I'd not declined the dates. I'm not particularly fond of them, in fact, but I was going to eat them all on principle.

'It's Porteus that I feel sorry for,' he went on presently, when

Marcellinus had toddled over with the ball. 'All those debts that he's been lumbered with! Well, he should have remembered that the buyer must beware. He is liable, because he did the ordering, though Florens wrote and asked him to, under the lictor's seal. And he still has that daughter to find a husband for!'

I nodded stickily. 'It won't be easy now. She won't have much of a dowry after this.'

Marcus gave a grunt. 'And he won't be able to afford to be a candidate for Imperial priest. That was what Florens was working for, of course – they were always rivals for the Servir's post. If Porteus wasn't such a pompous idiot, I could feel quite sorry for the man.'

I didn't answer. I hadn't quite forgiven the councillor for what he'd done to me.

Marcus didn't notice. 'I don't think that awarding him the lictor's flat is going to compensate him much, and of course he won't get anything from Florens's estate. That's all gone to the Imperial purse. Alcanta offered him the steward, I believe, but that's no use at all. Calvinus wouldn't fetch a quadrans at the slave-market after what they put him through.'

'I wonder if Florens feels guilty about that? He must have known the servants would be the first to take the blame.'

Marcus rose, yawning, and threw the ball again. It went about an arms-length and fell into a pool. He sat down with a laugh. 'We'll no doubt find that Calvinus was impolite to him. Florens was vindictive, I told you that before. That's why – when the opportunity arose – he tried to imply that you had been involved. Not that he had anything against you person-ally, but he knew that by indicting you he would embarrass me.' The slave had fetched the ball and rolled it to his feet. Marcus kicked it back, remarking lazily, 'Well, he won't be trying to embarrass me again. By sundown he'll have had to leave the Empire for life.'

'It's lucky that Alcanta didn't suffer the same fate.' I licked my fingers delicately, as I'd seen my patron do.

Marcus laughed, slapping his hand against his thigh. 'There was never any chance of that, I think. Of course, she had a representative to speak for her in court, since being a woman she couldn't speak herself, but she lowered her lashes at the magistrate and looked properly contrite, and managed to convince him that she'd been overruled by men. He even volunteered to act as guardian himself. Titus Flavius – the man's a recent widower. I think she'll be all right.'

I had to laugh at this assessment of Alcanta's charms. 'She's persuaded him to buy that pavement, too. I thought I was going to make a loss on that.'

'Speaking of women, how's your charming wife?' Marcus was doing his best to flatter me. 'She's a doughty woman, too. You know she came here the other night to plead your cause? Wanted Julia to persuade me to speak for you in court. I had to promise that I'd do it if you really needed me. Combined their wiles against me, though I didn't have to do it in the end.' He glanced towards the gate. 'Ah, and here they come! With that new slave of yours. Funny little fellow. What's his name again?'

'We call him Brianus,' I answered. 'And it's worked out splendidly. My son and his family have been looking for a slave and Brianus will suit them very well. It's sometimes difficult to make him understand that I am not his master and he works for Junio, but he is young and willing and no doubt he'll learn. Now that he's eating better, he is gaining strength as well. He told me he had never been so happy in his life.'

'Well,' my patron said, heartily, 'I'm very pleased myself. You did very well to sort this problem out. They would never have caught the murderer if it had not been for you.'

Marcus was not good at compliments and I appreciated this. 'Oh, it was nothing, patron,' I told him modestly. 'At first I made a number of mistakes. The only thing I really did was focus on the farm.'

He smiled benignly. 'Come to think of it, I suppose that's true. Anyone might have worked the rest of it, if they'd happened to be there.' He looked over at the plate which had been set for me, picked up the last date and ate it daintily. Then he got to his feet. 'Shall we go and greet the ladies? I believe a light refreshment may have been prepared.'